Double Agents 2+2=0

Double Agents 2+2=0

Anthology

Rodney James White

Printed in Australia
ISBN 978-0-6451599-2-9 (paperback)
ISBN 978-0-6451599-3-6 (ebook)

Cover art: Laila Savolainen - Pickawoowoo Publishing Group
Interior Layout: Pickawoowoo Publishing Group

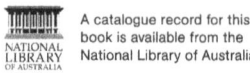

A catalogue record for this
book is available from the
National Library of Australia

CONTENTS

CONTENTS

CONTENT SYNOPSIS

This anthology is a compilation of the stories by Rodney James White about the Mi5 agents Bill Parsons , Jack ' Dumpey ' Delaney and Rebecca James an Australian from Sydney.

1) Double Agents 2+2=0 , tells of their action packed escapade on the trail of Russian double agents. Their quest takes them around the world , supported by government agencies and the latest in military hardware. They also need to get into the minds of the Russian double agents.

2) More Double Agents - Never Trust a Spy ! Parsons and Delaney are back ! Again they are on an action packed adventure checking out double agents and spies in St. Petersburg, Russia. Rebecca James , the Australian , is there also giving her expertise and knowledge to trap the double agent Jim Middleton and bring him to justice.

3) Are There Any More Spies Out There ? Another action packed adventure with Mi5 agents Bill Parsons , Jack Delaney and Rebecca James on the trail of any spies who are out there. They trip to Vladivostok ,

Russia and trap and prison the Russian agents Christian Jansen and Hilary Jacobsen in America.

4) Never Fall in Love With A Spy ! It is summer in London , England and the Mi5 agents Bill Parsons and Jack Delaney are at Lord's cricket ground watching the first day of the Ashe's Test between England and Australia where they meet the Australian Mi5 agent Rebecca James in the bar. At the cricket they see the spies Michael Leung and Jason Cheung from Hong Kong and Caroline Kusinski and Vladimir Hotinski who are Soviet spies. They duly entrap the Chinese and Russians and bring them to justice.

5) What Does A Spy Think And Do Next ? Once again the Mi5 agents Bill parsons , Jack Delaney and Rebecca James are on the trail of spies , this time in Scotland at St. Andrews Golf Course and Club. The Russian spies Dmitri Kosov and Anastasia Sochi are keen golfers and staying at the same accommodation at No.14. Problems arise with North Sea Oil and refineries in Britain which are to be attacked by Russian KGB High Command. War is declared between Britain and Russia. Britain defends itself at whatever cost and

the Mi5 agents enjoy Britain's victory with some drinks at the Rose and Crown Pub.

6) Well I Didn't Expect That ! Bill Parsons , Jack Delaney and Rebecca James , all Mi5 agents are drinking Champagne and eating scones with strawberry jam and cream at the men's singles Wimbledon final of 2020 between Roger Federer and Novak Djokovich. There are a couple of suspected Russian spies by the names of Alexis Uson and Miranda Barton who C instructs them to keep under 24/7 surveillance.The spies seek asylum in the Russian Embassy and the Embassy , it's staff and the spies are expelled to Russia with a complimentary move by the Russians to the British Embassy in Russia.

7) Back In The U.S.S.R. Boys! The Mi5 agents Bill Parsons , Jack Delaney and Rebecca James are in the head of Mi5's (C) office and he is sending them to Russia. They are suspicious of a mole in Mi5 , Mi6 and SOE. They trail the Russian spies Nikita Volgo and Karolyn Caribou. After being in a bit of bother whilst being under attack from the KGB , C sends in six Harrier jump jets to get rid of the KGB and the Russian spies.

8) Afghanistan Is For Afghans And That Doesn't Mean Only The Dogs ! The three Mi5

agents are sent to Afghanistan where they reside at the Safir Landmark Hotel in Kabul.They observe some Afghani drug runners dealing with some North Americans who are proprietors of a dodgey pharmaceutical company called Trusty Proprietary Limited based in Michigan , USA , who are also implicated in the supply of illegal cocaine and heroin. The agents hire a red Shelby GT Mustang convertible and drive Route 66 and then up to Vancouver , then fly back to Chicago where they engage lawyers to prosecute the US Multinational pharmaceutical company. They trip back to England and engage the Australian lawyer Geoffrey Robertson QC et al. to prosecute Trusty P/L which he does and wins.

9) Southward Ho ! Another book in the series by Rodney James White about the Mi5 agents Bill Parsons , Jack Delaney and Rebecca James who are again on the trail of Russian agents. Their journey takes them to Sydney , Australia and to the Southern Continent Antarctica.

10) In and Out of Africa ! Another action packed adventure from Rodney James White. The three Mi5 agents , Bill Parsons , Jack Delaney and Rebecca James venture into

Africa. They stumble across a couple of German big game and ivory hunters and two Russian KGB agents who are about to take over South Africa's nuclear facilities. However we won't tell you any more , you must read it for yourself !

11) I Love To Go To America ! Bill Parsons and Jack Delaney are finally retired and decide to trip to the U.S.A. and Canada. They decide hire a red Mustang Shelby GT convertible again and relive their drive across Route 66 East to West and come back on Canadian Pacific National Railway to Levis , Quebec. They meet up with Rebecca James and decide to go snow skiing. They then decide to go to South America and note that quite a few Nazi war criminals went to South America includ-ing Helmuth Rasmussen , Gerhard Somner , Alfred Stark and Aglimanto Daclide.

Whilst in Buenos Aires they find out from C that Rasmussen is the VW agent and Somner and Daclide are Mercedes agents. Whereas Stark is in the Atlantic Coast.

Subsequently the Buenos Aires' police arrest and charge Rasmussen , Sommer and Daclide and they are tried and sentenced to life im-prisonment as Nazi war criminals.

They then trip to Santa Cruz in Argentina and deal with Stark who is sentenced to life imprisonment.

12) Arctic , Arctic , Arctic It's Cold , Cold , Cold At The North Pole! The Mi5 agents Bill Parsons , Jack Delaney and Rebecca James along with the CIA operative Jack O'Halloran , have another action packed adventure this time in Anchorage, Alaska and the wild lands of Alaska. The U.S of A's largest state. This time they foil the plans of some German neo- Nazis and then continue with their retirement , whilst Rebecca James marries Jack O'Halloran in Alaska.

13) Between Morocco And A Hard Place ! This is the latest adventure about Mi5 agents Bill Parsons , Jack Delaney and Rebecca James. Another action packed adventure that takes them to Morocco and across the U.S.A. and back to England on the trail a Moroccan Terrorist Group with links to Al Queda.

14) Once A Spy Always A Spy ! This adventure about the Mi5 agents Bill Parsons , Jack Delaney and Rebecca James takes them to the environs of Kensington , London where they uncover a dentist who is also a KGB agent and a Spy.

VULCAN BOMBER

DOUBLE AGENTS by Rodney Tim White

HARRIER JUMP JET

SOVIET CRUISE MISSILES

2 # 2.0

VLTAVA RIVER

PRAGUE

1

DOUBLE AGENTS 2+2=0

PREFACE:

This book was inspired by the writings of the legendary espionage writer David John Moor Cornwell (1931-2020) who lived for 89 years and was better known by his pen name of John le Carre' and he will put pen to paper no more. Le Carre' means 'the square' which is fitting for him, being bordered by four equal sides enclosing MI5, MI6 and Special Branch within the elitist educational and class system of Britain which includes Eton school, Oxford and Cambridge universities. He had first-hand knowledge of spying having worked for MI6.

Even though this story is inspired by le Carre' it in no way tries to emulate him for he was the ultimate character builder, describer and assassinator of people.

For the younger reader a double agent is a person employed by a government to discover information about enemy countries, but who is really working for one of these enemy countries – if you like two spies in one – the perfect spy! Which, incidentally, le Carre' wrote a novel about called The Perfect Spy. MI5 is Military Intelligence Section Five. Its principal function is national security in the United Kingdom. It identifies, investigates and contains threats to national security, as well as threats to the economic wellbeing of the United Kingdom which arise from overseas.

MI6 is Military Intelligence Section Six. Officially known as Secret Intelligence Service (SIS), its role is to obtain intelligence on the activities of its enemies and potential enemies. It is an arm of the Foreign Office and its boss, known as C – for Control – is answerable to the Foreign Secretary. It used to be said that MI6 agents worked abroad and MI5 within the United Kingdom but nowadays that is not the case.

Up until a decade ago the main threat was from the Soviet Union and other Warsaw Pact countries. The Warsaw Pact was a defence treaty signed between the Soviet Union and seven other Eastern bloc socialist republics of Central and Eastern Europe in Warsaw, Poland, in May 1955 during the Cold War. The strategy behind it was driven by the desire of the Soviet Union to prevent Central and Eastern Europe being used as a base for its enemies. The members of the Warsaw Pact were Albania, Bulgaria, Czechoslovakia, East Germany (but on October 2, 1990, they withdrew), Hungary, Poland (withdrew June 4, 1989), Romania (withdrew December 29, 1989) and the Soviet Union. The Cold War was a period of geopolitical tension between the Soviet Union and the United States and their respective allies after World War II. The Cold War is considered to have been at its most heated between 1967 and

1991 though it started in 1947. The term cold is used because there was no large-scale fighting directly between the two superpowers. After the collapse of the Soviet Union its main focus was on the Irish Republican Army (IRA). But since September 11, 2001, its focus has been Muslim extremists.

SPECIAL BRANCH is the British police force which works mostly for the security services, especially MI5. Formed in London in 1885, its main function is to collect evidence and arrest the enemies of the United Kingdom who live on home territory. Historically, these have been the IRA, Soviet or Russian intelligence agents and Islamic extremists and terrorists.

SPECIAL OPERATIONS EXECUTIVE (SOE) was a secret British World War II organisation. It was formed on July 22, 1940, from existing secret organisations under the control of the Minister of Economic Warfare, Hugh Dalton. Its purpose was to conduct espionage in occupied Europe against the Axis powers (and later, also in occupied Southeast Asia), and to aid local resistance movements.

Few people were aware of SOE's existence. Those who were part of it or liaised with it were sometimes referred to as the "Baker Street Irregulars", after the location of its London headquarters. It was also known as "Churchill's Secret Army "or the "Ministry of Ungentlemanly Warfare"

I do hope you enjoy his story and that it inspires you to write some of your own.

RJW.

RODNEY JAMES WHITE

February 2, 2021

DOUBLE AGENTS 2+2=0

He was tall and dark, with a black moustache. He walked with a slight limp.

You just knew he was a double agent – he had that look about him!

I first saw him outside the Bookshop Café in Prague sipping coffee and talking with one of the most attractive females you've ever seen. She had blonde hair and spoke English with a Russian accent. Another double agent?

While they were there a message came over the public address system asking for a Ms Ursula Popovich to attend reception. Shortly thereafter the blonde stood and moved toward reception. She then returned to her table and companion and finished her coffee.

I watched them and listened as best I could until they kissed and moved on in opposite directions. His limp got more pronounced as his gait increased. She moved easily and swiftly.

The weather was worsening, the sky sullen and grey but windless, and rain was starting to fall so everyone outside raised and opened their umbrellas.

I couldn't follow them both, so I decided to follow the male and rang Jack Delaney, another MI5 agent, to tag the woman. Jack replied, "OK Bill I'm onto her, delighted actually! I'll ring you later."

My quarry walked to a unit on the second floor of a

dilapidated block of units by the river. Despite the buildings the view was superb, up, down and across the river to the snow-capped mountains in the hinterland.

I followed up the creaky stairs, his door was closed, and I heard him talking in muffled tones with what I thought was a Russian accent saying this phone may be bugged so meet me at the usual at the usual time.

I knocked at the door, but there was no answer just the sound of the phone hanging up and the click of what I assumed was a revolver hammer being engaged, probably a Luger, ready to go.

So I went downstairs to the lobby and waited and waited.

My mobile rang whilst I was seated downstairs in the lobby. It was Jack. "She's here at the Bookshop Café sitting outside."

"Good, I'll be there in a jiffy!" I said.

Then my quarry's door opened and out he came. He limped down the creaky stairs and past me to the outside world.

I followed him at a distance then rang Jack to tell him to keep a watch and an ear on them at the Book Café as I did not want to blow my cover.

Jack rang ten minutes later and said that after having a coffee – he had a flat white, she had a double espresso – they both went into the bookshop and opened a book titled 'Stalin.' They opened it to reveal an enclosed box into which they both inserted a set of keys. They then kissed and departed. I followed him and Jack followed her.

I contacted MI5 saying that we needed backup for these two as Jack and I can't do it 24-7.

"Sure, thing mate!" Control said.

He limped back to his room, and she walked back to hers. After five minutes he came out and grabbed his blue and white Peugeot bicycle out of the apartment's back shed. It was a nice bike with an aluminium frame and Reynolds strengtheners, 12-speed with a triple chain ring but he still had to pedal.

It was a sunny windless day and I thought how can I keep up with him, so I ran to the shed and pinched someone's bike, a white Cervelo – nice bike too!

So off we rode with me trailing behind, not drafting, but at a visible distance riding along the cycle path of the Vitava River.

He rode for about fifteen minutes until he reached the eighth bridge across the Vitava where he alighted and parked his bike in a rack. The woman was on the bridge waiting. Jack too, at a distance. Jack saw me and acknowledged with a wink.

We couldn't hear what they were saying but they embraced, kissed, and departed.

Jack and I split – I followed him, and Jack shadowed her.

As he went back to his unit, I heard the receptionist call him Mister Curtis. On another occasion I sat in the lobby and was having breakfast and a coffee when Curtis came down the creaky stairs and asked if he could join me as there were no other places available. "Sure, "I said. We then introduced ourselves and I said, "Here's my phone number in case you need to contact me, "and he gave me his. After breakfast he ventured outside, hopped onto his bike and headed south-east to the Bohemian Forest where he met a man of short stature dressed in a grey greatcoat with semi-brogue black shoes and a black hat. They talked in what appeared to be a rather gruff manner and then departed.

Curtis then rode to Stalin's monument in Letna Park and met and talked with the blonde, but they did not hug and kiss before they departed.

He then rode north-east across Bohemia away from the wild water and eighteenth bridge across the Vitava to the entrance of the Czechoslovakian nuclear warhead and rocket factory which was deceptively called the Bata Shoe Factory. He entered after showing his pass to the guard at the boom gates where the guard acknowledged him as 'Viktor'.

Viktor Curtis (more likely, Viktor Cransky, thought Parsons) then sat down on a nearby bench seat and slowly reached to the left inside pocket of his fawn double-breasted suit and pulled out a packet of Peter Stuyvesant cigarettes. He tapped the upended packet with his right index finger and out fell a cigarette which he picked up in the fingers of his left hand and he then flicked open a stainless steel cigarette lighter with the initials VC engraved on both sides. Viktor then pursed his moustachioed upper lip, placed the cigarette between his lips, flicked the cigarette lighter on, lit the Stuyvesant and inhaled three deep breaths before blowing out two excellent smoke rings.

Curtis rose and proceeded to the forbidden area where an

attendant greeted him, looked at his passes and allowed him through with his lit cigarette.

Viktor surreptitiously crept towards the top-secret area that housed the section on nuclear warheads and cruise missiles, although the cigarette smoke was a bit of a giveaway!

Viktor then slowly sifted through the papers, found what he wanted and placed them inside his left sock and slowly proceeded outside puffing on his cigarette. Once outside he hopped on his Peugeot and cycled back to his unit. Jack followed on his Specialized.

Jack rang Parsons and related what Curtis had done whilst he was watching him outside the building.

Jack and Parsons then met up and both tailed Curtis back to his unit and observed Ursula Popovich arrive.

Shortly afterwards Curtis rang Parsons and said they needed to meet in front of Lenin's statue in Letna Park, Prague at 10am.

Bill, followed by Jack at a distance, proceeded to Stalin's statue where he was met by Curtis and Popovich. Curtis said he was going to London tomorrow.

Before Parsons left Prague he woke early on a beautiful sunny day and was sitting in the lobby restaurant at his hotel when down came Rebecca Joyce, a tall beauty with dark hair down to her shoulders and a figure that most women would die for. She is an MI5 agent who had come over to help keep a tag on Curtis and Popovich but had since been assigned to Prague. She was an Australian from Sydney.

"Hi Bec, "said Bill. "How's things? "

Rebecca replied, "G'day Pars, things are fine with me. How's about you?"

Bill replied, "Good. I was thinking it's such a beautiful day that I thought I might go for a drive through the Alps. I've got a car on hire that I pick up at ten. I'll grab it, then come and pick you up if you want ".

"Sure thing Pars. See ya soon!"

At 9:30 Parsons left the hotel on foot and arrived at Miocevich's car hire at 9:45. Outside was this gorgeous Jaguar E Type Zero open two-seater in British racing green with two yellow drag stripes and tan leather seats and interior trim. Parsons thought there's not a better-looking car in the world than the 'E'.

He showed his papers and passport and paid a deposit before receiving the keys. He started it up and said to Joe Miocevich who was standing nearby, "Where's the noise?"

"You know it's electric don't you? "Joe said. "Flick the synthesiser button if you want noise!"

Bill drove back to the hotel and picked up Rebecca who was standing outside waiting. She hopped in and he fiddled with the radio till he got the BBC World Service. They then headed for the Alps.

The road was narrow and winding, just barely wide enough for two cars going in opposite directions but the view was superb down to the valley and the snaking wild water of the Vitava, whenever Parsons decided he could take a glimpse away from the mountain pass road.

Not too far along the way there was the honk of a car

horn behind them. Parsons looked in his rear view and side view mirrors.

"It's a Monza, "they both said. Sure enough it was a red Ferrari Monza SP2 convertible and it was being driven by a male with a female passenger.

"Crikey! That's the two Russian spies I was tailing in Prague, "Rebecca said. "They're probably headin' for Russia, those Commos."

Parsons pulled over and allowed the Ferrari to pass. "OK, we'll tail them. I know this Zero is fast and handles well, so let's find out for sure!"

Bill put his foot down and was keeping up with the Monza until they came to a section with switchbacks and hairpins.

The Ferrari driver then floored it with a squeal of tyres and smell of tyre smoke that left the Zero in its wake.

Bill and Rebecca gave chase and were gaining on them when suddenly they came to a tight hairpin and there was no Ferrari ahead of them just the smell of burnt rubber and black tyre marks heading over the edge. They slowed and glanced to the right and then stopped. There careering down the mountain slope was the red Ferrari which eventually came to a halt, rolled and caught on fire.

"Strewth!" said Bec.

"Well Bec, I guess we've dealt with those Russian spies!" Bill said.

"Too right Pars, they're cactus!"

Once back in his room, Curtis picked up his mobile and Googled the number for Flight Centre, Prague, and booked a flight from Va'clav Havel International Airport Prague to Heathrow leaving at 7am European time.

One hour and fifty minutes later the tall frame of Curtis limped down the walkway to the arrival lounge and waited for his bag to arrive on the carousel. The lounge was crowded with what looked like Jamaicans, African Americans and Caucasians who in reality were probably POMEs. (That's Australian for Prisoners Of Merry England – but in fact the POMEs became Australians.)

Viktor Curtis then rang Bill Parsons and said, "Meet me in the lobby of the Grosvenor Hotel near the Waterloo Station at eight A.M"

They met at the said time where Viktor took some papers out of his sock and gave them to Parsons with apologies.

The MI5 agent perused them quickly and said thanks as he pocketed them inside his double-breaster then twirled his black moustache. He then asked Curtis where he was staying. Curtis replied, "At the Wellington!"

Bill Parsons then twirled his moustache again and thought this is one for Control at MI5. Next thing he's sitting opposite Control with his huge presence and stentorian voice showing him the papers and relating his story.

"Well mate, we've got to get rid of these warheads and missiles somehow, "Control said. "Let me think about this!" He lit up a Havana cigar, which, unknown to them at the time would turn out to be quite prophetic and took a few slow puffs.

"Well mate, "said C, "we'll have to take them out somehow,

but it will probably start World War Three! Oh well, C'est la vie!!"

Control then contacted the Home Secretary, SOE and the Prime Minister and got the OK to take them out. They alerted and mobilised their defence forces and checked with the meteorological office.

Three Vulcan bombers and ten Harrier jets scrambled from an undisclosed air base at 3am and proceeded to Russia east of Prague.

The bombs and the incendiaries were dropped, and the cruise missiles were taken out and the nuclear warheads exploded releasing plutonium into the atmosphere and stratosphere as the prevailing winds sent it east across Russia and Siberia.

The Russian Prime Minister, Breheny, was quickly on his hot phone to the United States of America's President, Mike Owen, the British Prime Minister, Graham Mitchell, the Canadian Prime Minister, Chuck Davis, Australian Prime Minister, John Whitney, and the New Zealand Prime Minister, Jessica Page, telling them about the situation and saying they were at war with them. The Allies consulted one another and said, "We're in!"

Parsons and Delaney deliberated, and Parsons said, "Well you know Jack there are more nuclear warheads and cruise missile bases in Russia and we had better deal with them too, pronto!"

Parsons then had a characteristic twirl of his moustache and a puff on his cigarette and told 'Dumpey' Delaney what was happening.

Parsons then rang Graham Mitchell, the British Prime Minister, to say more bombers and jets were needed to take out the rest of the Russian warheads and missiles. Mitchell approved. Game on! – but this is not a game!

Bill said to Delaney, "I need a drink! Let's go to the local!"

At the Rose and Crown, they sank a couple of pints of dark ale in the smoky public bar. Parsons said, "You know Jack, we had better get Curtis tied down before he runs, you know the typical agent running theme."

"Yeah Bill, I'll get armed and grab a crew and nab him!" Delaney responded.

The MI5 crew arrived at Curtis's abode, two covered the back door with revolvers drawn and cocked and three at the front door with guns at the ready.

Inside were Curtis and Popovich. With a knock at the door they were alerted and dived for their Lugers.

"MI5 here, open up, "yelled Parsons. Nothing happened.

"Righto boys, batter it down!"

Meanwhile, Vulcans and Harriers were winging it to Russian nuclear warheads and cruise missile sites. On entering Russian airspace, they copped a hammering, and one Vulcan went down with all aircrew killed.

The door to Curtis's unit was bashed down accompanied by a barrage of bullets from Curtis and Popovich but the MI5 agents stood aside initially and then hit the deck and fired up at Curtis and Popovich hitting and killing them accompanied with desperate cries and a flood of blood.

"Well, I guess that's the end of them, "Parsons said, "but

there 'll be more Russian double agents, there always are. Our job is to find them and trap them.

"You know Jack, what we need to do with this Vulcan going down is to find some way to block their radar or tracking systems – let's get onto Special Branch and the boffins at Croydon House and see what they come up with."

"Righto Bill, let's get onto it!" Delaney replied.

Croydon House is a big imposing structure, formerly a castle, with ramparts, battlements, and gargoyles atop its third storey, with a Union Jack fluttering on a flagpole atop it all. It is set in an estate of 20 acres with lush grassland and huge oak trees with deer grazing and the occasional visible fox and rabbit. Jack had contacted the staff and arranged a meeting with them for Parsons and himself.

At the meeting were two of the Croydon House staff – Dennis Jackson, the head, and Trevor O'Hehir his second in command.

"Well gents what's this all about? "Asked Jackson.

"Well, "Parsons begins, "you probably heard about the Ruskies shooting down our Vulcan – well we don't want that to happen again! What can you guys come up with to prevent it? I'm thinking along the lines of blocking their radar and tracking devices so we can get in and out again!"

Jackson murmured to O'Hehir, "You know more about this side of things than I do, so over to you."

O'Hehir was a wiry muscley character about six foot two inches tall with longish blond hair, who spoke with a broad Irish brogue and twang.

"Top o' t day t ya gents!" O'Hehir started. "Well, t be shore oi'll haf t giv tis sum taught. Radar blockage tis nought on t cards. You know, I tink we need t take anutter truk wit tis. We need t go t high tech...India avoidin' Russia!"

By 9:15am we were in the air leaving Heathrow aboard Singapore Airlines flight S22. The flight was pleasant enough, just a bit of turbulence over Iran – where I believe there was a bit of turbulence on the ground too – and a bit of turbulence over the Himalayas. The service, meals and drinks were superb with a lovely Cabernet Merlot from Leeuwin Estate of Margaret River in Western Australia.

Touchdown in Delhi was a bit of a shock to the senses of Delaney and Parsons. Delhi is a thriving metropolis of 17 million people, a teeming mess of people, cows, cars, rickshaws, scooters, two-stroke motorbikes humming, buzzing, screaming, and polluting. The stench is overwhelming, occasionally masked by the smell of cinnamon and cardamon and burning sandalwood around the souks.

Delaney and I travelled in a ramshackle red Tata Motors four-wheel-drive past the New Delhi Arch to the University of Delhi where we had a meeting planned with Doctor Mahatma Singh – Doctor of Philosophy (Cambridge) in information technology, Master of Arts (Cambridge) and Bachelor of Science (Delhi), the lower degrees all with first class honours.

Singh's office was situated in the staff block and had an imposing wooden door carved with amazing geometric patterns with rhesus monkeys climbing up them.

Singh was tall, dark, and handsome, incredibly so, and spoke in impeccable English. Despite his caste he did not wear the traditional headwear, and despite the heat and humidity – which had Parsons and Delaney sweating – he appeared cool, calm and collected. Before they had left England O'Hehir had said, "Oi'll bet ya a Guinness he speaks wit a noddin' head,"– and he did!

"Welcome to India gentlemen, "Dr Singh said warmly. "Thank you for your email. However, I think you're on the wrong track with blocking radar and tracking devices with the Soviets. They'll be onto that like a shot, I think you'll be better off with this new computer technology, but it'll cost you three million Euros up front and three million in a week. Your other options are to fly much higher than the American Gary Powers who was shot down and captured in his Central Intelligence Agency U-2 spy plane in 1960 flying at seventy thousand feet, by the Soviets. At present the highest manned flight by an aeroplane is 314,688 feet achieved by the American Robert White in an X-15 in 1962. The other option is to fly faster and that would have to be in a Lockheed SR-71 Blackbird at 2193.2 miles per hour, the fastest manned flight in an aeroplane!"

Parsons says, "OK, I'll just need to check with Treasury first."

"OK then, "the doctor says. "These computers will need to be fitted to all your recon. planes, bombers and fighters that are to go into Russia and what they will do will be to alter the reading on their radar and trackers to give the aircraft's position as two hours ahead or behind its actual position – whatever you want. These computers are exclusively yours."

"OK, sounds good to me!" Parsons says.

Parsons then contacts the British Chancellor of the Exchequer and receives the affirmative for the money.

Within three weeks the computers were fitted to the British aircraft, six Super Hornets supplied by Australia and ten supplied by the yanks.

So, it's game on again!

Vulcans, Lancers and Tempest bombers, F34 B Lightnings, MQ9 Reapers, F35B Lightnings, Panavia Tornado fighter bombers and six Super Hornets from Australia and ten Super Hornets from the US were loaded with armaments, air crew assembled and cleared for take-off.

They scrambled from various airports in Britain and were quickly entering Soviet airspace as the Russian radar tracked them flying over the North Atlantic Ocean from west to east towards Ireland.

The Russians were most surprised and amazed when they heard and saw this armada of aircraft bombing their nuclear warhead and cruise missile bases. They scrambled their MIGs and fired their Ak-Ak guns and missiles, but it was to no avail – they were doomed.

Meanwhile, British PM Mitchell had received notification from US President Owen that the Indians had sold the computer technology, similar to that of the Allies, to the Cubans.

Apparently, Dr Singh had been nodding his head saying 'no' but his larynx was saying 'yes'.

Parsons thought this was typical of the Indians who he thought were always out to make a quid.

So, now we have another Cuban crisis similar to the Kennedy-Khrushchev missile crisis of 1962. Game on in Cuba!

Britain instituted legal proceedings against Dr Singh. He retorted, "You can do what you like, take me to the International Court in Geneva or any court you like but I won't be paying you a brass razzoo!"

Parsons put his hand on Jack's shoulder and said, "Well mate, looks like we're off to Silicon Valley in sunny California to soak up a bit of sun and surf and possibly some snow skiing whilst the Yankees sort out this Cuban crisis!"

Delaney booked two tickets with United Airlines, and they were in the US the following day and California the next. Sporting sunnies and baseball caps, they walked into the sumptuous offices of Blyton Inc.

"Well Tex, "said Parsons, "the situations like this, "and he runs through it with Tex Simpson – a tall, gangly, bald Texan with a full beard and a big Stetson on his desk.

"You've got two options as I see it, "Tex started in his slow Texan drawl. "One is to sue the hell out of Singh, and two is to give us five million US and see what we come up with."

"We've tried option one and that was negative, "Parsons replied. "Option two means we lose five million US and have to have blind faith in you! And we've also got our hands full in Europe!"

Tex Simpson assembled his thinkfield panel of another four North Americans James Savage, Daisy Jeffries and Melanie Thompson from the US, and Frank Green, with the amiability, friendliness, and broad shoulders of a man of the land, from Canada. They were all in the high echelon of Blyton Inc.

After two days of deliberation with his panel Tex rang

Parsons – who had been hitting the slopes of Mammoth Mountain one day and Squaw Valley the next with Dumpey – to make an appointment to meet with him and Delaney.

"It's like this fellas, "Tex says. "We think you've got to fly in your bombers and fighter jets and bomb the hell out of those Commo Cuban missile bases and airports!"

"We paid you five million US for that!" Parsons murmured through his moustache.

"Yehhh, but yewl have our backin'!" Tex adds quickly.

"OK, but it'll have to be a lot of backing for five million!" Parsons concludes.

So, the Allies' over-stretched air forces are loaded with bombs and are winging it towards Cuba. Squadron leader White, a matter of fact sort of bloke, says, "This weather is not looking good with a tropical storm and hurricane predicted by meteorology over Cuban airspace. However, there is a good side – the Cubans won't be expecting us!"

White then hears from his radioman that it is MISSION ACCOMPLISHED in Russia – "Goodoh!" he says. "Let's make this MISSION ACCOMPLISHED too!"

Vision was not good in the Panavia Tornados and the turbulence was unpredictable but White knew they were undetectable by the Cubans unless the Cuban's had the new computer technology. Singh had said he thought not, so White believed they'd catch the Cuban's unaware. The Yanks were also coming from the other flank to add to the Cuban's downfall.

White says, "We're ready here! Bombardiers get ready!"

The bombs were dropped in a fusillade of fire and frenzy,

picturesque from the air but not so good if you were on the ground. The Yanks came in from the other side and gave their five million bucks worth. Their planes circled Cuba. "MISSION ACCOMPLISHED", said White with a slight smile on his face. "Let's all head for home!"

Parsons and Delaney got word and they both said together, "Let's head for home!"

The two MI5 agents got back to Heathrow and headed for their respective houses and families. When Parsons got home, he said hello to his wife and kids and gave them all a kiss and put on a CD of Dire Straits playing "Going Home".

They all lived happily ever after, never to spy again!

MORE

DOUBLE AGENTS

NEVER TRUST A SPY

ANOTHER SPY THRILLER

LONDON

2

MORE DOUBLE AGENTS – NEVER TRUST A SPY

PREFACE:

KGB (Komitet Gosardarstvennoy Bezopasnosti) translates into English as the Committee for State Security and was the main security for the Soviet Union from 13/3/1954 until 3/12/1991. It was feared in Russia as its primary role within Russia and the satellite republics of the Soviet Union was to quell dissent, by first identifying dissidents promoting anti-communist political and /or religious ideas and then silence them. To do this task the KGB agents often used extremely violent means even occasioning death / murder at times.

This story is inspired by the network of Russian spies that has existed for some time. Some of the most famous and notable are described below but by no means all of them because we probably don't and will never know all of them.

VLADIMIR PUTIN

The present Russian President, Vladimir Putin was a KGB agent for fifteen years before entering politics. After studying law at Leningrad State University, Putin joined the KGB and spied on expatriates in St. Petersburg. In the early 1980's he moved to the KGB's foreign intelligence division in East Germany, where his job was to identify East Germans -professors, journalists, skilled professionals – who had plausible reasons for travelling to Western Europe and the United States and send them to steal intelligence and technology from Western countries.

Putin returned to Russia at the end of the 1980's and worked as a university assistant for a year, which was really a cover for clandestine work with the KGB. His days as an official KGB agent came to an end when he became an advisor to St. Petersburg's mayor Anatoly Scback. He also has been widely criticised for ordering the deaths of Alexander Litvinenko, Sergei Skripal, Anna Politkovskaya and Dmitri Sergei.

Putin has recently made and passed a law that he remains Russian President for another fifteen years (could that be a dictator rather than a President?). He can also handle himself as he has a black belt in Judo.

ALEXANDER LITVINENKO

Litvinenko made headlines for what some call courageous whistleblowing – and others, the reckless bravado that may have earned him an ugly untimely death.

Litvinenko - joined the KGB in 1988 and worked as a

counter - intelligence spy until the Soviet Union dissolved. He then joined the most secret division of the FSB (Federal Security Service) – the domestic successor to the KGB.

He was a British naturalised Russian defector and former officer of the Russian FSB who specialised in tackling organised crime.

On 1/11/2006 Litvinenko suddenly fell ill and was hospitalised in what was established as a case of poisoning by Plutonium 210. He died on 23/11/2006.

He was poisoned by Dmitry Kovtun and Andrei Lugovoi under secret orders from Vladimir Putin.

Litvinenko met Lugovoi and Kovtun at the Pine Bar at the Millennium hotel in Mayfair where he took a few sips of green tea, laced with Polonium 210.

Within Russia's FSB Litvinenko was regarded as a traitor for accusing the agency both of colluding with the Mafia and of being behind the apartment bombings that helped precipitate the Chechen war.

But there was also, the Owen inquiry found, "undoubtedly a personal dimension to the antagonism between Litvinenko and Putin. The bad blood went back to 1998, when the then FSB officer met with the newly appointed director of the agency to protest about corruption with little effect. It only intensified in the following years, culminating in July 2006 when Litvinenko wrote an article claiming Putin was a known paedophile who had used his power as FSB chief to destroy videotapes of himself having sex with underage boys.

Just days before his death. Owen notes, Litvinenko was pointedly accusing Putin, by then Russian President, of being responsible for murdering the journalist Anna Politkovskaya, who was shot dead in Moscow in early October 2006.

BORIS HARPICHOV

He was a double agent and still lives in London.

OLEG LYALIN

She is famous for a defection to British Security Service, or MI5 which led to the discovery and deportation of 105 Soviet officials who were accused of spying in Britain.

VASILY MITROKAN

Mitrokan was a career KGB agent whose secret project – smuggling devices out of the KGB archives – became the subject of the 1999 book "The Sword and the Shield" which he collaborated on with the British author Christopher Andrew.

For 12 years, Mitrokan smuggled thousands of documents from the archives, stuffing them in his shoes before he left each night. He then hid the documents in milk cartons and buried them in his garden or under the floorboards of his house, not even telling his wife what he was doing.

ALDRICH AMES

For Americans, Ames is perhaps the most infamous KGB

spy, having worked as a mole in the CIA for nine years until he was tried and convicted for treason.

In 1985, Ames offered the names of three double agents to a KGB contact, thinking that what he was doing was not treasonous since they were technically KGB agents. All told, Ames disclosed the identities of 25 CIA operatives, 10 of whom were sentenced to death. He became the world's highest paid spy earning roughly $4 million for turning on his colleagues.

ANNA CHAPMAN

Was in a network of Russian sleeper agents whose apparent aim was to infiltrate high – end social and political circles. Anna was born in the Russian city of Volgograd; she was daughter to a senior KGB official and was a very attractive looking woman.

THE RUSSIAN SPACE SHUTTLE BURAN – Russian secret police the KGB stole the US shuttle design in the 1970's and 80's. The theft permitted the Soviet Union to build its own carbon copy of the US shuttles, called the Buran. It flew only once in 1990.

The story of the space shuttle is really the story of the competition between the two great space superpowers in microcosm, complete with all the Cold War intrigue and paranoia, mirror image competition and all manner of spies, both human and electronic. It may also be the first example of spying online.

The Mikoyan MiG -31 is one of the world's fastest jets and one of the only ones to be able to fire long-range air -to-air missiles.

The Mikoyan MiG -35 is a huge upgrade of the Mig-31 with precise targeting and is compatible with AESA radar. (AESA radar – Active Electronically Scanned Array. These radars can spread their emissions across a wide range of frequencies, which make them more difficult to detect over background noise, allowing ships and aircraft to radiate signals while still being more resistant to jamming. It is an electronically scanned array which is a computer-controlled array antenna in which the beam of radar waves can be electronically steered in different directions without moving the antenna.

The SUKHOU-Su -57 is a stealth fighter with a range of 3,500 Km. and cruises at Mach2. It is built with composite materials which reduces the number of parts and overall weight. It features a blended wing body fuselage and brings together the functions of a fighter jet and a strike aircraft. The high manoeuvrability and supersonic cruise capability are expected to give the fighter an upper hand in dog-fight scenarios.

Mach 1 is the speed of sound

Which is 340.3m/sec. or 761.23 mph. Mach 2 is twice the speed of sound which is 680.6 m/sec. or 1522.46 mph.

RUSSIAN SUBMARINES: -

The submarines in the Soviet Navy were developed by numbered "projects ", which were sometimes but not always given names. During the Cold War, NATO nations referred to these classes by NATO reporting names, based on intelligence data, which did not correspond perfectly with the projects.

Most Russian and Soviet submarines had a number "personal "name, but were only known by a number, prefixed by letters identifying the boat's type at a higher level than her class. Those letters included:

- K – cruiser
- TK – heavy cruiser
- B – large
- C(S) -medium
- M-malaya, "small"

Any of these prefixes could have C(S) added to the end, standing for (spetssialnaya) and meaning 'designed for special missions.

DIESEL ELECTRIC SUBMARINES Attack submarines- Project NATO REPORTING No.

- 611 Zulu class
- 613 Whiskey
- 615 Quebec
- 617 Whale
- 633 Romeo
- 641 Foxtrot
- 6415 COM catfish Tango
- 690 Kefal Mullet Bravo

- 877 877KB 877b Kilo
- Paltus (turbot)
- 636. 636M Improved Kilo
- 677 Lada Goddess of love
- 1650 the Amur River Lossos (Salmon.)

GUIDED MISSILE SUBMARINES – 4th GENERATION

- 885 Yassan ASu – Svererodinsk

BALLISTIC MISSILE SUBMARINES

- 667A
- 667AM

GUIDED MISSILE SUBMARINES

- Project
- P613
- 644
- 668
- 651

BALLISTIC MISSILE SUBMARINES

- V611, 611AV
- 629, 609,601,
- 668, 619

- 4th GENERATION
- 661Anchar Papa
- 667AT Yankee Notch
- 667M (Andromeda the constellation) Yankee Sidecar
- 670Ckam (skat, ray) Charlie 1
- 670M Ckam-M(Skat-M ray) Charlie11.

4th GENERATION

- 885(Yasen – ash) Severodvinsk

AUXILLARY SUBMARINES – 940

- 1710
- 1840

NUCLEAR POWERED

- Attack submarines – 4th GENERATION
- Project JE21971
- Project 8851(Yassan)

BALLISTIC MISSILE SUBMARINES

- 667A Yankee 1
- 667AM Yankee 11
- 6675 Murina eel Delta1
- 6676 Kal'mon squid Delta11
- 6675 PM dolphin Delta IV

- 4th Generation – 965Borei Borei

KGB WEAPONS :-

AK-47, officially known as the AUTOMAT KALASH-NIKOVA is a gas operated 7.62 x 39 mm assault rifle developed in the Soviet Union by Mikhail Kalashnikov in the aftermath of WW11. The number 47 refers to the year in which it was finished.

Even after seven decades, the model and it's variants remain the most popular and widely used rifles in the world because of their reliability under harsh conditions, low production cost compared to contemporary Western weapons, availability in virtually every geographic region, and ease of use. The AK-47's accuracy has always been considered to be "good enough"to hit an adult male torso out to about 300 m(328 yards.)

The MAKAROV PM is a simple and sound design which is considered to be one of the best compact self- defence pistols of all time.

While not extremely accurate and lethal at ranges beyond 15-20 meters it is still a formidable and reliable self-defence weapon.

A BALLISTIC KNIFE is a specialised combat knife with a detachable, self-propelled blade that can be ejected to a distance of several metres by pressing a trigger or operating a lever or switch on the handle. Originally developed as a weapon for Soviet and Eastern Bloc military special forces, the ballistic knife was not adopted by the military forces of other nations.

SPETSNAZ SPECIAL FORCES (Spetsnaz are comparable to the US ARMY RANGERS.) COMMONLY USED WEAPONS: -

1. Some versions of the 5.45 mm AK-47 rifle, the AK-47 weighs about 8 pounds and has a 30-round magazine capacity.
2. Short barrelled AKS-744 Carbine. Also known as the "KRINK". It has a nifty side-folding stock.
3. Some have a slightly different AKM fitted out with a GP-25 grenade launcher. The AKM is a modernised version of the AK-47 firing 7.62mm rounds up to 383 yards.
4. Although it's less commonly used today, some still prefer the SVD DRAGUNOV which fires 7.62 rounds and can hit a target up to 1312 yards out.
5. Another rifle used by Spetsnaz snipers is the SVDS DRAGUNOV, which is an advanced, lighter version of the SVD with a folding stock. It was originally designed for Russian paratroopers - the VDV.
6. The bolt -action SV-98 sniper rifle, which the Spetsnaz has been using more frequently. It usually has a scope with a range of about 1,110 yards.
7. For stealth missions Spetsnaz are more likely to carry

the VSS VINTOREZ silenced sniper rifle. It fires a heavy 9 x 39 mmm round but is not as accurate at long-range shots.

8. The PKP PECHENNES general purpose machine gun is Spetsnaz' main squad weapon. It fires a 7.62 x 54 mm round and began to be used by the Russian military in 2001. The PKP is similar to the US M249 machine gun.

9. Another rifle the Spetsnaz carry is a 9 mm AS VAL. It fires subsonic rounds, which means the bullet travels below the speed of sound and conceals the snapping sound of supersonic bullets.

10. They also use the SR-3 which is a shortened version of the AS-VAL. It fires a 9 x 39 mm subsonic round and can be fitted with a suppressor.

11. For sidearm Spetsnaz operations generally carry the 9mm GSL-18b. It's made for close combat, has an 18 round magazine and bullets that can pierce body armour.

BRITISH WEAPONS: -

Generally, MI5, MI6, Special Branch and SOE agents did not carry weapons unless they were on dangerous or special missions which may have been considered dangerous.

- ENFIELD No. 2 Mk7 REVOLVER
- WEMBLEY REVOLVER
- BROWNING FN – INGLIS PISTOL No.11 Mk 1

- COLT M1911A1
- WEMBLEY No. 1 Mk.1
- WELLROD SUPPRESSED PISTOL
- SMITH and WESTON MODEL 10
- COLT NEW SERVICE.
- .303 RIFLE
- .22 RIFLE

DISCLOSURE: Information has been obtained and quoted from Wikipedia. I-P, Airforce Technology, Business Insider and Google.

MORE DOUBLE AGENTS – NEVER TRUST A SPY

Parson's mobile phone rang and on the other end was the thunderous voice of Control. "Mate, you and Delaney are coming out of retirement. Come into my office tomorrow at 8:00 A.M.".

Parsons and Delaney were there at 7:50 A.M. Parsons took out a Marlboro cigarette, lit it and had a few puffs. Delaney says to Parsons "What's this all about Bill?"

Parsons replies "I don't really know Jack, except that we're apparently coming out of retirement, but I guess we'll find out soon enough!"

As Control's secretary says, "You can go in now gentlemen. " Parsons stubs out his cigarette in the adjacent ashtray.

Control says "Well, my good mates you're both coming out of retirement whether you like it or not! Tomorrow you've got a passage booked on a freighter to take you to St. Petersburg arriving on Friday. There you are to investigate a couple of Russians whom we are not sure whether they are double agents or not. We know they are Russian spies for sure! Their names are Alexis Ivanov and Anastasia Petrov, and their addresses are 55 Gorokhovaya Street and 78 Voznaxensky Avenue, near the Winter Palace, respectively. Do you have any questions?"

Parsons says "Yes, how long do you expect this to take because we've got a family trip to Australia planned for eight weeks' time? "

Control replies "Well, it depends on how long your piece of string is mate!"

Control then hands Parsons and Delaney their tickets for the freighter "Northward" leaving at 10:00 A. M. Friday.

The passage was calm and consequently quick with St. Petersburg in view by 4:00 P.M.. They steamed along the shores of the Neva Bay in the Gulf of Finland and islands of the river delta. They noticed that the elevation of St. Petersburg was in places no higher than 13 feet and reasoned that this was probably the reason for its numerous floods before the St. Petersburg Dam was built.

"Did you know that Vladimir Putin was from St. Petersburg and was a Russian spy. He probably still is, I don't think they ever stop. Once a spy always a spy I say. Never trust a spy – I reckon not even their own governments should trust them!" Parsons says to Delaney.

"Yeh, I reckon you're right on the ball there Bill. Never trust a spy - I like that. You know you and I are spies!" replied 'Dumpey' Delaney.

"Righto, let's get onto the job in hand. I think I had better contact C to get a few more agents onto this one as there is a lot of to- ing and fro-ing in St. Petersburg Jack".

"You can say that again!" Retorts Jack.

"Did you hear where Joe Biden is calling Putin a killer "says Jack to Bill.

"Yeh, well, it's an established fact that he ordered the poisoning of Alexander Litvinenko and the murder of Anna Politkovskaya, Dmitri Sergei and Sergei Skripal and they're just the four that we know of for sure!" Replies Parsons.

"O. K. let's get started on this one Jack. You know the sooner we get started the sooner we finish, and I can get to Oz and watch the Ashes where they'll probably thrash us again!" States Parsons.

Delaney replies "Yeh, they'll no doubt thrash us in the sledging department as well!"

"Well, I suggest we don't nab Ivanov and Petrov here in St. Petersburg or we'll have an international incident on our hands and probably end up in a Gulag in Siberia somewhere, although the Ruskies reckon they don't have them anymore, but I'll bet they still do!" Stated Parsons.

"Darn Tootin!" Replied Delaney.

"O.K. let's just observe them for a while and see what gives "says Parsons.

"You know what Bill, they always send their agents out as couples and the females are always drop dead gorgeous, maybe the blokes are too, I don't know about that!" Replies Dumpey.

"You're right about that Jack, I suppose we do the same with ours, come to think of it. Actually, that Aussie Rebecca James who was back in Prague is a bit of all right if you ask me. The only problem is she speaks Australian!"

"They also seem to make their agents work together in infiltrating high end political and social groups, so we better get ready for some inconsequential chit-chat Bill "Delaney says.

"Yeh, righto! That's easy to get ready for "Replies Bill.

The next day Parsons and Delaney were looking out of the window of their hotel room when they noticed Ivanov and

Petrov standing in the Palace Square accompanied by another male figure.

"Jack would you please hand me those field glasses as that other bloke looks strangely familiar."

"Holy hell!" says Parsons. "That's Jim Middleton from MI6. Now we've really got our work cut out and we're gonna need those reinforcements for sure!"

So, it's GAME ON IN ST. PETERSBURG!

Parsons and Delaney donned their overcoats and pulled their collars up high to disguise their faces as much as possible and also put on their bearskin hats with earmuffs for the same reason as well as to combat the cold as snow was falling on the Winter Palace and in the Palace Square.

"Bloody Hell, I'll be glad when this is all over and I can get to Oz for a bit of warmth and sunshine and a pint of good cold Fosters "mumbles Parsons through his blue lips.

"Yeh, I wouldn't mind coming with you Bill if I can get a leave pass!" Replies Delaney.

"Bring the missus with you" retorts Parsons.

"Yeh, I suppose I could it just doubles the expense".

"Forget the expense you are gonna need a break after this little episode" states Parsons.

"Yeh, I guess you're right again. "Jack replies.

"Hey Jack, I think on the strength of seeing Middleton I think we need a drink. Let's find a pub around here!" Says Parsons.

"Sure thing Bill, I thought you'd never ask, although I've heard Russian beer is crap, that's why they drink so much

Vodka and also to stay warm. Jeez it's cold here!" States Delaney.

"Let's try this one, the Bluzhdayushhiy Forward. With a name like that it's got to be Russian, and it might be warmer. "says Bill as the snow tumbles down accompanied by some heavy sleet.

They open the heavy doors to the pub and trudge inside and it is indeed warmer, and noisy and smoky and Parsons suspects there is a fair amount of marijuana in it too.

They order a couple of pints of Hoegaarde White and take a smell and a sip.

"It's not too bad "says Jack "I'm sure I've had worse somewhere, but I can't recall where!"

"Yeh, you're right "says Bill" I think we'll hold back on the Vodka for a while".

"Now with Middleton I think we'd better inform C to see what he wants us to do. Hopefully he'll give us some information and contacts so we can get into the social circles of Ivanov and Petrov so we can suss them and Middleton out". "States Bill.

After another pint of beer, this time Zogovor Algorithm Maple plus Caramel, just for a change, the two MI5 agents retired to their room in the Petr.

"Jack, you know – even though C said that Middleton was O.K. as he was here working for MI6 I think we should be wary of him as I've always thought he was a supercilious prat of the first order and I wouldn't trust him as far as I could throw him!" Parsons blurts to Delaney.

"D'accor!"Replies Dumpey.

"I don't think we'll get up too early tomorrow before we go out as I think it's best to let the sun get up a bit before we venture out and I assume the Ruskies and Middleton will be doing the same!" exclaims Parsons.

"I'm with you there" replies Delaney.

"O.K. lights out I'm hittin' the sack Jack" says Parsons to end the day and night.

In the morning Parsons checked his phone and C had texted the details they required for the social contacts for Ivanov and Petrov, he also said I'll see if I can arrange a meeting.

Delaney questions Parsons with"How's your Russian as I presume Ivanov and Petrov will be speaking Russian? "

"Yeh, well mine's passable, I did that crash course at King's College before we left.What about you ? Come to think of it I didn't see you there" states Parsons.

Delaney replies" No, I came down with a dose of 'flu and was still contagious and didn't have time to do it. Anyway, I'll record what I can and you can translate it!" exclaims Delaney.

The next day a text appears on Parsons phone from C stating that he has arranged a meeting with the Mayor of St. Petersburg the American politician Richard David "Rick "Kriseman who is the 63rd mayor of St. Petersburg inside the Winter Palace at 10:00 A.M. tomorrow.

The day dawned and the two MI5 agents had their breakfast at the Petr hotel and then trudged slowly across the snow and ice of the Palace Square and entered the Winter Palace.

"Crikey Bill, no wonder they had a revolution!" Delaney exclaims to Parsons as they walk towards the Armorial Hall and the Ambassador's staircase of the Winter Palace." I've never seen so much gold and gold leaf in my life" continues Jack.

They check their watches and then Rick Kriseman arrives.

"Hello Rick, nice to see you again" starts Bill.

"Yeh, likewise Bill it must be at least a couple of years since we met in London" says Kriseman in his American drawl.

"Sorry, Rick this is my MI5 colleague Jack "Dumpey" Delaney who I've been through hell and high water with, and we're still together." states Parsons.

"Glad to meet you, Jack. "replies Kriseman.

"Now, what can I help you guys with?" questions Kriseman who is also a CIA agent as well as a politician.

"As you no doubt know from CIA we are here to check out Alexis Ivanov and Anastasia Petrov and also Jim Middleton and his relationship with them" says Parsons.

"Yeh, yeh, yeh CIA have told me all that !"says Kriseman somewhat irritatingly.

They then started to ascend the stairs to the upper floor of the Winter Palace when what sounded like three gunshots reverberated through the building.

"Bloody Hell!" exclaims Kriseman as Ivanov and Petrov race helter-skelter down the stairs with their Lugers smoking.

The British agents and Kriseman ran up the stairs to the upper floor where they saw the body of a man lying on the floor with bullet wounds in his forehead and blood oozing onto the floor. Parsons attended to him to no avail as there was no pulse. After assessing that he could not be revived

Parsons looked through his coat for some sort of ID but there were no papers not even a wallet.

He said to Kriseman" Do you know this bloke Rick?"

Kriseman answers "Well sort of. I've seen him around town a bit and I think he's Vadim Bakatin who was head of the KGB from about August 1991 till December 1991 for a period of 96 days." replies Kriseman.

"Well in that case what's this all about? I can only assume Bakatin knew something about Ivanov and Petrov that they didn't want revealed" says Parsons.

"I think I'll check with C and probably best if you check with Langley, Virginia and see what they come up with as well." commands Parsons.

Meanwhile Jack had run out into the Palace Square following the two Russians. Once outside they placed their Lugers inside their coats and met up with Jim Middleton. Delaney got as close as he could without being suspicious. He overhears Ivanov say to Middleton in English "We've just got rid of that traitor Bakatin before he revealed to the Brits that we are Soviet spies and I'm a bit suspicious of you Middleton. So, we'll be watching you, so don't do anything stupid. Do you know what I mean?" Ivanov states forcefully.

With that Middleton pulls up his coat collar and says I'm going to retire it's too damn cold out here for me! I'll see you later.

Petrov cuttingly remarks "Oh, that's funny I thought the heat was just being turned on James!"

Meanwhile Jack couldn't hear what the threesome were

saying, but shortly afterward he followed them to their hotel where he waited in the lobby for some time until Middleton came out into the lobby.

Delaney says "Hi Jim! What are you doing here?"

"Mornin' Jack I was just talking and catching up with a couple of friends who are over from Australia. "Lies Middleton.

Parson says "Where abouts in Australia do they come from? Because I'm going over there when this is finished!

"I think they're from Perth on the West Coast!" Lies Middleton again.

"Yeh, it's the most isolated capital city in the world, which is good when we have a pandemic "says Parsons.

"Would you like a coffee? There's a good café in the square?" Parsons says to Middleton.

"O.K., sounds like a good idea" replies Middleton.

The three of them – Parsons, Delaney and Middleton sit and order their coffees from the waitress at the café where Parsons thinks he'll bait Middleton to see if he can catch him hook, line and sinker as he knows he is lying.

As they take a few sips of their coffees Ivanov and Petrov walk past them without acknowledging Middleton.

Parsons says to Middleton "Aren't they your two Australian friends Jim? "says Bill.

"Yeh, that's them" replies Middleton.

"It's rather funny that they didn't acknowledge you isn't it?" questions Bill.

"Oh I think they're pretty shy" lies Middleton again.

"O.K. but I heard them talking in the square earlier and

I thought that their accents were more Russian than Australian. How do you explain that? "says Bill.

"Dunno!" exclaims Middleton.

"Well I think I'm going to have a serious talk to C about you James and we'll see what comes of that. "says Bill knowing that it would blow his cover and send him running.

Parsons rings C and explains the situation about Middleton. C says "Well mate I think that you and the other agents better keep tag on Middleton 24/7 and go wherever he goes"

Delaney and Parsons arose at 5:00 A.M. and had breakfast at the hotel breakfast bar which looked out onto the square opposite Middleton's hotel. After a while a young attractive female came down for breakfast and it was Rebecca James.

"Hi fellas I heard you two were here. I've been assigned here with you as things have quietened down in Prague since you two cockatoos left!" she says.

Parsons replies "Great to see you again Bec. Tell me would you do me a favour and go across to the hotel opposite and ask if a Jim Middleton, you may know him from MI6, is in. If he's not in ask them where he is today, "requests Parsons.

"Sure thing Pars. I'm onto it like a limpet. "Quips James.

She promptly walks across to Middleton's hotel and almost as quickly returns and says that Middleton was not there and he didn't say where he was going.

Delaney says "looks like he's done a runner, probably to Moscow!"

"O.K. well what do we do for the rest of the day? questions Bill.

Rebecca says "Well I'm going out sailing in the bay for

a few hours soonish and you can come with me!" exclaims Rebecca James.

So the threesome venture down to the harbour where they board a lovely sixty foot catamaran yacht made by Alumarine in France called "CAT-CH US IF YOU CAN".

The day is fine but cold with a breeze of about fifteen knots coming from the North. The Neva Bay had started to freeze partially in places and there was the occasional small iceberg floating in the bay.

"All aboard!" declares Bec. "Do any of you have sailing experience?" she asks.

Parsons replies. "Yeh I've sailed for a number of years around Devon and Cowes."

Delaney replies. "Me too. I was a deckie in the 2000 Sydney to Hobart. We didn't come anywhere but it was great fun sailing with the Aussies!"

"Okey Dokey!" says James." We should be Ridgie – Didge then, so long as we don't do a Titanic! Tally Ho! Off we go! Cast -off!"

So off they sailed all rugged up into a stiff northerly. Rebecca was the skipper and she ordered a round of rum for everyone on board which was greatly received by one and all. After manoeuvring around a couple of icebergs they then had to counteract an outgoing freighter, although technically power should give way to sail, but James decided that it was bigger than them and so gave way.

As it passed she noticed a familiar figure on the deck holding onto the rail and smoking a cigarette.

"Hey fellas, that's Jim Middleton unless I'm mistaken and I'd bet my last wombat that I'm not!" she exclaimed.

Shortly after the Aleutian passed Parsons yelled " We can't grab him here in Russian territory and waters, not even if we get Interpol onto it pronto, so we'll have to get onto C and see if the Brits can get him in International or British waters."

"How about another round of rum Jack? It warms the cockles of me heart!" she says.

Bill immediately rings C and explains the situation.

C says "We'll most certainly try and do that as soon as they enter international waters. What's the name of the vessel?

Parsons says "It's the Aleutian!"

C replies "O.K. we're onto it mate!

A couple of Navy gunboats and a fast destroyer were dispatched straightaway from Edinburgh to engage and board the Aleutian.

Shortly after the Aleutian hit the international waters it was engaged by a shot across its bows by one of the British gunboats and one of the officers cried out over a megaphone." Cut your engines and prepare to be boarded forthwith !"

Parsons said to Delaney" This is exactly what we didn't want to precipitate - an international incident. Now we have one!"

"Yes, well we had better try and mitigate it as best we can. "says Delaney.

The Aleutian immediately turned hard to starboard and headed back towards Russian waters to get out of international waters at full steam and speed. As the Aleutian started to turn to starboard a Russian 'Charlie 'class submarine surfaced on its port side with five officers on deck shortly, all armed with AK-47 Kalashnikov's and a PKP PECHENNES machine gun at the ready, after it surfaced.

Also, as the sub. surfaced a Kamov helicopter arrived overhead the Aleution.

The Aleutian was of course no match for the British gunboats, but the British knew their restrictions as far as maritime law was concerned and didn't sail into Russian waters.

The captains and crew of the gunboats watched this through their binoculars and observed a person being winched aboard the Kamov Ka-15.

The Naval commanders in Britain were notified and this was subsequently relayed to C, who let Parsons and Delaney know.

On receiving the news from C Parsons said to Delaney "That'll be Middleton and he might be hard to track from here. We best get our radar tracking this one and find out where it lands and get Jamesey to track Middleton from there and report back."

Meanwhile, back in St. Petersburg, the mayor, Rick Kriseman was trying to get some justice about the killing of Vadim Bakatin by Ivanov and Petrov in the Winter Palace, but he knew it was going to be a hard road as they were KGB agents and the KGB would oppose it with all their might. Nevertheless, he fought it as hard as he could. His councillors told him not to be stupid as the KGB were not averse to bumping of people, even if they were mayors of St. Petersburg.

Back at sea the Kamov Ka-15 had started its flight back.

Rebecca James had guessed that it would land at the Russian naval base on Kotlin Island at Kronstadt and so had it under surveillance. Her guess was correct. However, on landing Middleton was whisked away by a Mikoyan MiG – 35 long range jet plane to an unknown destination which kept Rebecca James on her toes with even more surveillance.

Rebecca is with Parsons and Delaney in the Palace Square when she exclaims "Crikey, strewth I'm as dry as a dead dingo's diaphragm, let's pop into the rubbidy and sink a pint or two of Foster's."

To which parsons replied "Crikey, strewth you Aussies do have a good turn of phrase!"

They lined up the first set of Fosters and Rebecca downed hers in quick smart time. Whereupon Delaney comments "Geez Bec you didn't waste any time downing that one !"

"Just normal back in Oz when the heats on Dumps. Let's line up the next lot and get rid of them!" states James.

After doing so Rebecca says "Please excuse me fellas I've got to go – Japanese bladder or something!"

She locates the Ladies and enters where she walks into one of the cubicles and sits and takes out her mobile phone and Googles information about the Mikoyan MiG-31 and -35 and the Sukhou - Su -37 as she didn't have any knowledge of them.

Google said the Mikoyan MiG- 31 is one of the fastest fighter jets in the world and also one of the only ones able to fire long-range air-to-air missiles.

The Mikoyan MiG-35 is a huge upgrade of theMiG-31 with precise targeting and is compatible with AESA radar.

The Mikoyan MiG-35 is a stealth fighter with a range of 3,500 Km. and cruises at Mach2 which is twice the speed of sound. (Mach 1 is 340.3m/sec.or 761.23 mph. Mach 2 is therefore 680.6m/sec. or 1522.46 mph.)

The Sukhou Su-57 is a stealth fighter with a range of 3,500 Km. It can cruise at Mach2 and is built with composite materials which reduces the number of parts and overall weight. It features a blended wing body fuselage and brings together the functions of a fighter jet and a strike aircraft. The higher manoeuvrability and supersonic cruise capability are expected to give the fighter the upper hand in close-range dogfight scenarios.

So, Rebecca James thinks O.K. Middleton can be whizzed away at supersonic speed for a distance of 3,500 Km. without having to refuel. She also thinks well where can he go? The most likely is England, probably London or maybe even Berlin or Madrid to try and put us off the scent.

James observed Middleton at the departure flight desk at St. Petersburg Clearwater International Airport purchasing an electronic ticket. She then saw him board an Aeroflot flight whose destination was Heathrow, London.

She immediately rang C and told him about Middleton's movements.

C replied "O.K. mate we'll nab him when he lands, Thanks!"

The Aeroflot flight landed at Heathrow after three hours and forty minutes and Middleton was seized by Special Branch officers.

He was subsequently tried and imprisoned for life for

espionage and for being a doble agent. Which just goes to show one should NEVER TRUST A SPY.

Parsons and Delaney landed at Heathrow on a Virgin flight and said goodbye to one another and smiled as they both said in unison "MISSION ACCOMPLISHED, GAME OVER IN St. PETERSBURG!"

They then arrived at their respective homes to retire from MI5 never to investigate spies and double agents again.

Or is it so?

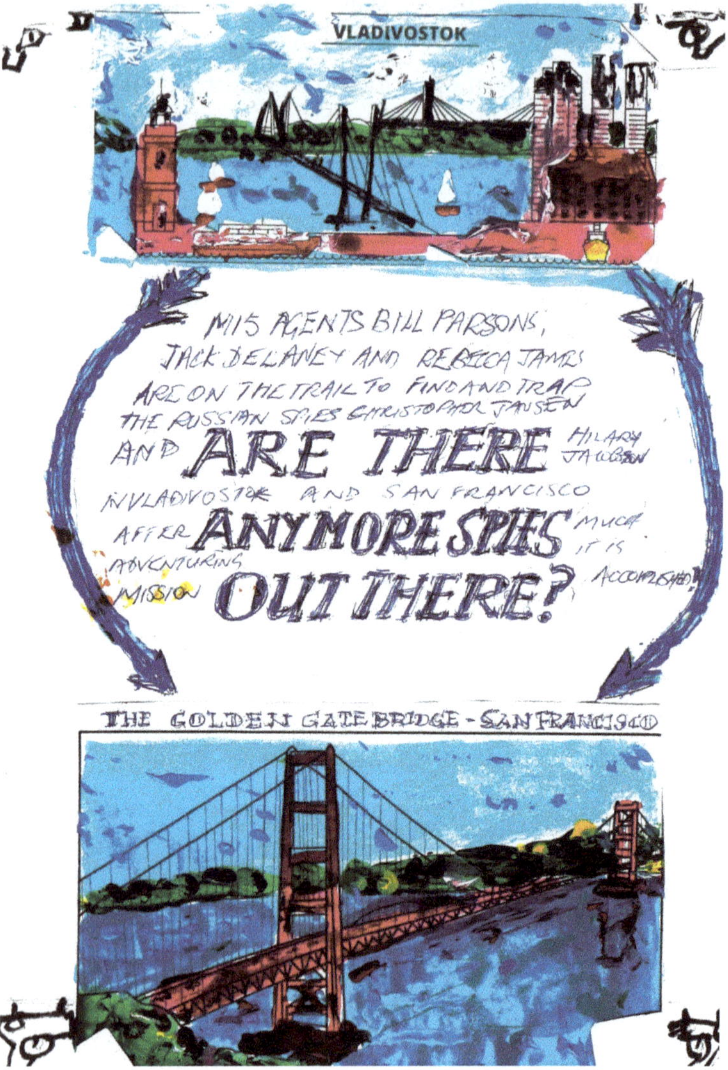

VLADIVOSTOK

MI5 AGENTS BILL PARSONS, JACK DELANEY AND REBECCA JAMES ARE ON THE TRAIL TO FIND AND TRAP THE RUSSIAN SPIES CHRISTOPHER JANSEN AND HILARY JACKSON IN VLADIVOSTOK AND SAN FRANCISCO AFTER ADVENTURING MISSION MUCH IT IS ACCOMPLISHED

ARE THERE
ANY MORE SPIES
OUT THERE?

THE GOLDEN GATE BRIDGE - SAN FRANCISCO

3

ARE THERE ANY MORE
SPIES OUT THERE?

PREFACE:

There have been countless spies and double agents through-out history. They have existed since ancient times. Spies were present in the Greek and Roman empires. During the 13th and 14th centuries, the Mongols relied heavily on espionage in their conquests in Asia and Europe.

Feudal Japan often used SHINOBI to gather intelligence. The SHINOBI or NINJA was a covert agent or mercenary in feudal Japan. The functions of the Ninja included espionage, deception and surprise attacks. Their covert methods of waging irregular warfare were considered dishonourable and beneath the honour of Samurais.

SAMURAIS were warriors that belonged to the noble classes of Japanese society. On the other hand, Ninjas would often belong to the lower classes of Japanese society.

A significant milestone in spying was the establishment

of an effective intelligence service under King David IV of Georgia at the beginning of the 12th century or possibly even earlier. Called 'mstovaris', these organized spies performed crucial tasks, like covering feudal conspiracies, conducting counter - intelligence against enemy spies, and infiltrating key locations, like fortresses, castles and palaces.

Aztecs used Pochteas, people in charge of commerce, as spies and diplomats, and had diplomatic immunity. Diplomatic Immunity is a form of legal immunity that ensues diplomats are given safe passage in the country they are stationed in and are considered not susceptible to lawsuit or prosecution under the host countries laws although they may still be expelled from that country.

Many modern espionage methods were established by Francis Walsingham in Elizabethan England. His staff included the cryptographer Thomas Phellipes, who was an expert in deciphering letters and forgery and repairing seals on documents without detection.

The 18th century saw a dramatic extension of espionage activities. It was a time of war: in nine years out of ten, two or more major powers were at war.

France under King Louis XIV (1643-1715) was the largest, richest and most powerful nation. It had many enemies and few friends. During the American Revolution (1775 -1783), American General George Washington developed a system to detect British locations and plans. Washington has been called "Americas First Spymaster."

Britain, almost continuously at war with France (1793-1815), built a wide network of agents and funded local elements trying to overthrow governments hostile to Britain. Napoleon made heavy use of agents, especially regarding Russia.

Modern tactics of espionage and dedicated government intelligence agencies developed over the course of late 19th century. The establishment of dedicated intelligence organisations was directly linked to the colonial rivalries between the major European powers and the accelerating development of military technology.

Integrated intelligence agencies run directly by governments were also established. The British Secret Service Bureau was founded in 1909 as the first independent and interdepartmental agency fully in control over all government espionage activities.

By the outbreak of the First World War in 1914 all the major powers had highly sophisticated structures in place for the training of spies and for the intelligence information obtained through espionage.

Two new methods of intelligence collection were developed over the course of the war – aerial reconnaissance and photography and the interception and decryption of radio signals. The British rapidly built up great expertise in the newly emerging field of signals intelligence and codebreaking.

In the Second World War Winston Churchill's order to "Set Europe ablaze "was undertaken by the British Secret Service or Secret Intelligence Service, who developed a plan to train spies and saboteurs. Eventually this would become the SOE or Special Operations Executive, and to ultimately involve the United States in their training facilities.

DISCLOSURE: Information has been obtained and quoted from Wikipedia and the Irish Times.

ARE THERE ANY MORE SPIES OUT THERE?

Parsons and Delaney were both at their homes in London when Bill's mobile rings, so he answers it and says "Hi Jack – I won't say that when we're onboard a plane. What's up!"

"Oh I just thought I'd like to catch up. How about an ale at the local?"

"Sure thing! I'll see you there in about ten. I've just got a few bills to pay first. "says Parsons.

After Bill has paid his bills he and Delaney meet at the Rose and Crown hotel. They order a couple of pints of Guinness from Rosie, the affable barmaid and she brings them over to them where they are seated in the hotel lounge.

Jack says "How'd you get on Down Under Bill as I haven't heard from you since then?"

"Yeh, we had a great time down there. We watched the Ashes Tests where the Aussies trounced us two nil with one drawn match. They've got a pretty good attack with Cummins, Starc, Patterson, Behrendorf, not to forget the perennial workhorse Peter Siddle as well as Nathan 'Gary' Lyon to spin us out. "says Bill.

"Yeh, and their batting line-up is not too shabby with Smith, Warner, Cam Green and all the others. Actually, they can bat right through!" states Jack.

"Have you heard anything from MI5 lately, as I haven't?" enquires Jack.

"Nah, it's been all quiet on the Western Front, but I suspect that won't last for too much longer!" says Bill.

"You know what Bill, I was wondering if there are any more spies out there? "asks Jack.

"There always are Dumps but they never catch the good ones – they're too smart. I actually wonder If the Russians, and us of course, have sacrificial spies to sort of throw us off our guard?" questions Parsons.

"That's quite possible Bill, actually I'd never thought of that. Mmmmm!" muses Jack.

"You know we traditionally think of spies as British, Russian or German, but I've made out a list and they come from almost all over the world and I guess they've always got to get paid by someone, that would make for a very interesting money trail by gee!" states Parsons.

"What's the list Bill? "asks Jack.

"Rosie, let's have another round please pet" asks Bill.

"After Rosie brings the drinks I'll let you know!" says Parsons.

Parsons reaches into the right hand pocket of his brown corduroy trousers and pulls out a piece of paper with his list of spies.

"It's quite lengthy Jack, but I guess you've got time!" states Bill, after giving a characteristic twirl of his black moustache.

He goes on "These are not in any particular order:-
Sir Francis Walsingham.

- Christopher Marlowe.
- Mata Hari.

- Julius and Ethel Rosenburg.
- Melita Norwood.
- Virginia Hall.
- Fritz Joubert Duquesne.
- Klaus Fuchs.
- Belle Boyd.
- Sidney Riley.
- Harold 'Kim 'Philby.
- Oleg Gordievski.
- Aldrich 'Rick 'Ames.
- Ursula Kuczynski.
- Benedict Arnold.
- Rose O'Neill Greenhow.
- Nathan Hall.
- Carl Lody.
- Elizabeth van Lew.
- Richard Sorge.
- William G. Sebola.
- Rudolf Abel.
- Sir William Stephenson.
- Larry Wu-Tahi-Chin.
- John Walker Jr.
- Lhi Mack.
- Noshia Gowadi.
- Robert Hansen.
- Ana Montes.
- Alexander Litvinenko.
- Edward Snowden.
- You Xiarong Shannon You.

- Vladimir Putin.

"Phew!" Exclaims Parsons.

"Like me you probably know a few of them. The rest you had better Google "Parsons suggests.

"Yeh, well I've heard of a few of them – Putin obviously, Snowden, Ames, Fuchs, Philby, Reilly, Mata Hari, Walsingham but I did not know that Marlowe was a spy. what did he do?" quips Delaney.

"The Irish Times said that while there is no direct evidence that Marlowe was a spy, there is plenty of circumstantial evidence. Along with long absences from university, accounts from the university show that he spent lavishly on food and drinks at a time when his own income would not have supported it. He was also arrested in 1592 for his involvement in the distribution of counterfeit coins in the Netherlands. He was sent to be dealt with by the Lord Treasurer but there was no charge or imprisonment. This may have been because it was another of his spying missions. If we add to this his reputation as a drinker, a brawler who was often in trouble with the law, and a lady's man Marlowe starts to sound like an Elizabethan James Bond. "recites Parsons.

"Righto then. I didn't know that!" remarks Jack.

"By the way, it looks like there were a lot of females spies. I counted about ten in that list "comments Jack.

"Yes, I think you're right there Jack, Very interesting, Mmmm" thinks and says Bill.

"By the way who spied on Adam and Eve when they committed the 'original sin' whatever that was! Thinking about it, it must have been our God, but how would he have told a human unless the human had an epiphany, or more likely an erroneous illusion that a God told him. Don't get me started on religion. It's caused some good in the world but it's also caused a lot of hatred and wars and the deaths of millions of people!" goes Bill.

"Sure thing!" replies Jack.

"I might ring C and make an appointment to see him sometime. Do you want to be in it? "says Parsons.

"O. K. and I'm pretty flexible time wise at the moment "comments Delaney.

Parsons rang C's secretary and arranged an appointment for a couple of days' time at 9:00 a.m. He then texted Jack and told him. Jack texted back and said "That's fine."

Bill and Jack were both in C's office at 8:55 and Bill pulled out a fag and offered one to Jack who replied "No thanks, trying to give them up!"

C's secretary contacted C and said that Bill and Jack were there and he replied "send them in!"

They entered and C greeted them and asked how they were. They both replied that they were fine.

"Well then what can I do for you!" states C.

"We were both thinking it's been pretty quiet since the Middleton episode and surely there must be something going on as there are always spies out there somewhere "replies Parsons.

"Actually, there are some covert episodes going on at the moment and Rebecca James is onto it in freezing Vladivostok! 'says C.

"She reckons it's bigger than Ben Hur over there and wants some reinforcements, so I'm afraid you two are coming out of retirement again. Take it as a compliment, because I can't think of any better agents in MI5, MI6, Special Branch or SOE to send. Just as well you had your time down under mate as Bec says it's damn cold, she actually said "Frigid as an icy pole" Damn Aussies you've just got to love them!" said and thought C.

"Any way it's pretty cold there as they get winds from Eurasia and the Himalayas, so make sure you rug up. Although there's plenty of action with Vlad. being a port for the Pacific region and end / start for the Trans-Siberian "informs C.

"I've got your air tickets to Vlad. Leaving with Cathay Pacific from Heathrow at 9:00 a.m. so it's a comfortable hour to start, except for getting through the traffic, but presumably you'll be getting a cab and they know how to get through it!" exclaims C.

"How long is the flight to Vladivostok?" enquires Parsons.

"All going well, with a tail wind it should be twelve hours thirty minutes, but don't ask me what time it lands with time zones and all! Although I'll have to look into it because I'll need to know. Actually I'll just ask Jean and then we'll all know "says C "I'll just phone her now".

Jean, C's secretary replies quickly "Sir, the flying time is 12hours 46 minutes and London is nine hours behind making arrival in Vladivostok midnight!" reports Jean.

"Thanks Jean!" says C. "Righto then my old mates I suggest you get a cab from the airport to your hotel. At least the cab will be heated "says C.

So Parsons and Delaney get the cab from Heathrow and all the time in it Parsons is thinking "Damn the no smoking in these cabs, but I can see the reasons why."

However as soon as they get out of the cab, he lights up a cigarette and has a few drags before entering the airport terminal. Delaney refrains.

"O.K. lets order a cab to the hotel, I'm knackered!" States Parsons.

They actually didn't have to order one as there was a long line of Lada taxis outside the terminal.

"Bill, you do the talking as your Russian is better than mine. "says Jack.

"Mmmm "replies Parsons.

He approaches the first cab and speaks to the driver.

"Pree-vyet, pa- zhai-staot vezi nas v otel 'Lotte. Spa see-ba "says Bill.

Meaning "Hello, please drive us to the hotel Lotte".

Whereupon the cab driver says "Certainly Sir!" in perfect English.

Delaney is looking up his Lonely Planet guide and he recites it to Parsons as they travel in the cab to the hotel.

"Vladivostok was founded in 1850 as a Russian military outpost and was named Vladivostok (variously interpreted as "Rule the East "or" Lord of the East" or" Conquerer of the East)" It's forward position in the extreme south of Russia inevitably led to a role as a port and naval base. It has a cool climate due to winds from the vast Eurasian landmass in winter, also cooling the ocean temperatures. Summers are warm, humid and rainy due to the East Asian monsoon. Average rainfall is 840 mm (33 in). Winters are dry. The city's main industries are shipping, commercial fishing and the naval base. A very important employer and a major source of income is the import of Japanese cars".

They arrive at the hotel Lotte, pay the cabbie, enter the sumptuous hotel, check in and retire for the night in separate rooms.

The next morning C rang Parsons and said "Bill we believe there are a couple of Russian agents who are in Vladivostok en route to the US. Their names are Christian Jansen and Hilary Jacobson and they are staying at your hotel, room fifty five I believe. Rebecca James is also staying there but she hasn't given me her room number yet, and I think she knows Jansen and Jacobson from Prague."

"O.K. "says Bill "We'll keep them under surveillance!"

Bill and Jack caught up with James over lunch and after finishing they all took a cab to the port.

It was a fine sunny day with a slight zephyr but it still had a pretty high wind chill factor. so they found a café with some shelter and despite the cold they sat outside where they could get a better view of the port entrance. When they had finished their coffees they checked their mobile phones and James looked up and there were Jansen and Jacobson, who were accomplices of Popovich and Curtis, but they were only small fry then and since then they've been dealt with these two have moved up in the world of espionage.

So, the MI5 agents decide to follow and observe the Russians. Jansen and Jacobson moved to the cruise ship Costa Serena which is the biggest ship to berth at Vladivostok and can take over three thousand passengers. It was due to embark for San Francisco shortly.

The MI5 agents watched them board and Parsons texted C and told him of the Russian's plans.

C texted back and said "O.K. you guys better fly to San Francisco and watch them there."

During the flight aboard Aeroflot Delaney asks Parsons "What do Russian spies do in America now?"

Bill replies "I think they want to disrupt Western life and destroy NATO. They have also tried to influence the American Presidential elections for example in the 2016 Trump campaign the Russians created false accounts that favoured Trump and disparaged Clinton and in 2018 the Trump administration expelled sixty alleged Russian spies and closed the Russian consulate in Seattle as they believed the consulate was serving as a key base for Russian intelligence operations. Also in the 2020 Presidential Election Russia denigrated Biden's candidacy."

"All right, so it does still go on!" exclaims Jack.

They landed at San Francisco airport and got a cab to the Marriott hotel at Fisherman's Wharf and checked in there.

Bill, said "I'm knackered Jack. I'll see you in the morning."

"Righto mate, I'll see you then "replies Jack.

In the morning the three MI5 agents gather for breakfast at their hotel. They all order porridge followed by scrambled eggs on toast and flat white coffee.

Bill says to Rebecca "Hey Bec, C says that Jansen's a bit of a womaniser"

She replies "That's interesting, maybe I can play him along and get a few secrets out of him if he takes the bait."

"Well it's worth a try, not really much to lose only your life!" quips Jack.

"Yeh, and what's a life worth now. Probably not even a pinch of pelican poop!" says Bec.

"Oh, you Aussies are laughable" states Jack.

"Righto Bec, how are we going to arrange this. I think you can sit at the café outside table and when he comes out ask him for a light and take it from there Bec. "says Bill.

"Yeh, sounds like a plan Stan!" replies Bec.

The next day Bec starts to carry out the plan. Jansen arrives and lights up her cigarette and then he says "I notice you're alone. Do you mind if I join you?"

Bec says "No, it's most certainly lonely here in San Fran. For a single girl from Oz."

Jansen replies "Oh, I thought I detected an accent, but I didn't know whether it was Australian, New Zealand or South African.

"Geez mate! I don't mind you calling me a Kiwi, but a bloody South Afreekan! I draw the line at that. You might as well have said that I'm from Timbuktu and I can't even buck one let alone two and my name's Rebecca not Tim!" says James trying to put him in his place.

"Oh, well now I know where I stand !" says Jansen with a smile on his face.

"What are you up to for the rest of the day? "He questions.

"Nothing really, what do you suggest? "asks Bec.

"Oh, I thought maybe we could hop on a train and go to Alaska" He says with a cheeky grin on his face.

Bec thinks to herself I'm starting to like this bloke even though he's a Russian spy. He's not bad looking either. But, I had better watch it as that is not a good sign and he's as sharp as a tack and a womaniser to boot so he has probably been in this territory many times before. Bec thinks 'Make a note to myself – Watch it mate! '

They hopped on a cable car and travelled over the Golden Gate Bridge and were amazed at the skyscape with the towering Salesforce building at 326 m and the Transamerica building at 260 m and wondered what would

happen if San Francisco had another earthquake like the one in April 1906, although they supposed the buildings had been designed and built to withstand earthquakes of a higher magnitude since then. They were also impressed with the expanse of the bay and the amount of traffic on the roads and could also see the fog starting to drift in around the island of Alcatraz.

They get out of the cable car and because it was a hot summers day they headed for the Lucky Chances Casino in the hope of air conditioning and a lunch time meal.

As they walk towards the casino Jansen puts his arm around Rebecca's shoulder. She doesn't rebuff him but thinks 'This is nice, I think I might ply him with a few drinks and maybe he'll unwittingly unload a few Soviet secrets. '

They enter the plush casino and the comfort of the air conditioning.

Bec says "You probably don't think about it much Chrissy being Scandinavian but this aircon. even though it makes things cool inside it makes things hotter outside and so adds to global warming or is it GLOBAL WARNING!" She emphatically states.

She carries on before Jansen can reply "However, you know there has been global warming and ice ages before – they come and go, it's just that man has speeded up the warming."

Jansen replies, now that he has the chance, "Yeh I guess you're right there Bec. However, the abolition of internal combustion engines and using electric cars should help."

Bec counters with "I don't know about that one as I wonder how much energy is used and how much pollution is produced in making the batteries."

Jensen parries with "Fair point Bec however the powers that be are thinking of putting all our polluting manufacturing on another planet and that should help us!"

Bec almost explodes with infuriation "Well I'll be damned!, What ? We'll pollute the rest of the universe in the process. Why not start at home and pollute less by using alternative energy sources?"

"O.K., I don't have a problem with that, but I'm not the one you have to convince. I think it's the multinational capitalists and governments that you've got to deal with!" replies Christian.

"Don't get me started on a philosophical discussion / argument about the pros and cons of capitalism and communism! All I'll say at this stage is that communism doesn't work very well because people in general are greedy. I think it only exists now in Cuba and look at them. They drive cars that are about sixty years old and have old, dilapidated buildings and ramshackle casinos. To their credit they do have good Havana cigars and I suppose in the main they are mostly happy with their lot. Fini, at the moment" exclaims James.

Bec carries on with "Stone the crows and starve the lizards I'm as dry as a dead dingoes diaphragm, I think I'll line up a few rounds of Fosters!" with the intention of getting Jansen inebriated.

Jansen replies with "You wouldn't be from Down Under would you?"

"Too right!" replies Bec quickly.

She then goes across to the bar tender and says "We'll have a couple of rounds of beers, a full strength Fosters for the bloke and a Heineken Zero for me followed by a bottle of Xanudu merlot from Margs. And two glasses please mate "The bartender questions" What and presumably where is Margs. madam? "

She thinks "You imbecile!" but doesn't say it, instead she says politely" Why it's Margaret River in Western Australia, sir !"

"Oh yes, they do make fine wines there, especially reds I believe" He replies.

She thinks "You better believe it kiddo, much better than your Nappa Valley stuff!"

She thinks Jansen will be pretty well done by the time he finishes his two glasses of full-strength beer and two glasses of wine. And he was done!

"Howsh itsh goinsh Becsh?" says Christian.

"Pretty good Chris, howsh yoush goinsh?" she answers.

"Neversh beensh bettersh matesh!" He attempts to say.

She then baits him with "Suppose if you were a Russian spy, what would you be doing in America mate?"

"Welsh Aushie Iish thinksh Iish wouldsh bring downsh thatsh Biden Bloke andsh getsh Trumpsh baksh cosh he'sh easier to handleshhh."

Bec then says "Why don't you and Hilary come here for dinner tomorrow night at 7:00 p.m. and I'll see if Bill Parsons can join us too."

"Okey Dokey Becsh "replies Jensen.

After departing the casino and finding their own ways home Rebecca James rings C and tells him what is happening.

C replies "Well my old mate I think we'll get MI5, the FBI and CIA to give them a very warm welcome!"

Seven O'clock rolled around and the four of them are seated at their table having drinks when they are interrupted by a contingent from MI5, FBI and CIA who subsequently handcuff Jansen and Jacobson and take them away.

They were subsequently tried, convicted and sentenced to life imprisonment in the Federal Penitentary for being Soviet spies and agents.

Bec, Parsons and Delaney all said "MISSION ACCOM-PLISHED!" and also "Let's head for home!"

Bill and Jack added "And retirement!"

HONG KONG

NEVER FALL IN LOVE WITH A SPY

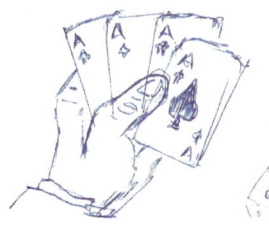

| 7 | 7 | 7 |

4

NEVER FALL IN LOVE WITH A SPY

PREFACE:

The sport of cricket has a known history beginning in the late 16th century, having originated in south-east England, it became the country's national sport in the 18th century and developed globally in the 19th and 20th centuries. Cricket is the world's second most popular sport after association football (soccer).

Governance is by the International Cricket Council (ICC)which has over one hundred countries and territories in membership although only twelve currently play Test cricket.

Cricket was probably created during Saxon or Norman times by children living in Weald, an area of dense woodland and clearings in south – east England that lies across Kent and Sussex. The first definite reference to cricket is dated Monday, 17th January 1597 ("Old Style "Julian date, the year equating to 1598 in the modern calendar.)

There have been several speculations about the game's origins, including some that it was created in France or Flanders. The earliest of these speculative references is dated Thursday, 10 March 1300 and concerns the future King Edward II playing at "creag and other games "in both Westminster and Newenden. It has been suggested that "creag" was an Old English word for cricket, but expert opinion is that it was an early spelling of "craic ", meaning "fun and games in general". Cricket was possibly derived from bowls by the intervention of a person with a bat trying to stop the ball from reaching its target by hitting it away.

A number of words are thought to be possible sources for the word "cricket. "The name may have been derived from the Middle Dutch krick (-e), meaning a stick, or the Old English crice or cryce meaning a crutch or staff, or the French word "criquet "meaning a wooden post. Heiner Gillmeister says it derives from the Middle Dutch phrase for hockey, (kriik ket) (i.e. "with the stick chase.")

Cricket was introduced to North America via the English colonies in the 17th century. It was introduced to the West Indies by the colonists and to India in the first half of the 18th century. It arrived in Australia almost as soon as colonisation in 1788. New Zealand and South Africa followed in the early 19thcentury.

The game continued to spread throughout England. The original form of bowling (i.e. rolling the ball along the ground as in bowls) was superseded sometime after 1760 when bowlers began to study variations in line, length, pace, swing and spin. The first international cricket game was between the US and Canada in 1844.

In 1859 a team of leading English professional cricketers set off to North America on the first ever overseas tour and, in 1862, the first English team toured Australia. Between May and October 1868, a team of Aboriginal Australians toured England in what was the first Australian cricket team to travel overseas.

Lords cricket ground, commonly known as 'Lords ', is a cricket venue in St. John's Wood, London. Named after its founder, Thomas Lord, it is owned by the Marylebone Cricket Club (MCC) and is the home of Middlesex County Cricket Club (MCCC), the England and Wales Cricket Board (ECB), the European Cricket Council (ECC) and, until August 2005, the International Cricket Council (ICC).

Lords is widely referred to as "The Home of Cricket" and is home to the world's oldest sporting museum.

Hong Kong, officially known as the HONG KONG SPE-CIAL ADMINISTRATIVE REGION OF THE PEOPLE'S REPUBLIC OF CHINA (HKSAR) is a metropolitan and special administrative region of the People's Republic of China on the eastern Pearl River Delta of the South China Sea. With over 7.5 million residents of various nationalities in a 1,104 square kilometre (426 sq. miles) territory. Hong Kong is one of the world's most densely populated places.

Hong Kong became a colony of the British Empire after the Qing Empire ceded to Hong Kong Island at the end of the First Opium War in 1842.

The Opium Wars were two wars waged between the Qing

Dynasty and the Western powers in the mid-18th century. The First Opium War which was fought between 1839 and 1842 between the Qing and Great Britain, was triggered by the dynasty's campaign against the British merchants who sold opium to Chinese merchants.

The Second Opium War was fought between the Qing, Britain and France, 1856-1869. In each war the European forces modern military technology led to easy victory over the Qing forces with the consequence that the government was compelled to grant tariffs, trade concessions and territory to the Europeans.

The wars and the subsequently imposed treaties weakened the Qing dynasty and Chinese government and forced China to open specified treaty ports (especially Shanghai) that handled all trade with the Imperial powers. In addition, China gave sovereignty over Hong Kong to Britain. The colony expanded to the Kowloon Peninsula in 1860 after the Second Opium War and was further extended when Britain obtained a 99 - year lease of the New Territories in 1898. As a special administrative region, Hong Kong maintains separate governing and economic systems from that of mainland China under the principle of "one country, two systems."

Originally a sparsely populated area of farming and fishing villages, the territory has become one of the world's most significant financial centres and commercial ports.

It is the world's tenth largest exporter and ninth largest importer. Hong Kong has a major capitalist service economy characterized by low taxation and free trade, and it's currency, the Hong Kong dollar, is the eighth most traded currency in the world. Hong Kong is home to the second highest number of billionaires of any city in Asia, and the largest concentration of ultra – high – net worth individuals of any city in the world. Although the city has one of the highest per capita incomes per se, severe income inequality exists, as well as growing housing unaffordability and shortage among the population. Hong Kong is a highly developed territory and ranks fourth on the UN Human Development Index. The city has the largest number of skyscrapers of any city in the world, some of which are:- (1) The International Commerce Centre 484m, 1588 feet and is the 12th tallest building in the world. (2) Two International Finance Centre 415.8m, 1364 feet. (3) Central Plaza 373.9m, 1331feet. (4) The Center 346m, 1227 feet. (5) Bank of China Tower 315m, 1135 feet. (6) Cheung Kong Centre 292.8m, 928 feet are some of the tallest buildings in Hong Kong. Its residents have some of the highest life expectancies in the world. The dense space led to a developed transportation network with public transport rates exceeding 90%. Crime in Hong Kong is generally low. Crime in Hong Kong is often associated with the Triads. Common triad related crimes include extortion, illegal gambling, drug trafficking and racketeering. One of the world's largest triads 'SUN YEE ON ", was founded in Hong Kong in 1919 and is reported to have 55,000 members worldwide. Sun Yee On's rival organisation, '12K Triad' was formed in Guang-zhou, Guandong China in 1945 and relocated to Hong Kong in 1949.

British organised crime groups known as the 'WIDE

AWAKE FIRM 'and the 'INNER CITY JIBBERS 'specialize in jewelry thefts and pickpocketing operate in Hong Kong.

China – officially The People's republic of China is a country in East Asia. It is the world's most populous country with a population of 1.4 billion. China covers an area of approximately 9.6 million square Kms. It is the world's third largest country: -

- President – Xi Jinping Trending
- Capital – Beijing
- Gross Domestic Product – 14.34. Billion US Dollars
- Currency -Renminbi
- China is divided into 23 Provinces with two special administrative regions – Hong Kong and Macau.

Chinese authorities have been criticized by political dissidents and human rights activists for widespread human rights abuses including political repression, mass censorship, mass surveillance of their citizens and violent suppression of protests. China is the world's fastest growing major economy. It is the world's largest manufacturer and exporter. The nation has the world's largest standing army – the People's Liberation Army with a reserve personnel of 510,000 and 660,000 paramilitary.

China is first in the world in total number of millionaires and second in millionaires.

KGB WEAPONS: -

1. AK-47 later adapted as the KALASHNIKOV automatic rifle. it is officially known as the AUTOMAT KALASHNIKOVA and is a gas operated 7.62 x39 mm assault rifle developed in the Soviet Union by Mikhail Kalashnikov in the aftermath of World War Two. The number 47 refers to the year it was finished.

   Even after seven decades, the model and it's variants remain the most popular and widely used rifles in the world because of their reliability under harsh conditions, low production cost compared with Western weapons, availability in virtually every geographic region, and ease of use. The AK- 47's accuracy has always been considered" good enough "to hit an adult male torso out to 300m (328 yds)

2. VSS – special sniper rifle.

3. THE KAKAROV PM is a simple and sound design, which is considered to be one of the best compact pistols of all time. While not extremely accurate and lethal at ranges beyond 15-20 metres it is still a formidable and reliable self – defence.

4. A BALLISTIC KNIFE is a specialized combat knife with a detachable self-propelled blade that can be ejected to a distance of several metres by pressing a trigger or operating a lever or switch on the handle. Originally developed as a weapon for Soviet and Eastern Bloc military special forces.

5. 2B25 'silent '82mm MORTAR SYSTEM.

6. SPETSNAZ SPECIAL FORCES are similar to the US

Army Rangers. It is a Russian umbrella term for Special Forces which is used in numerous Russian speaking post-Soviet states. Historically, the term referred to special operation units controlled by the new military intelligence service the GRU. It is the primary elite unit of the Russian military forces.

Their commonly used weapons are: -

1. Some versions of the AK-47 rifle. The AK-47 weighs about 8 pounds and has a 30 round magazine capacity.
2. Short barrelled AKS -744 Carbine. Also known as the "KRINK". It has a nifty side folding stock.
3. Some have a slightly different AKM fitted with a GP-25 grenade launcher. The AKM is a modernized version of the AK-47 firing 7.62 mm rounds up to 383 yards.
4. Although less commonly used today, some still prefer the SVD DRAGUNOV which fires 7.62 mm rounds and can hit targets up to 1312 yards out.
5. Another rifle used by the Spetsnaz is the SVDS DRAGUNOV, which is an advanced, lighter version of the SVD with a folding stock. It was originally designed for Russian paratroopers – the VDV. The Russian Airborne Forces or VDV is a separate branch of the armed forces of the Russian Federation. First formed before World War Two, the force undertook two significant airborne operations and a number of smaller jumps during the war and for many years after 1945 was the longest airborne force in the world.

6. Troops of the Russian Airborne Forces have traditional sky blue berets and blue striped tops and are called 'Desent 'from the French 'Descente'. There are 72,000 + paratroopers.

7. The bolt action SV-98 sniper rifle, which the Spetsnaz has been using far more frequently. It has a scope with a range of 1,100 yards.

8. For stealth missions Spetsnaz are more likely to carry the VSS VINTOREZ silenced super rifle. It fires a heavy 9x39 mm round but is not as accurate at long-range shots. Also called the "THREADCUTTER "it is a marksman's rifle featuring an integral sound suppressor originating from the Soviet Union, it was developed for clandestine operations. It is a gas operated select -fire rifle. It uses a sub-sonic9x3mm cartridge to avoid sonic boom, the bullet is very effective at penetrating body armour. For carriage and concealment, the rifle is dismantled into three main components carried in a special briefcase.

9. The PKP PECHENNES general purpose machine gun is Spetsnaz's main squad weapon. It fires a 7.62x54 mm round and began use with the Russian military in 2001. the PKP is similar to the US M249 machine gun.

10. Another rifle the Spetsnaz carry is a 9 mm AS Val. It fires subsonic rounds which means the bullet travels below the speed of sound (343meters per sec.) and conceals the snapping sound of supersonic weapons.

11. They also use the SR-3 which is a shortened version of the AS Val. It fires a 9x39 subsonic round. It is

intended for concealed carry and can be fitted with a sound suppressor.

12. For a sidearm Spetsnaz operations generally carry the 9 mm GSL-18. It is made for close combat, has an 18 round magazine and bullets that can pierce body armour.

DISCLOSURE: Information has been obtained and quoted from Wikipedia and Business Insider.

NEVER FALL IN LOVE WITH A SPY

It is the summer of 2021 in London, England and Jack 'Dumpey' Delaney, a MI5 agent, rings Bill Parsons, another MI5 agent.

"G'day Bill I was thinking that I might go to Lords today and watch the first day of the first test between us and the Aussies, are you up for it? "questions Delaney.

"Sure thing!" replies Parsons "How about you come around here and we'll catch the tube to Lords."

"O.K. I'll see you soon" replies Jack enthusiastically.

They duly arrive at Lords cricket ground and enter the Taverners bar attired in their Lords blazers and red and yellow ties.

They approach the bar and notice Rebecca James, who is an Australian and another MI5 agent, at the bar with a couple of male companions.

Bill whispers to Jack

"One of those blokes looks vaguely familiar. Do you know any of them?

"Nope!" replies Dumpey.

They approach Bec and say hello to her.

Bec replies. "G'day fellas, turned out nice again. By the way this is my dad Russell and a mate of his from New Zealand, Graham Andrews."

They all shake hands and ask how they are to the reply of fine thanks.

Russell James then asks Bill and Jack "What'll it be fellas?"
They reply "A pint of dark ale thanks Russ."

"Bec explained earlier that you guys work with MI5. Sounds like interesting work. "says Russell James.

"Oh yeh, it has its moments." replies Bill.

"What line of work are you guys in?" enquires Jack.

"Oh, I'm with Interpol in Australia and Grahams with SIS that's their Secret Intelligence Service, although it's not too secret if you ask me!" retorts Russell.

"Well, you're pretty well on the ball there Russ. "Answers Andrews.

"Well, you know Rebecca James then, she's been working on a couple of assignments with us recently and I must say you're damn good too Bec. "Bill reports.

"Yeh, well you're right there and for sure she's the bees knees. Mind you, you got a bit emotionally involved with that spy Jansen, but luckily you realized and snapped out of it. You now reckon that one should NEVER FALL IN LOVE WITH A SPY!"

"Too true mate!" says Bec.

"Well enough about work. "says Graham Andrews. "How do you think the cricket's going to go?"

"I don't really know" says Bill.

"The Aussies have got a pretty good attack with Cummins, Pattison, Starc, Abbott, Hazlewood and Lyon to spin us out and their batting line-up is not too shabby with Dave Warner, Tim Paine, Cam Green, Travis Head, Moise Henriques, Steve Smith. Geez, where does it end, they can bat right through!"

"Yeh, but they have had some monumental batting collapses too" exclaims Russell James.

"That's true. "says Bill

"Well it should be an interesting game!" continues Bill.

"It's my shout! The same again thanks love. "he says to Jaquie, the affable bar maid with the rosy cheeks.

Before the start of play Bill has a look at his program and sees that the English Test squad has thirty seven players.

He passes his program to the Kiwis and says "whom of these do you know?"

They peruse the program and reply "Not many actually, on Joe Root, Eoin Morgan, James Anderson, Jonny Bairstow, Stuart Broad, Chris Jordan, Ben Stokes and Chris Woakes. How many is that? I think eight out of thirty-seven. There must be some unknown quantities in your squad, not like the Aussies!" emphasizes Russell James.

"You could say that" says Bill "but I reckon that we've got a home ground advantage and the weather might help us out too." Delaney pops up with.

"Hey, there's Justin Langer walking into the Aussie's change rooms. He adds a lot of experience and calmness to the Aussies. I think he's a West Australian to boot too! says Rebecca.

"Yeh, you're right there Bec. Funny how you always notice the good-looking blokes, isn't it?" questions Andrews.

"Yeh, well you're correct there. However, I've noticed you're not too bad with the girls too!" responds Bec.

"Touche!" replies Andrews.

Graham Andrews buys another round and they then proceed to sit in their allotted seats to watch the match.

The Aussies won the toss and have sent the Pommies into bat and have them reeling at three for ten after four overs.

Bec says "Geez, the Aussie attack is pretty impressive they've got that ball moving at 140 to 150 miles per hour and that's on a dead English pitch!"

Parsons replies "Yeh and they have removed some of our best batsmen."

By the norming drinks break England had recovered somewhat by putting on another fifty runs but had lost another wicket to be four for sixty.

The Australian captain, Tim Paine, made a courageous decision to bring the spin bowler Nathan Lyon on at an early stage with Lyon taking another two wickets, both LBW's, for ten runs, bowling in tandem with Mitch Starc who had eight runs hit off his bowling.

At the lunch break Australia had England nine for 176 and were almost ready to have their openers padding up.

Russell James says "I'm just going to point Percy at the porcelain, I'll see you all at the bar for lunch shortly!"

Bec says "Sure thing, I'll just go and Powder my nose. "Which means the same thing as her father except they're in separate toilets!

After eating an enjoyable lunch washed down with a lovely Shiraz from Margaret River Estate, Western Australia they watch the start of the afternoon session of play.

After a little while Bec looks into the crowd and notices a

group that includes two Asian males and a blonde female and a male with pale complexions.

She says "That's funny, I didn't think that Asians apart from Indians, Packies and Bangladeshians were interested in cricket!"

"Yeh. "states Bill "Maybe they've just come to bet, some of the Chinese are mad gamblers!"

"That's true" says Bec" I think I might take a photo of them and send it to MI5 and see if they know them" which she does straight away.

A reply comes back almost immediately saying that the two Chinese men are Michael Lee and Jason Cheung who are spies from Hong Kong and the other couple are Caroline Kusinski and Vladimir Hotinski who are Soviet spies.

Include in the message was "Track them" Which they duly do.

Parsons then contacted C to tell him what was going on and also to say that they will need reinforcements to track the four of them 24/7.

C replies "No problem mate. 'I'll get it organised now!"

C organises Rebecca and Russell James and Graham Andrews and Steve Jacobs, another Kiwi to help with tailing the Chinese and the Russians.

Parsons and Delaney say in unison "GAME ON IN HONG KONG!"

C organises for MI5to find out which airline and what time the Chinese and the Soviets are leaving London for Hong Kong and texts Parsons, Delaney and Rebecca James.

They are leaving with Cathay Pacific Flight CX254 departing at 10:45 p.m. in first class which arrives in Hong Kong at 6:05 p.m. Hong Kong time says the text from MI5.

Parsons then arranges seats for himself, Delaney, Rebecca and Russell James, Graham Andrews and Steve Jacobs in first class with good access to view the Chines and Soviets.

The next evening, they all depart Heathrow aboard Cathay Pacific flight CX25 at 10:45 on a direct flight to Hong Kong. They have a good view of the Chinese and the Soviets. After a supper break in which Parsons and company had cups of tea and the Chinese also but the Soviets had a couple of stiff Vodkas, nothing much seemed to happen except their quarry fell asleep so Parsons lot thought they may as well do the same and they did.

After two hours Bill awoke and as he had an aisle seat, he thought he would stretch his legs and go for a bit of a walk. In doing so he passed the Chinese and the Soviets and noticed that they were all fast asleep and that Vladimir Hotinski was snoring quite loudly on occasions. He proceeded to the rear of the plane where he ordered a flat white coffee from one of the air hostesses who he found was an Australian from Sydney and her name was Katie Barlow. She was a tall attractive brunette who had done a swap through Qantas and Cathay Pacific with one of their hosties.

The rest of the flight into Hong Kong was uneventful and they flew into Kong Kong airspace at 6:00 p.m. Hong Kong time and had a fantastic view of Hong Kong harbour with its numerous skyscrapers. On landing at Hong Kong

International Airport, they disembarked and Katie Barlow thanked them for flying with Cathay Pacific and wished them a pleasant stay in HK.

They then grabbed a taxicab to their hotel which was the Venetian Casino Resort, which is one of the world's largest casino resorts featuring a premier shopping mall, gondolas and gondoliers, with canals running alongside mock Italian streets and more than 3,000 rooms. It also has well trained dealers and appetizing snacks and drinks from the bars.

Whilst Parsons, Delaney and Rebecca James were having breakfast next morning Katie Barlow came and joined them.

Bill asks her what she does for a living and she replies "Oh, I work for Interpol and ASIO, the hostie bit is a cover and I understand you are all with MI5 and are on the trail of Lee, Cheung, Kusinski and Hotinski. Well, I've been after them for a while too. They have been tripping to Hong Kong for some time now, but I haven't been able to ascertain what they are on about yet. However I'll bet my last dollar and platypus that they are up to no good! I can tell you that from HK they fly up to China quite regularly and stay for a few days before flying back to HK and then back to Moscow."

Whilst they were having their coffees Cheung, Lee, Kusinski and Hotinski walked past them and entered the hotel lobby. Parsons and company hastily put their coffee cups down and followed the Chinese and the Russians into the lobby area where they overheard them saying they would like to order a ferry to Macau this morning. Parsons, Delaney, Rebecca and Russell James, Steve Jacobs and Graham Andrews all jumped into a Maxi Taxi and said to the driver "Follow that cab!

They all ended up at the ferry terminal to Macau and boarded it just before it embarked for Macau. As the conditions were calm and the ocean flat, they were in Macau in fifty minutes where they all disembarked. Parsons whispered to his people "We had better watch it in trailing this lot, so that they don't notice us on their trail I think it may be best if we split up say with Jack and I, Steve and Graham and Bec and Russell so it won't look so obvious."

So that was how they trailed the spies in Macau.

After disembarking the Chinese and the Russians headed for the Casino Babylon at Fisherman's Wharf.

"I told you those Chinese are mad gamblers" States Jack.

"Well these two most certainly are!" says Bill.

They watched as Lee and Cheung gambled away for some time on the roulette and blackJack tables and noticed that they had a few minor wins to add to some larger losses whilst the Soviets were more interested in drinking Vodka.

Shortly after this there was a confrontation where one of the Soviets pulled out a ballistic knife which he threw at Parsons and the other Russian pulled out a GSL-18 revolver which was fired at Delaney, confirming their suspicions that the Russians were KGB and Spetsnaz agents. Parsons and Delaney immediately and instinctively dropped to the ground and rolled, as they were trained to do, and intuitively reached for and fired their Enfield No. 2 Mk7 revolvers in a frenzied fusillade of fire. Bill and Jack were luckily unscathed, but Vladimir Hotinski was killed on the spot and was left lying in a pool of his blood. The Chinese and the remaining Soviet then hurriedly left the gambling area and Jack Delaney noticed a piece of paper on a nearby table which he quickly confiscated and read, Gill Parsons observed this and asked Jack what it said. Jack replied "Hardcastle.

"What in the Dickens does that mean? "Questions Bill.

"Damned if I know! I think I'll have to Google that one" replies Jack.

Which he promptly does and after sorting out the wheat from the chaff he comes up with the Hardcastle family history which states that it is an English (Yorkshire) habitational name from a place name in Middle English 'hard, difficult, inaccessible, impregnable, or perhaps cheerless plus castel, castle, fortress, stronghold. "Perhaps Hardcastle Garth in North Yorkshire or Hardcastle Crags in West Yorkshire, although either or both of these could be from the surname. It has been suggested that the surname could have come from a Roman fort forming part of Hadrian's Wall in Northern England.

"Well what do you think of that!" exclaims Jack.

"They're our options are they with this Hardcastle thing? I'm really none the wiser. Perhaps time will tell "answers Bill.

"Yeh, they say all things come to pass. Which reminds me, did I tell you the one about that, "says Jack.

"No!" replies Bill.

"O.K., there's this Emir in Saudi Arabia and he gathers all his wise men and says to them 'What is a saying that I can use on all occasions?' After some deliberation they say" All things come to pass !" And so, it is my friends – all things come to pass. "States Jack.

"So be it! That could be another one "says Bill.

Bill then says "This Hardcastle thing has got me stumped.

I'm damned if I know what it's all about. I think I'll ring C and see if he knows anything."

He rings C and after a short delay due to the time difference between England and Macau he tells C about the Chinese and the Russians and the note they left on the table at the casino.

C replies "Mmmm, if you had asked me yesterday I also would have had no idea mate but I heard from one of our spi--, err agents in Beijing. It's funny though, all the so called world super powers and even smaller nations and countries have espionage and I suppose it keeps us all in a job and keeps the wolf from the door so it can't be all bad. Any how our agent in Beijing reckons that 'Hardcastle 'is an affiliation with the triad Sun Yee On and as well as gambling, drug trafficking, racketeering and sex exploitation you can now add espionage and no doubt murder."

Bill then says to C "Well how do we handle this?"

C replies "Don't ask me, you guys are the so-called experts. Just use your initiative!"

"O.K. then we'll do that!" says Parsons somewhat per-plexed and dumbfounded.

He mutters softly to himself, but it was overheard by Delaney "Hmph – use your intuition."

Jack says to him "What does that mean?

Bill replies "Damned if I know.I think I'll ask Barlow and see if she has any clues."

They subsequently meet up with Katie Barlow at breakfast and question her about Hardcastle.

She replies "Yeh, I do recall something about Beijing and

being involved with Sun Yee On. Apparently Hardcastle is a cover for all the Chinese spies so they can contact one another and the Chinese government without supposedly gathering any suspicion."

"Yeh, well it almost worked with us!" exclaims Parsons.

"If Jack hadn't seen that note that they supposedly left unintentionally on the table at the casino we wouldn't have known about Hardcastle. Mmm, you know I also wonder if it was unintentional and wonder if one of their spies wants to come in from the cold and defect to Britain or the United States. I think C should know about this possibility. "Parsons states forcibly.

He immediately rings C and with the time difference C answers somewhat confusedly "What, what and what do you want and who is it calling at this time of night? "

"Sorry sir it's Parsons and I forgot about the time zones, however I thought this may be important and MI5 may have to act on it soon if it comes to fruition."

"O.K. O.K. Out with it man!" says C now that he has found his senses and his voice.

"Sure, sure Sir, you know how the Chinese left that note about Hardcastle at the casino?"

"Yeh, yeh man get on with it!"

"Well, I thought it may have been intentional by one of them and they may want no defect but I don't know who it is or if there is more than one. If I am correct in my assumption, then no doubt we will be contacted. I just thought it best to advise you and you can think about making the necessary arrangements and maybe try and keep it away from the Press." says Parsons.

"Yeh, well keeping it out of the Press is sometimes easier said than done. So maybe we had better not converse on this matter anymore unless it is absolutely essential 'advises Control.

For some time, Rebecca James had been aware that Steve Jacob was having a relationship with a Chinese girl by the name of Susan Lee. Rebecca thought that she may be a Chinese spy and advise Steve of this and said "NEVER FALL IN LOVE WITH A SPY!" She also spelt out her reasons for this and this put an end to the relationship.

The following day Parsons had a phone call from Jason Cheung asking if they could meet at a nearby café at 10:00a.m.

Bill said "Surely. I'll see you there at 10:00."

They met at ten o'clock and Bill set the conversation in motion by asking "What's this about Jase?"

Cheung slowly reached into the inside pocket of his coat, which had Bill in a reflex action moving his right hand toward his Remington revolver. Cheung then slowly pulled out a page of paper, to Parsons relief, and started by saying "It's about my defection and this sheet of paper has a list of all the spies and double agents that I know of so hopefully my asylum will be granted."

He hands the sheet of paper to Parsons who peruses it methodically and says "O.K. you're in from the cold mate. Welcome!

He then texts C who alerts MI5, MI6, SIS, SOE and Special

Branch agents who had flown in to arrest Cheung, Lee and Kusinski and to also arrest as many of the spies and double agents on Cheung's list. Some of these had got wind of what Cheung was up to somehow or another and had vamoosed to Beijing and the protection of the Chinese government and so were considered untouchable by the British.

However, a sizeable number of them were arrested and jailed in Hong Kong, with 'never to be released 'stamped on their papers.

At the conclusion of all this Bill Parsons, Jack Delaney and Rebecca James all said unison

"MISSION ACCOMPLISHED, GAME OVER IN HONG KONG AND CHINA, LET'S HEAD FOR HOME!"

5

WHAT DOES A SPY THINK
AND DO NEXT?

PREFACE:

G OLF: Golf is a club and ball sport in which a player uses various clubs to hit a ball into a series of holes on a course in as few strokes as possible.

Golf unlike most ball games, cannot and does not utilise a standardised playing area, and coping with varied terrains encountered on different courses is a key part of the game. It is usually played over 18 holes, although a shortened version can be played over nine holes. Each hole on the course must have a teeing ground to start from, and a putting green containing the actual hole or cup 4,1/4 inches (11cm.) in diameter. There are other standard forms of terrain in between, such as the fairway, rough (or long grass), bunkers (or sand traps), and various hazards (water, rocks, trees, sloping lies, uphill and downhill) but each hole on a course is unique in its specific layout and arrangement.

Golf is played for the lowest number of strokes by an individual, known as stroke play, or the lowest score on the most individual holes in a complete round by an individual team, known as match play.

The modern game of golf originated in 15th century Scotland. The 18 hole round was created at the Old Course at St Andrews in 1764. Golf's first major, and the world's oldest tournament in existence, is The Open Championship, also known as the British Open, which was first played in 1860 at Prestwick Golf Club in Ayrshire, Scotland. This is one of the four major championships in men's professional golf, the other three being played in the United States: The Masters, the US Open, and the PGA Championship. Most countries have their form of an open championship, such as The Australian Open, The New Zealand Open, The Malaysian Open and The South African Open etc. The games ancient origins are much debated. Some historians trace the sport back to the Roman game of 'paganica ', in which participants used a bent stick to hit a stuffed leather ball

Others cite chuiwan ("chui "means striking and "wan "means small ball) as the progenitor, a Chinese game played between the 8th and 14th centuries.

THE STEAM ENGINE: -

A steam engine is a heat engine that performs mechanical work using steam as its working fluid. the steam engine uses the force produced by steam pressure to push a piston back and forth inside a cylinder. This pushing force is transformed, by a connecting rod and flywheel, into a rotational force for work. In general usage, the term 'steam engine 'can refer to either complete steam plants (including boilers etc.) such as railway steam locomotives and portable engines or may refer to the piston or turbine machinery alone, as the beam engine and stationary steam engine.

Reciprocating piston type steam engines were the dominant source of power until the early 20th century, when advances in the design of electric motors and internal combustion engines gradually resulted in the replacement of reciprocating (piston) steam engines in commercial use. Steam turbines replaced reciprocating engines in power generation, due to lower cost, higher operating speed, and higher efficiency.

The five most famous steam engine railway locomotives are 1) The Mallard, 2) The Flying Scotsman, 3) The Big Boy, 4) The Fairy Queen, 5) Stevenson's Rocket.

LNER is the London North-eastern Railway and is a British train company owned by the Department of Transport. It operates the Inter City East Coastline providing long-distance inter-city services on the East Coast Main Line from London's Kings Cross to Yorkshire, NE England and Scotland.

THE LEAR JET: -

The Lear jet is a Canadian - owned aerospace manufacturer of business jets for civilian and military use based in Wichita, Kansas, United States.

Founded in the late 1900 's by William Lear as Swiss

American Aviation Corporation, it has been a subsidiary of Canadian Bombardier Aerospace since 1900, which markets it as "The Bombardier Lear Jet Family. "The 3,000th Lear jet was delivered in June 2017.

In February 2021, Bombardier announced the end of production for all Lear jet aircraft but with the continuation of support and maintenance for aircraft currently in service.

HISTORY – Lear jet was one of the first companies to manufacture a private, luxury aircraft. Lear 's preliminary design was based upon an experimental American military aircraft known as the MARVEL, substituting fuselage mounted turbojet engines for ducted fan turboshaft engines. However, that preliminary design was abandoned for an abortive 1950 's Swiss ground-attack fighter aircraft, the FFAP-16.

The basic structure of the Swiss P-16 aircraft was seen by Bill Lear and his team as a good starting point to the development of a business jet and they formed the Swiss American Aircraft Corporation, located in Altenhein, Switzerland and staffed with design engineers from Switzerland, Germany and Britain. The aircraft was originally intended to be called the SAAC-23. The wing with its distinctive wing tip fuel tanks and landing gear of the first Lear jets were little changed from those used by the fighter prototypes.

Although building the first jets started in Switzerland the tooling for building the aircraft was moved to Wichita, Kansas in 1962. Bill Lear Junior stated that it took too long to get anything done in Switzerland despite the cheaper labour cost.

Lear jet was in a temporary office which opened in September 1962 while the plant at Wichita's airport was under construction. On February 7, 1963, assembly of the first Lear jet began. The next year, the company was named the Lear jet Corporation.

The original Lear jet 23 was a 6–8-seater and first flew on October 7,1963 with the first production model being delivered in October 1961. Just over a month later Lear jet became a publicly owned corporation. Several derived models followed with the model 24 first flying on February 24th,1966. On September 19th,1966 the company was renamed Lear jet Industries.

MERGER WITH GATE'S AVIATION:

On April 10, 1967, Bill Lears' approximately 60% share of the venture was acquired by the Gates Rubber Company of Denver, Colorado, for US $27,000,000. Lear remained on the company board until April 2, 1968, when the company was renamed Gate's Lear jet Corporation. In 1971 the first model 25 powered by a Garret TFE731-2 turbofan engine was flown. The aircraft later became the successful Lear jet 35. That year the company was awarded the President's "E "award for export sales.

In 1974, the world's Lear jet fleet had exceeded the one million flight hours mark and in 1975 the company produced its 500th jet, both industry firsts. By late 1976 the company increased monthly aircraft production to ten.

On August 24, 1977, the Lear jet 28 made its first flight. It was based on the Lear jet 25 but received a completely new wing fitted with winglets. These resulted in both improved fuel economy and performance and inspired the name "Longhorn "for the short-lived Lear jet 28/29 and for some of the more successful models that followed.

On April 19,1979 the prototype of the model 54/55/56 series made its first flight, and on July 7, 1983, a standard production model 56 set six new time - to - climb records for its weight class.

In 1984 Gates Lear jet announced the start of their Aerospace Division, a high technology endeavour. However, by the end of the year the company had ceased production of its commercial jets in an effort to reduce inventories. This lasted until February 1986 when the company headquarters were transferred to Tucson, Arizona, and production was restarted both in Wichita and Tucson.

On September 10, 1986, the Aerospace Division was awarded a contract to produce parts for the Space Shuttle main engine. In 1987 Gate's Lear jet was acquired by Integrated Acquisitions and the next year the name was changed to Lear jet Corporation. By January 1989 all production had been moved from the Tucson facility back to Wichita with an employment of 1,200.

ACQUISITION BY BOMBARDIER:

In 1990, Canadian company Bombardier Aerospace purchased the Lear jet Corporation. The aircraft were marketed as the "Bombardier Lear jet Family "On October 10, 1990 the Lear jet 60 mid-sized aircraft had its first flight, followed on October 7, 1995 by the Lear jet 45. In October

2007 Bombardier Lear jet launched a brand-new aircraft programme, the Lear jet 85. It was the first FAR Par1-25 all-composite business aircraft.

Bombardier celebrated the 45th Anniversary of the first flight by a Lear jet with 2008's Year of the Lear jet Campaign. One of its highlights was British Formula One driver Lewis Hamilton racing a Lear jet and winning an event at Farnborough Air Show.

On October 28, 2015, Bombardier announced cancellation of the Lear jet 85 programme. On October 11, 2021, Bombardier announced the end of production of all Lear jet Aircraft.

Bombardier also announced that they would continue to fully support the Lear jet fleet well into the future and launched the Lear jet RACER re- manufacturing programme for the Lear jet 40 and 45 aircraft.

- The Lear jet 75 Bombardier features: -
- The first private Executive suite on a jet aircraft.
- Honeywell TFE731-40BR engines Take-off thrust of 3850 lb ft Long - range cruise speed
- Range 2080 nautical miles
- Capacity – up to nine passengers
- Top Speed Mach 0.81 (Mach 1 is the speed of sound = 340.3metres per second {1,234.8 km. per hour} or
- 761.23 miles per hour)
- High Speed Cruise Mach 0.79 Typical Cruise Speed Mach 0.76
- Operating Altitude Maximum 51,000 feet

- Intra Cruise Altitude 45,000 feet.
- CODES: -
- Morse
- Huffman
- Genetic - DNA
- messenger RNA --proteins -genetic code
- Godel Code in mathematics
- Traffic lights and other colour coded objects.
- Acronyms.

THE ENIGMA CODE:

The enigma code was invented by the German engineer Arthur Scherbuis at the end of World War One. The enigma machine was a famous encryption machine used by the Germans during WWII to transmit coded messages. It allowed for billions and billions of ways to encode a message, making it incredibly difficult for other nations to crack German codes during the war – for a time the code seemed unbreakable.

Bletchley Park is an English country house and estate in Bletchley, Milton Keynes (Buckinghamshire) that became the principal centre of Allied codebreaking during the Second world war.

Bletchley Park celebrated the work of three Polish mathematicians who cracked the German Enigma Code in WWII – Marian Rejewski, Henryk Zygalski and Jerzy Rozyski.

The enigma code machines were a facility of portable cipher machines with rotor scramblers. The code was broken by the Polish General Staff Cipher Bureau in December 1932 with the aid of French-supplied intelligence material obtained from a German spy.

The enigma code worked as it has an electromechanical rotor mechanism that scrambles the twenty-six letters of the alphabet. In typical use, one person enters text on the enigma keyboard, and another writes down which of the twenty six lights above the keyboard lights up at each press.

During WWII, the estate held the Government Code and Cypher School (G C and C S) which regularly penetrated the secret communications of the Axis Powers – most importantly the German Enigma and Lorenz cyphers. Amongst its most notable early personnel the team of G C and C S team of codebreakers included Alan Turing, Gordon Welchman, Hugh Alexander, Bill Tutte, and Stuart Milner- Barry.

The nature of the work there was secret until many years after the war.

The main focus of work at Bletchley Park was in cracking the enigma code. The enigma machine was a type of enciphering machine used by the Germans to send messages securely.

Some historians estimate that Bletchley Park's massive codebreaking operations, especially the U-boat enigma, shortened the war in Europe by as many as two to four years.

It was so hard to crack as it was so sophisticated, and it amounted to what's now called a 76-byte

encryption key. One example of how complex it was: typing the same letters "H-H "(for "Heil Hitler ") could result in two different letters, like" L-N". That type of complexity made the mechanics impossible to break by hand.

The enigma code was so important as the Germans were convinced that enigma output could not be broken so they used the machine for all sorts of communications – on the battlefield, at sea, in the sky, and significantly with its secret services.

The British described any intelligence gained from enigma as "ULTRA "and considered it TOP SECRET.

WINSTON CHURCHILL: -

Sir Winston Laurence Spencer Churchill KG, OM, CH, TD, DL, FRS, RA, (30/11/1874 – 24/1/1965) was a British Statesman who served as Prime Minister of the United Kingdom from 1940 - 1941 during the Second World War and again from 1951 - 1955. Although best known for his wartime leadership as Prime Minister, Churchill was also a Sandhurst - educated soldier, a Nobel Prize winning writer and historian, a prolific artistic painter and one of the longest serving politicians in British history. Apart from two years between 1922 and 1924 he was a member of parliament from 1900 to 1964 and represented a total of five constituencies. Ideologically an economic Liberal and Imperialist he was for most of his career a member of the Conservative Party, which he led from 1940-1955, though he was also a member of the Liberal party from 1904- 1923.

Of mixed English and American parentage Churchill was born in Oxfordshire to a wealthy, aristocratic family. He joined the British Army in 1895 and saw action in British

India, the Anglo-Sudan War, Cuba and the Second Boer War, gaining fame as a war correspondent and writing books about his campaigns.

As First Lord of the Admiralty during the First World War, he oversaw the Gallipoli Campaign but after it proved a disaster he was demoted to Chancellor of the Duchy of Lancaster.

Widely considered as one of the 20th Centuries most significant figures,

Churchill remains popular in the U.K.

and Western World where he is seen as the victorious wartime leader who played an important role in defending Europe's liberal democracy against the spread of fascism. He was also a social reformer; however, he has been criticised for some wartime events – notably the bombing of Dresden when he vowed to set

'Europe ablaze ', and also for his imperialistic views including comments on race.

Churchill drank a lot of alcohol, and he could be defined as a "high- functioning alcoholic."

He also suffered from depression, and some said he suffered from bipolar disorder.

He also smoked a lot of cigars. His love of cigars began when he was serving in Cuba. He smoked as many as ten cigars a day and he believed cigars helped calm his nerves.

WHAT DOES A SPY THINK AND DO NEXT?

It is cold! It is wet! It is dark! It is Miserable! It is 2022! It is January! It is London!

In fact, it is the coldest wettest winter in history, but i don't want to spoil a good story by telling the truth or giving you facts, so i won't. However, it is windless so parsons and Delaney thank their lucky stars

Mi5 agents bill parsons and Jack Delaney are on another

Adventure but they don't know it

Yet but you the readers do!

They are seated in the London city gate hotel whose website says it is situated 0.4 metres from the gates of Kings Cross Station.

Bill says to Jack "well I'll go and Heave if that's 0.4 metres, I reckon it's got to be at least

Fifteen!" "yeh, you've got no opposition from me there" replies Jack.

So, they sit in the pub and wait for the next train to Edinburgh.

They order a couple of coffees then have their cold cuticles circle the Caldor cups of coffee to try and warm parts of them.

"You know c said that mi5 and 6 reckon there are a couple of Russian spies up at St Andrews

And we've got to check them out "states Jack. Yeh, i know but what i don't

Know is when we are going to

Take our retirement."

"Damned if I know, probably when we die is my guess!" remarks Jack.

They finish their coffees and look at their watches and both say, "it's almost time to jump on that train."

Whilst walking to their platform Jack says, "Hey Bill did you know that Kings Cross Station was built in 1852 by Great Northern Railway."

"No!" Replies Bill "That's a bit of trivia I could've lived without, but I can't now!"

Once at their platform which just happens to be the platform used by Harry Potter, that is platform 9 and ¾ they look at a wall sign showing the route from London to Edinburgh. It shows: - London, Peterborough, Doncaster, Hull Paragon, Leeds, Harrogate, Newcastle, Sunderland and Edinburgh and at the end of the line is Inverness.

They board their train at 10:00 a.m., not the Hogwarts Express but The Flying Scotsman which is a sleek Red and Yellow Azuma capable of travelling at 125mph.

The train immediately leaves Kings Cross them plunges into the short Gas Works and Copenhagen tunnels. It then accelerates through the outer London suburbs.

A few minutes after leaving Kings Cross it passes Emirates Stadium the home of Arsenal Football Club. Alexandria Palace with its large radio and TV mast is on the left ten minutes after leaving Kings Cross.

Jack then proceeds to give Bill a running description from his guidebook of what they can see on their journey.

"Soon suburbia will give way to open country, woods and

fields as the train powers up to 125 mph. It's a four track line but all trains have to squeeze into just two tracks to cross the Welwyn Viaduct which is something of a bottleneck. The woods and fields eventually give way to the flat Cambridgeshire fenlands.

As you approach Peterborough and cross the River Neve, 76 miles from Kings Cross the squat towers of Peterborough Cathedral are visible on the righthand side.

A few miles further south of Grantham is a sign which says the LNER A4 locomotive MALLARD set the world speed record for steam trains of 125.88 mph, a record which still stands today.

York Station 188.5 miles from London should now become visible."

Jack glances across to Bill and notices that he has fallen asleep. Jack thinks 'Oh well, I'll keep on reading aloud in case he wakes '.

So, he continues. "A blur at 125mph is the famous London to Edinburgh halfway sign on the right about seven miles from York.

At Durham the train crosses a viaduct giving superb views of Durham city

with its castle on the right-hand side.

As the train approaches Newcastle, the Angel of the North is just visible high up on a hill on the right hand side, It's a 66 feet high contemporary steel sculpture by Sir Anthony Gormley erected in 1998.

At Newcastle the train slows and rumbles across the River Tyne into Newcastle Central, 288 miles from London.

The train races across the Royal Border Bridge over the River Tweed approaching Berwick. Designed by Robert Stephenson, this impressive 659-metre-long viaduct was opened by Queen Victoria in 1800. Just beyond the bridges over the Tweed the river flows into the North Sea.

Two and a half miles north of Berwick the train crosses the English – Scottish border marked by a colourful wooden board with the English and Scottish flags next to the track on the right-hand side.

The train is now rolling along the lovely Northumberland Coast right by the cliffs with the sea breaking on rocks below."

Jack then decides he may as well close his eyes as well and does so for a while and then wakes.

Jack wakes Bill and says "We'll soon be in Edinburgh mate!"

Bill replies "Sorry, I must have dozed off. That send-off we had last night must have caught up with me. C was plying me with the Balvene all night. He was having a few too but I guess he's a pretty big boy in more ways than one and can put it away!"

They alight from the train and head for the nearest car hire place where they hire a red Aston Martin DB 11 convertible which has a turbocharged 4 litre V8 with 503hp and 513 ft-lb of torque and has a top speed of 311 km./ hr.

They jump into the Aston with Bill in the driver's seat.

"O.K. Bill, let's head for St. Andrews and these spies and see what they are thinking of and figure out what they are up to next!" Says Jack.

"Yeh who knows what a spy is thinking and what they are up to next!" says Bill.

"You do realise we are spies Bill? "Questions Jack.

Bill starts her up and heads off towards St. Andrews occasionally opening up the DB11 and hitting 250 when he could on the narrow twisting road, so

they were soon at the seaside town of St. Andrews.

They immediately head for their accommodation at the No.14, that is number 14 Abbey St. St Andrews whose website says it offers accommodation with free WIFI, 500 metres from St Andrews East Sands Beach, 500 metres from St Andrews University and 300 metres from St Andrews Cathedral. It features four bedrooms, a flat screen TV, an equipped kitchen with a dishwasher and a microwave, a washing machine and four bathrooms with showers.

They turn into the driveway of No. 14 in the Aston Martin DB11, alight and head for reception where they show their credit cards and check into unit 2.

Jack quips to Bill "Hey, this is all right we should have brought our wives - they could have cooked our meals and done the washing up!"

"I don't think I'll tell them that you said that! Jack."

Meanwhile Bill's phone indicates that a text has arrived. It's from C saying that the two Russian spies are Dmitri Kosov and Anastasia Sochi, whom he supplies photos of, and says that they are staying at the same accommodation as them and they are also keen golfers.

Bill replies to C saying that he had better send Rebecca

James up as she is a good golfer, and they are only mid-week hacks.

C replies "I've already done that mate!"

They catchup with Beccie outside their unit and say they are off to the golf course as C has texted that the Russian spies are about to have a game of golf.

Bec says "I'll be there in about thirty.

I'm just going to pick up Katie Barlow at the airport. She's staying with me for a while. "The weather is fine with no wind, but there is still a bit of a nip in the air as St Andrews is further north than London. Bill and Jack think this will be ideal for golf after they rug up a bit.

Rebecca James and Katie Barlow arrive at the course and meet up with Bill and Jack.

"Do you want to join us and make up a foursome. If you're quick, we can tag along behind this couple who as you are probably aware are Dmitri Kosov and Anastasia Sochi!" says Bill.

They do so and tee off at the first at St Andrews and much to their amazement they all hit their ball onto the fairway with Bec's ball about forty yards out in front.

Bec says to Bill "I wonder what spies think about on a golf course? "

Bill replies "I don't really know but maybe it just gives their minds a bit of a break and they just think of hitting the ball and overcoming obstacles ahead "

"Yeh, in a way it's a bit like life!" .

"Mmmm, I hadn't thought of it like that, but I suppose you're right "says Bill.

Any how the game unfolds and transpires so they retire to the 19th hole, The Jigger Inn, and sit at a table next to Kosov and Sochi.

Bill leans across to his left and says to the Russians. "How did you go? Get your money's worth?"

Kosov replies "Yeh, sure did Sir. It was most enjoyable. How did you go? I noticed your female comrades hit a nice ball, Bill!"

Kosov saying Bill's name left Bill a bit perplexed as it seemed to him that the Russians knew who they were and that Kosov had let his guard down a bit. Bill thought let's see what gives from here.

"Yeh, they sure do. Sorry, I'm Bill Parsons and this is Jack Delaney,

Rebecca James and Katie Barlow. "Kosov thinks to himself 'Yeh I already know that the KGB informed us before we left Moscow. '

Jack then gets up to get drinks from the bar and says to Kosov and Sochi "Can I get you guys a drink? "

"Nyet, thankyou Jack we've got a vodka and a vodka and orange on order."

Bill and Katie are writing up their score cards when Jack returns with the drinks. "Thanks Jack!" Say Bill, Bec and Katie.

"How'd we score? "Questions Jack. "Not too badly. You guys both had

105's which off a handicap of 20 gives you 85 which is not too bad for St. Andrews. Katie had 82 minus 8 which gives her 74 and I had a 77 which off a five gives me 72 which is par here today!" says Bec.

After imbibing a couple of rounds they decide that it's time to leave and step outside just as an aeroplane fly overhead.

"Well stone the crows, starve the lizards, wobble the wombats derrier and fair crack of the whip that's that Liberty Bombardier Lear jet that was out at the airport today."

Dmitri Kosov retorts "You Osssies, the things you say!"

Bec responds with "You RUSSIANS, we could probably write a song about you!"

Bec says. "I think it's owned by Azeri Oil's Nasib Hasanov and that Jeremy Huch the first CEO and former president of B.P. Russia is on board.

As the Lear jet starts to head over the North Sea there is an almighty bang, and the aircraft explodes into a fiery ball of about a million pieces.

"Bloody Hec!" Exclaims Bec "What in the world's going on here!"

The remains of the plane hit the ocean 's surface and quickly disappeared with all members on board doing the same going down into Davey Jones Locker never to be seen again.

Shortly afterwards three Russian TUPOLEV Tu-95 bombers appear out of the sun (The Tupolev -95 {Russian Tynones tu-95} NATO reporting name "Bear". Is a large four – engine turbo prop strategic bomber and missile platform.)

Six (which is Russia's full contingent of these) MIKOYAN Mi -35 fighter jets also appear and then the Tupolev Tu- 95 and the Mikoyan Mi-35's proceed to strafe and bomb six oil rigs in the North Sea in close proximity to them.

Bec says "I'd better inform C of this pronto! It looks like World War Three's about to happen!" And she does. C answers Bec by saying "Well there's probably not much more that you can do! Just keep your head down and try and stay alive you're more use to me alive than dead! Let me know if you guys need any reinforcements for this one."

They all then walk to the 'Seafood Ristorante 'which is a modern glass

building with panoramic views of West Sands Beach and serves local seafood with an Italian twist.

They are seated at their table and order beers for the men and the ladies order a G and T. After perusing the menu Anastasia Sochi says, "I've heard the risotto with clams and scallops is to die for."

Bec quickly replies "I'm not planning to die for anything real soon".

Anastasia replies almost as quickly "You can't be too sure about that darlink!" As a statement not a question.

Rebecca James 'phone then pings indicating an incoming text, so she quickly glances at it and is perplexed by what she sees.

"This is all gobbledy- gook it might as well have come out of an Emu's beak at Jabiru!" she exclaims. She then shows it to Katie Barlow who whispers to Bec. "You know it could be some sort of code meant for those Russian spies which you have inadvertently intercepted. It does happen, that's why we need to be so careful with these mobiles and computers, nothing is secure! What we need to do is crack this code somehow. Do you remember The Enigma Code, well that gave the Brit's a bit of a headache until they deciphered that one?"

"Bill and Jack who do we get onto for this one? I suppose C will know?"

"Yeh he will no doubt know and he'll probably put you onto the boffins at Croydon House namely Trevor O'Hehir, T'.B. sure, T'.B.sure!" says Bill with a chuckle.

So Bec sends the undeciphered text off to O'Hehir at Croydon and asks if they can decode it for her, but she also said not to send his reply by phone or e- mail for security reasons.

O'Hehir immediately texted Bec back saying "What's your address? "

Bec texted back number 14 Abbey St. St Andrews.

That afternoon an Mi5 agent knocked on number 14's door and said to Rebbeca "Here's an envelope with a note for you from C".

After the agent had left, she opened the envelope and read its contents.

It said the decoded message said.

"TOP SECRET FROM RUSSIAN KGB HIGH COMMAND. ALL AVAILABLE AIRCRAFT ARE TO ATTACK BRITAIN'S NORTH SEA OIL RIGS AND WIPE THEM OUT AND ALSO ATTACK THEIR LAND BASE SUPPLIES AND OIL REFINERIES IN BRITAIN AND SCOTLAND."

Then Bec, Parsons and Delaney all say in unison "GAME ON IN ST ANDREWS AND THE GAME ISN'T GOLF!"

Bec says "Holy Hell, this is going to be World War Three, I'm goin' back to Oz as soon as I can!"

Bill says "I think you'll be grounded by MI5 and C!" "Yeh, well we'll see about that my wallaby friend!" Bec replies.

They are then confronted with six VDV paratroopers landing in front of them with Kalashnikov AK-47's blazing and spurting out a fiery fusillade of bullets at them. The Russian spies Kosov and Sochi also grab their Makarov PM revolvers and start firing at the Brits.

Parsons, Delaney, James and Barlow instinctively hit the ground, roll and pull out their Enfield No. 2 Mk7 revolvers and fire at the Russian spies and paratroopers. Despite being down in numbers they get the upper hand and kill all the paratroopers and the Russian spies. Barlow is wounded with a shot to her right thigh but it is only in muscle and so readily treatable.

Meanwhile C had alerted Britain's military forces and had them on red alert for the Russian invasion. Their whole fleet of Lockheed F-38 Lightnings , Short 184 bombers, Bell Aircobras, Bristol Bowfighters, Eurofighter Tycoons, Hawker Harriers and Hunters, Boeing P-8 Poseidons and British Aerospace Hawk T1's scrambled from airfields around England and Scotland. As well the United States of America. Australian and New Zealand airforces and military were put on red alert.

SO, IT'S GAME ON WORLDWIDE!

Britain's First Sea Lord, Admiral Tony

Radakin commands all his fleet to be at the ready and sail

to engage Russia in the North Sea and surrounds. The fleet includes: -

- The Vanguard Class Warships – HMS 's Vanguard, Victorious, Vigilant, Vengeance
- Acute Class – Astute, Ambush, Artful, Audacious.
- Trafalgar Class – Trenchant, Tallent, Trump
- Surface Fleet – Aircraft Carriers
- Queen Elizabeth Class – Queen Elizabeth, Prince of Wales. Amphibious Warfare
- Albion Class – Albion, Bulwark
- Destroyers – Type 48 (Daring Class)
- Daring, Dauntless, Diamond, Dragon, Defender, Duncan
- Frigates -Type 23 (Duke Class) - Argyle, Lancaster, Iron Duke, Monmouth, Montrose, Westminster, Northumberland, Richmond, Somerset, Kent, Portland, St Albans
- Offshore Patrol – River Class – Tyne, Severn, Mersey, Forth, Medway, Trent, Tamar, Spey.
- Mine Countermeasures – Hunt Class – Ladbury, Cattistock, Brockelsby, Middleton, Chiddingfold, Hurworth, Penzance, Pembroke, Grimsby, Bangor, Ramsey, Blyth, Shoreham
- Coastal and Fast Patrol – P 2,000 or Archer Class – Archer, Biter, Sinter, Pursuer, Blazer, Dasher, Puncher, Charger, Ranger, TrumpeteR, Express, Example, Exploit, Tracker, Raider
- Scimitar Class – Scimitar, Sabre

You'd think with all these ships in the water that there wouldn't be room to move, but you'd be wrong!

They were all fuelled, armed and crewed and steamed out of different ports in England and Scotland towards the North Sea action.

Within ten minutes the F-38 Lightnings, the Eurofighter Tycoons the Harrier Hawkers and Hunters were engaging the Russian flying, fighting firepower over the North Sea. These aircraft included: - The Mikoyan MiG-29, 31 and 35, the Sukhoi Su – 24,25, 27, 30, 34, 35 and 57 jet fighters. Also the bombers – Tupolev Tu-160, 22M and 95 The AWACS (early warning and control aircraft.) Beriev A-50, Ilyushin Il -24, 80 and 82.

Electronic warfare planes – Antinov An- 30, Ilyushin I2-20, Myasishen M-55, Tupolev Tu-214,Tu-214R. Tankers – Ilyushin Il – 78.

Transport – Antonov An – 12, 22, 26,72,124, 140,148. Ilyushin Il -18,62, Let L - 410 Turbojet. Tupolev Tu- 134 and 154.

So, the battle went on, and on and on.

The British Prime Minister, after consulting his Allies, appeared on the BBC, looking as if he was having a bad hair day and said "We and our Allies are at war with Russia!" And being somewhat original he also said" We will fight them on the beaches, we shall fight them on the landing grounds, we shall fight them in the fields and in the streets, we shall fight in the hills; we shall never surrender and even if, when I do not for a moment believe this island or a large part of it were sub-jugated and starving, then our Empire beyond the seas, armed and guarded by the British Fleet, would carry on the struggle until in God's good time, the NEW World with all its power and might, steps forth to rescue as the liberation of the old.

We shall go to the end, we shall fight in France, we shall fight on the seas and oceans, we shall fight with growing confidence and growing strength in the air, we shall defend our Island, whatever the cost may be!"

Boris adds, almost as an oversight to most observers "With thanks to Winston."

So, the might and power of The United Kingdom was up against the might and power of Russia, or was it the other way around? Once again time will tell as all things come to pass!

So, Boris Johnston has Britain ready to fight anywhere. He also says that "The United Kingdom has fought battles everywhere and has won, not like the Americans who have started wars and usually lost them."

This sparked a quick call from Joe Biden on his hot phone from the White House.

Johnston then thought and muffled under his breath "You're just Biden, your time Biden and you're soon going to be trumped by Trump!"

So, the British nation fought on, the battles raged for months and countless oil rigs were lost in the North Sea and supply depots throughout the land, but the Brits eventually triumphed as they have a habit of doing. Bill, Jack Rebecca and Katie retired to the Rose and Crown in London and were having a drink or two when they all said together "GAME OVER IN ST ANDREWS, MISSION ACCOMPLISHED!"

WELL I DIDN'T EXPECT THAT!

BY RODNEY JAMES WHITE

MI5 AGENTS BILL PARSONS
JACK DELANEY AND REBECCA JAMES
ON THE TRAIL OF RUSSIAN SPIES.

6

WELL, I DIDN'T EXPECT THAT!

PREFACE:

Tennis is a racquet sport that can be played individually against a single opponent (singles) or between two teams of two players each (doubles). Each player uses a tennis racquet that is strung with cord to strike a hollow rubber ball covered with felt over or around a net and into the opponent's court. The object of the game is to manoeuvre the ball in such a way that the opponent is not able to play a valid return. The player who is unable to return the ball will not gain a point, while the opposite player will.'

Tennis is an Olympic sport and is played at all levels of society and at all ages. The sport can be played by anyone who can hold a racquet, including wheelchair users. The modern game of tennis originated in Birmingham, England, in the late 19th century as lawn tennis. It had close connections both to various field (lawn) games such as croquet and bowls as well as to the older racquet sport today called 'real tennis '.

The rules of modern tennis have changed little since the 1980's. Two exceptions are that from 1908 to 1961 the server had to keep one foot on the ground at all times, and the adoption of the tie-break in the 1970's. A recent addition to professional tennis has been the adoption of electronic review technology coupled with a point challenge system, which allows a player to contest the line call of a point, a system known as Hawk-eye.

A King Brown is 1) a 750 ml. bottle of beer often made in Darwin in the Northern Territory of Australia. 2) A species of highly venomous snake (Pseudechis Australis), native to northern, western and Central Australia. It is a robust snake up to 3.3m (11 ft) long. Its venom is not as potent as those of Australia's other dangerous snakes but can still cause severe effects if delivered in large enough quantities. Its main effect is on striated muscle tissue, causing paralysis from muscle damage, and also commonly affects blood clotting (coagulopathy). Often extensive pain and swelling occur, rarely with necrosis, at the bite site. Deaths from its bite have been recorded, with the most recent being in 1969. Its victims are treated with black snake (not brown snake) antivenom.

WELL, I DIDN'T EXPECT THAT!

Bill Parsons, Jack Delaney and Rebecca James are drinking champagne and eating scones with strawberry jam and cream at the men's singles Wimbledon final of 2022 between Roger Federer and Novak Djokovic who are having their warm-up hit.

Rebecca quips "I wonder if there are any spies here today. I think I'll text C and find out if he knows!"

Almost on cue her mobile pings indicating a text and it's from C saying "Bec, there are a couple of Russians at Wimbledon today whom we suspect are spies. Their names are Alexis Uson and Miranda Barton, I'll send photos of them and please keep them under surveillance 24/7. I'll send reinforcements with I.D., and I'll also send pictures of them for your reference."

After watching Federer defeat Djokovic in five sets, the MI5 agents decide to depart as they hadn't seen Usov and Barton. However, as they were passing through the exit gates Rebecca James spots Uson and Barton who were also leaving. She elbows Bill in the side and whispers "That's them!"

SO, IT LOOKS LIKE IT'S GAME ON AT WIMBLEDON AND THE GAME'S NOT TENNIS!

And the surveillance continues as the extra MI5 agents Jimmy Sommerville and Kerry Short are waiting outside the exit gates to greet Parsons, Delaney and James with their I.D. in hand.

So, surveillance is the name of the game and that's what the Mi5 agents do.

Parsons, Delaney, Sommerville and Short tail The Russians from the Wimbledon Tennis Club gates at a distance. Usov and Barton soon enter the Dog and Fox pub at 24 High St. in the heart of the Wimbledon Village. Likewise, the Mi5 agents enter and sit at a table near the Russians who are meeting up with another ten people, who they presume are Russians as well. Bec surreptitiously takes a photo of them and sends it to C and asks who they are.C texts back "They are Russian spies, so you have uncovered just about every Russian spy that we know of in England so something must be cooking. Be on you guard!"

Bec replies, "Righto Sir, but on the strength of this I think I'll have the contents of a couple of King Browns and I mean the bottles, not the snakes!"

"O.K. you do that Bec, you may as well get some enjoyment while you can and I think you are going to need more Mi5 agents to cover all these Russians although we are getting a bit stretched on agents to tell the truth!" says C.

James then approaches the bar and says to the bartender "I'll have a King Brown of VB thanks mate!"

The bar tender replies "This isn't exactly Earl 's Court matey but I'll see what I can do!"

After a quick search he says "Got one, how many glasses?"

Bec replies "Three thanks cobber!" She then grabs the bottle and the glasses and pours the golden amber into them with a generous head on all of them and says to Parsons and

Delaney. "Get you laughing gear around this my friends!" Which they duly do and reply together.

"Hey that's not too bad at all Bec, I can see why you drink it."

Jack in the meantime has secretly started his recorder on his mobile phone to overhear what the Russians are saying and of course will need Bill to translate it for him.

After ten minutes the Russians get to their feet and walk outside to the taxi rank and hop in a cab which departs. Jack Delaney, Bill Parsons, Rebecca Parsons. Jimmy Sommerville and Kerry Short all squeeze into the next cab on the rank and Bill says "Follow that Cab!" And Jack says rather disappointedly "Hey mate I've always wanted to say that!" To which Bill replies "Well you can!" And so, Jack naturally says "Follow that cab!" And the taxi driver does. They proceed down Bayswater Rd and Bill says "I think I know where they're heading. They're heading for the Russian Embassy unless I'm mistaken!"

Jack remarks "WHAT DID YOU EXPECT!"

Bill replies "Actually I expected the unexpected and this is not really unexpected as they are seeking political asylum. I think I had best contact C and inform him of this."

So, Bill rings C and tells him what is going on with the Russian spy ring.

C says to Bill. "Well mate I'd better get onto Boris and see what the government can do about this."

In a secret private conversation Boris Johnson said "About all we can do is to expel the Russians and their embassy and of course they will do the same to us in Russia, so be it!"

This with the passage of time transpired, which was what Bill and Jack expected as their cab rolled into 67 Kensington Palace Gardens which is the site of the Russian Embassy London. They then consulted a Mr K. Sokolov – Sherbachev who was outwardly seemed sympathetic to their cause, but Bill and Jack weren't so sure as they knew there would always be more spies, that they knew for sure! So they all retired to their local, the Rose and Crown and downed a few quiet ales and said together "GAME OVER, MISSION ACCOMPLISHED! and maybe it's retirement for us now."

BACK IN THE U.S.S.R BOYS!

Russia

Moscow

7

BACK IN THE U.S.S.R.
BOYS!

PREFACE:

The Soviet Union, officially the Union of Soviet Socialist Republics (USSR), was a socialist state that spanned
most of Europe and Asia during its existence from 1922 to
1991. It was nominally a federal union of multiple national republics; in practice its government and economy were highly
centralised until its final years. The country was a one-party
state prior to 1990 governed by the Communist Party of the
Soviet Union, with Moscow as its capital within its largest
and most populous republic, the Russian SFSR. Other major
urban centres were Leningrad (Russian SFSR), Kiev (Ukrainian SSR) Minsk (Byelorussian SSR), Tashkent (Usbeck SSR),
Alma-Ata (Kazakh SSR) and Novosibirsk (Russian SFSR). It
was the largest country in the world covering over 22,402,200
square kilometres (8,649,500 square miles) and spanning
eleven time zones. The Soviet Union's five biomes were tun-

dra, taiga, steppes, desert and mountains. Tundra is a type of biome where the tree growth is hindered by low temperatures and short growing seasons. The term Tundra comes from the Russian word for tundra and the KILDIN SAMI word tundar meaning "uplands ", "treeless mountain tract". Tundra vegetation is composed of dwarf shrubs, sedges, grasses, mosses and lichens. Scattered trees grow in some tundra regions. The ecotome (or ecological boundary) between the tundra and the forest is known as the treeline or the timberline. The tundra soil is rich in nitrogen and phosphorus.

A BIOME is a collection of organisms that have adaptions for the environment in which they exist. While a biome can cover large areas, a microbiome is a mix of organisms that co-exist in a small space on a much smaller scale e.g. the human microbiome is the collection of bacteria, viruses, fungi and other microorganisms that are present on or in the human body.

A BIOTA is the total collection of organisms of a geographic region for a time period. The biotas of the Earth make up the BIOSPHERE.

Russia's diverse population was officially known as the Soviet people.

The Soviet Union had its roots in the October revolution of 1917 when the Bolsheviks, headed by Vladimir Lenin, overthrew the Provisional Government that had earlier replaced the monarchy of the Russian Empire. They established the Russian Soviet Republic, beginning a civil war between the Bolshevik Red Army and many anti-Bolshevik forces across the former Empire, among whom the largest faction was the White Guard, which engaged in violent anti-communist repression against the Bolsheviks and their worker and peasant supporters known as the White Terror. The red army expanded and helped local Bolsheviks take power, establishing Soviets, repressing their political opponents and rebellious peasants through Red Terror. By 1922, the Bolsheviks had emerged victorious, forming the Soviet Union with the unification of the Russian, Transcaucasian, Ukrainian and Byelorussian republics. The New Economic Policy (NEP), which was introduced by Lenin, led to a partial return of a free market and private property; this resulted in a period of economic recovery.

The Bolsheviks from the Russian word 'majority' also known in English as Bolshevists, were a radical, far-left and revolutionary Marxist faction headed by Vladimir Lenin and Alexander Bogdanov that split from the Menshevik faction (the Mensheviks, also known as the Minority were one of the three dominant factions in the Russian socialist movement. The others being the Bolsheviks and the Socialist Revolution Revolutionists.)

The factions emerged in 1903 following a dispute with the Russian Socialist Democratic Labour Party (RSDLP) between Julius Martov and Vladimir Lenin. Martov's supporters who were in the minority in a crucial vote over a question of party membership came to be called Mensheviks derived from the Russian word for minority, while Lenin's adherents were known as Bolsheviks from the Russian word for majority.

Following Lenin's death in 1924, Joseph Stalin came to power. Stalin suppressed all political opposition to his rule inside the Communist Party and inaugurated a command economy. As a result, the country underwent a period of rapid industrialisation and forced collectivisation, which led to significant economic growth, but also led to a man-made famine in 1932-1933 and expanded the Gulag labour camp system originally established in 1918. Stalin also fomented political paranoia and conducted the Great Purge to remove his actual and perceived opponents from the Party through mass arrests of military leaders, Communist Party members, and ordinary citizens alike, who were then sentenced to correctional labour camps or sentenced to death. It is estimated that Stalin killed at least 20 million Russian people.

On 23 August 1939, after unsuccessful efforts to form an anti-fascist alliance with Western powers, the Soviets signed the non-aggression agreement with Nazi Germany. After World War II, the formally neutral Soviets invaded and annexed territories of several Eastern European states, including eastern Poland and the Baltic states. In June 1941 the Germans invaded, opening the largest and bloodiest theatre of war in history. Soviet war casualties accounted for the highest proportion of the conflict in the cost of acquiring the upper hand over the axis forces at intense battles such as Stalingrad. Soviet forces eventually captured Berlin and won World War II in Europe on 9 May 1945. The territory overtaken by the Red Army became satellite states of the Eastern Bloc. The Cold War emerged in 1947 as a result of a post-war Soviet dominance in Eastern Europe, where the Eastern Bloc confronted the Western Bloc that united in the North Atlantic Treaty Organisation (NATO) in 1949.

Following Stalin's death in 1953, a period known as de-Stalinisation and the Krush chev Thaw under the leadership of Nikita Krushchev. The country developed rapidly, as millions of peasants were moved into industrialised cities. The USSR took an early lead in the Space Race with the first ever satellite and the first human spaceflight and the first probe to land on another planet, Venus. In the 1970's there was a brief détente of relations with the United States, but tensions resumed when the Soviet Union deployed troops in Afghanistan in 1979. The war drained economic resources and was matched by an escalation of American military aid to Mujahideen fighters.

In the mid 1980's, the last Soviet leader, Mikhail Gorbachev, sought to further reform and liberalise the economy through his policies of glasnost and perestroika. Perestroika was a Russian political movement for reformation within the Communist Party of the Soviet Union during the 1980's widely associated with the Soviet leader Mikhail Gorbachev and his glasnost (meaning "openness ") policy reforms. The goal was to preserve the Communist Party while reversing economic stagnation. The USSR produced many significant social and technological achievements and innovations of the 20th century. The country has the world's second-largest economy and the largest standing military in the world. The USSR was recognised as one of the five nuclear weapons states.

Before its dissolution, the USSR had maintained its status as one of the world's two superpowers for four decades after World War II.

DISCLOSURE: Information has been sourced and quoted from Wikipedia and Google.

BACK IN THE U.S.S.R. BOYS!

The Mi5 agents Bill Parsons, Jack 'Dumpey 'Delaney and Rebecca Parsons, an Australian from Sydney, are in the head of Mi5's office. C, the head of Mi5 addresses them all by saying. "I'm sorry my old mates but your retirement is short lived again. You're all off to Russia in a couple of days, so get yourselves ready for action. Things may be a bit vigorous over there so you are all going to be armed and there will be a re-fresher course on self-defence and karate tomorrow at Jacob's Gym at 9:00 a.m. Don't be late!"

They all reply sarcastically "When have we ever been late!"

Jack follows on with "What's our schedule and how long do you expect this to take? Just so I can let the missus know!"

C Replies "It's a bit hard to say exactly but all going well I would expect it to take three weeks. You will leave tomorrow on separate flights to Moscow so as to try and avoid suspicion from our Soviet friends. The itinerary and information are contained in these envelopes which you shall read, memorise and destroy by burning!" He then whispers "This is because we are suspicious of a mole in Mi5, Mi6 and SOE Are there any more questions?"

They all reply "No sir!"

When they have arrived at their respective homes the MI5

agents open their envelopes, read the contents, memorise them and burn them and then break the ashes up with their fire pokers and dispose of them by burying them in their gardens. Bill Parsons says to his wife Jean "Well I'm of to Russia honey but I can't tell you where and for how long! Jean replies "That's O.K. Bill just so long as you leave those Ukraine, Moscow and Georgian girls alone!"

"No problem loves no female's going to be interested in an old fart like me! Except, maybe you!"

Bill departs Heathrow on Aeroflot flight 2583 leaving at 5:15 p.m. in a Sukhoi Superjet 100 with a full contingent of 87 passengers bound for Sheremetyevo International airport with a flight duration of 3 hours 45 minutes and expected time of arrival of 9:00 p.m. London time which is 11:00 p.m. Moscow time.

The three Mi5 agents arrive at Sheremetyevo International airport from different flights to avoid suspicion from the Russians and then meet up at Botanichesky Sad Station and travel by train together to Rostokino a town 9.5 km and 5.94 minutes from Moscow where Mi5 had instructed them to trail the Russian spies Nikita Volgo and Karolyn Caribout who lived there. Apparently the Mi5 agents, for some unknown reason thought that they would not arouse suspicion travelling together in Russia. Was this a mistake? Who knows? Read on and find out!

Once in Rostokino they found their accommodation at the Crown Plaza at ULITSA VILGELLA PIKA 14, North Eastern Administration Okrug Moscow 129323, that had been arranged by C and once checked in they got onto the trail of Volgo and Caribout. They figured a good place to start would be to sit at an outside table at the café opposite the Kremlin. On the first day their vigil turned out to be negative, however on the next day it was positive as they saw their prey coming out of the Kremlin and hail a cab for an undisclosed destination. The Mi5 agents immediately jumped into the taxi behind, and Bill exclaimed "Follow that cab!" emphatically. The cab containing the Russians ventured to a ramshackle old hut with moss and lichens growing on the roof and appeared to be a wood cutters refuge. Volgo and Caribout paid their cab driver, alighted and entered the cabin, peering outside around the corner of the cabin door before entering.

Parsons, Delaney and James arrived shortly afterwards but asked the cab driver to park behind some silver birch trees before they paid him and alighted and asked him to return to the cabin in 45 minutes. He replied "Nyet, Nyet!"

The Mi5 agents alighted with pistols drawn and crept guardedly towards the cabin. They opened the door and to their surprise they were confronted by Volgo and Caribout embracing and kissing. Jack exulted "Well, well, well, good morning to you both, you little love birds!"

Volgo answered with his strong Russian accent "Ahhh! am I glad to see you people from Mi5 as I 'm coming in from the cold and I will divulge all and sundry to you."

The cabin was cold, dank and had a musty smell, but it was quiet. That is until there was a sharp cracking sound of a Kalshnikov AK-47 being fired and the window splintered into about fifty pieces and then the sound of thud, thwack as a single bullet from a Kalashnikov AK-47 hit Volgo mid forehead and then a thud as he fell backwards and hit the wooden floor with blood oozing at first and then pumping from his forehead and then running all over his face and onto his sunken chest.. "Sniper!" Yells Parsons. "Hit the deck and roll! Looks like the KGB are on to us!" The Mi5 agents do this almost instinctively, but Caribout is a bit slower off the mark and cops a couple of rounds from the AK-47 killing her instantly.

Jack murmurs "I guess she won't be doing any talking either! However how in the heck are we going to get ourselves out of this hell hole?"

Rebecca James answers "With difficulty, mate!" Just as she says that they hear the sound of jet aircraft approaching rapidly and then the sound of rockets exploding and machine gun fire aimed at the KGB.

Previously Bill had texted C and told him of their coordinates and the situation they were in, and C had pre-empted the situation and ordered six Harrier jump jets to get The Mi5 agents out of trouble.

"Phew "sighs Bill "That's a relief! Now to get out of here!"

The taxi with its driver arrives spot on the 45-minute mark and picks them up.

They reverse their travel and end up in Heathrow and again say in unison "GAME OVER IN RUSSIA, MISSION ACCOMPLISHED".

Bill adds "I'm glad we're not BACK IN THE U.S.S.R. NOW BOYS!"

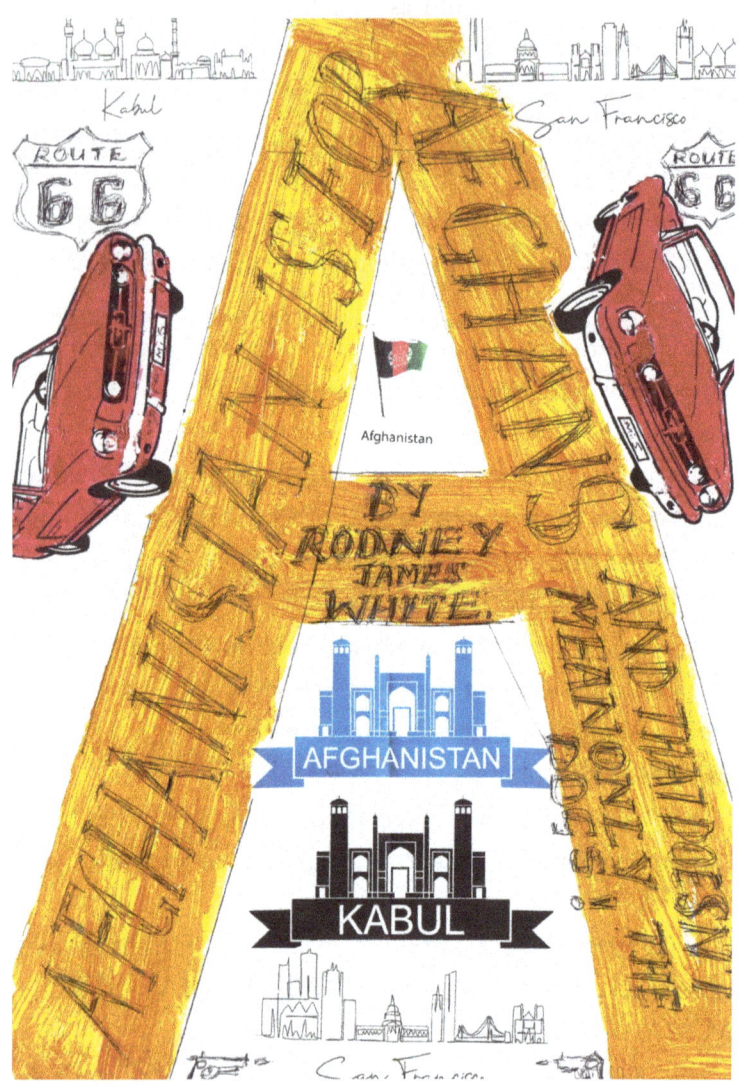

8 |

AFGHANISTAN IS FOR AFGHANS AND THAT DOESN'T MEAN ONLY THE DOGS!

PREFACE:

A fghanistan, officially the Islamic Republic of Afghanistan, is a mountainous landlocked country at the crossroads of Central and South Asia. Afghanistan is bordered by Pakistan to the east and south; Iran to the west; Turkmenistan, Uzbekistan, and Tajikistan to the north; and China to the northeast. Occupying 652,000 square kilometres (252,000 square miles) it is a mountainous country with plains in the north and southwest. Kabul is the capital and largest city. Afghanistan's population is around 32 million people, composed mainly of ethnic Pashtuns, Tajiks, Hazaras, and Uzbeks.

Humans lived in what is now Afghanistan at least 50,000

years ago. Settled life emerged in the region 9,000 years ago, evolving gradually into the Indus civilisation (Shotugai site), and the Helmand civilisation (Mundigak site) of the third millennium BCE. Indo-Aryans migrated through the Bactria-Margiana area to Gandhara, followed by the rise of the Iron Age Yaz I culture (ca. 1500 - 1100 BCE). The region, then known as "Ariana", fell to Achaemenid Persians in the 6th century BCE, who conquered the areas to their east as far as the Indus River. Alexander the Great invaded the region in the 4th century BCE.

In the First Anglo - Afghan War, the East India Company briefly seized control of Afghanistan, but following the Third Anglo - Afghan War in 1919 the country was able to become independent from foreign influence, eventually becoming a monarchy under Amanullah Khan, until almost 50 years later when Zahir Shah was overthrown, and a republic was established. In 1978, after a second coup, Afghanistan first became a socialist state, evoking the Soviet - Afghan War in the 1980's against Mujahideen rebels. By 1966, most of the country was captured by the Islamic fundamentalist Taliban, who ruled as a totalitarian regime; they were removed from power after the US invasion in 2001 but still control a significant portion of the country. The ongoing war between the government and the Taliban has perpetuated Afghanistan's problematic human rights records, with numerous abuses committed by both sides, such as killing and murdering of civilians, kidnapping and torture.

Afghanistan is a unitary Islamic republic. The country

has high levels of terrorism, poverty, child malnutrition, and corruption.

The root name "Afghan "is, according to some scholars, derived from the name of the Asvakan or Assakan, ancient inhabitants of the Hindu Kush region. Asvakan literally means "horsemen". "Horse breeders". or "cavalrymen".

The AKHAL-TEKE is a Turkman horse breed which has a reputation for speed and endurance, intelligence and a distinctive metallic sheen. The shiny coat of the breed led to the nickname of "Golden Horses. "They are adapted to severe climatic conditions and are thought to be one of the oldest existing horse breeds, from which the Thoroughbred breed was probably derived. There are currently about 6,600 Akhal-Tekes in the world, mostly in Turkmenistan.

Akhal is the name of oases along the north slope of the Kopet Dag mountains in Turkmenistan. It has been inhabited by the Tekke tribe of Turkmen.

Tribal people in Turkmenistan first used the horses for raiding. Due to its natural athleticism, it can be a good sporting horse, good at dressage, show jumping, eventing, racing and endurance riding. A noted example was the Akhal-Teke stallion,' Absent', who won the Grand Prix Dressage at the Summer Olympics in Rome in 1960. He went onto win the bronze individual in Tokyo in the 1964 Summer Olympics and won the Soviet teams gold medal at the 1968 Summer Olympics in Mexico.

Many empires and kingdoms have also risen to power in Afghanistan, such as the Greco-Bactrians, Indo-Scythians, Kushans, Kidarites etc.

Excavations of prehistoric sites suggest that humans were living in what is now Afghanistan at least 50,000 years ago, and that farming communities in the area were among the earliest in the world. An important site of early historical activities, many believe that Afghanistan compares to Egypt in terms of the historical value of its archeological sites.

In 1219 AD, Genghis Khan and his Mongol army overran the region. His troops are said to have annihilated the Kharazmian cities of Herat and Balk as well as Bamyan.

The Taliban emerged in September 1994 as a movement and militia of students (talib) from Islamic madrassas (schools) in Pakistan, who soon had military support from Pakistan. Taking control of Kandahar city that year, they conquered more territories until finally driving out the government of Rabbani from Kabul in 1996, where they established an emirate that gained international recognition from only three countries. The Taliban were condemned internationally for the harsh enforcement of their interpretation of Islamic Shariah Law, which resulted in the brutal treatment of many Afghans, especially women. During their rule, the Taliban and their allies committed massacres against Afghan civilians, denied UN food supplies to starving civilians and conducted a policy of scorched earth, burning vast areas of fertile land and destroying tens of thousands of homes.

In October 2001, the United States invaded Afghanistan to remove the Taliban from power after they refused to hand over Osama Bin Laden, the prime suspect of the September 11 attacks, who was a "guest" of the Taliban and was operating his al-Queda network in Afghanistan. Afghanistan is located in Southern - Central Asia, indeed the region particularly centred at Afghanistan is considered the "crossroads of Asia ", and the country has had the nickname "Heart of Asia".

The geography in Afghanistan is varied, but is mostly mountainous and rugged, with some unusual mountain ridges accompanied by plateaus and river basins. It is dominated by the Hindu Kush range, the western extension of the Himalayas that stretches to eastern Tibet via the Pamir Mountains and Karakoram Mountains in Afghanistan's far north-east.

The climate is a continental climate with harsh winters in the central highlands where the average temperature in January is below -15 degrees Centigrade, and hot summers where temperatures average over 35 degrees Centigrade and can go over 43 degrees Centigrade in some places. The country is usually arid in the summers, with most rain falling between December and April.

Law enforcement is the responsibility of the Afghan National Police (ANP), which is part of the Ministry of Interior Affairs. All parts of Afghanistan are considered dangerous due to militant activities and terrorism -related incidents. Kidnapping for ransom and robberies are common in major cities. Every year hundreds of Afghan police are killed in the line of duty. Afghanistan is also the world's leading producer of opium. Afghanistan's opium poppy harvest produces more than 90% of illicit heroin globally, and more than 95% of the European supply.

Agricultural production is the backbone of Afghanistan's economy and has traditionally dominated the economy, employing about 40% of the workforce. The country is known for producing pomegranates, grapes, apricots, melons, and several other fresh and dried fruits. It is also known as the world's largest producer of opium - as much as 16% or more of the nation's economy is derived from the cultivation and sale of opium. It is also one of the world's top producers of cannabis. Saffron, the most expensive spice, grows in Afghanistan, particularly in Herat Province. Production hit a record high in 2019 (19,469 kg. of saffron) and one kilogram is sold domestically between $634 and $1147.

The Afghan wars were about the internal conflict that began in 1978 between anti-communist Islamic guerrillas and the Afghan communist government (aided in 1979 - 87 by Soviet troops) leading to the overthrow of the government in 1992.

On September 11th, 2001, attacks on America killed nearly 3,000 people. Osama Bin Laden, the head of the Islamic terrorist group al Qaeda, was quickly identified as the man responsible.

The Taliban, radical Islamists who ran Afghanistan and protected Bin Laden, refused to hand him over. So, a month after 9/11, the US launched air strikes against Afghanistan.

As other countries joined the war, the Taliban were quickly removed from power, but they didn't just disappear -their influence grew back, and they dug in.

Since then, the US and its allies have struggled to stop Afghanistan's government collapsing and ending deadly attacks by the Taliban.

The Taliban first took control of the capital Kabul in

1996 and ruled most of the country within two years. They followed a radical form of Islam and enforced punishments like public executions.

Within two months of the US and its international and Afghan allies launching their attacks, the Taliban regime collapsed, and its fighters melted away into Pakistan.

A newly US backed government took over in 2004, but the Taliban still had a lot of support in areas around the Pakistani border and made hundreds of millions of dollars a year from the drug trade, mining and taxes.

As the Taliban carried out more and more suicide attacks international forces working with the Afghan troops struggled to counter the threat the re-energised group posed.

In 2014, at the end of what was to be the bloodiest war in Afghanistan since 2001, NATO's international forces – wary of staying in Afghanistan indefinitely – ended their combat mission, leaving it to the Afghan army to fight the Taliban.

But that gave the Taliban momentum as they seized territory and detonated bombs against government and civilian targets.

Afghanistan had been in a state of almost constant war for twenty years even before the US invasion. In 1979, a year after a coup, the Soviet army invaded Afghanistan to support its communist government. It fought a resistance movement – known as the Mujahideen that was supported by the US, Pakistan, China amongst other countries.

In 1989, Soviet troops withdrew but the civil war continued. In the chaos that followed, the Taliban sprung up.

There are at least four reasons why the war is still going on:

A lack of political clarity since the invasion began and questions about the effectiveness of the US strategy over the past 18 years.

The fact that each side is trying to break what has become a stalemate – and that the Taliban have been trying to maximise their leverage during peace negotiations.

An increase in violence by Islamic State militants in Afghanistan – they've been behind some of the bloodiest attacks recently.

The role played by Pakistan. The Taliban have their roots in Pakistan and were able to regroup there during the US invasion, although Pakistan denies it.

The Taliban have stayed so strong because they could be making as much as US $ 1.5 billion a year mostly from drugs - opium, heroin and marijuana which are grown in Taliban held areas.

Geoffrey Robertson A0, QC (born 30 September 1946) is a human rights barrister, academic, author and broadcaster. He holds dual Australian and British citizenship. He is a founder and joint head of Doughty Street Chambers. He serves as a Master of the Bench at the Middle Temple, a recorder, and visiting professor at Queen Mary University of London.

Robertson was born in Sydney, Australia, and grew up in the suburb of Eastwood. He went to Epping Boys High School and then attended the University of Sydney, where he graduated with a Bachelor of Arts in 1966 and a Bachelor of Laws with First Class Honours in 1970, before winning a Rhode's Scholarship to study at the University of Oxford, where he graduated with a Bachelor of Civil Law from

University College, Oxford in 1972. In 2006 he was awarded an honorary degree of Doctor of Laws by the University of Sydney.

He became a barrister in 1973 and was appointed QC in 1988. Robertson has appeared in cases before the European Court of Human Rights and in other courts across the world. Until 2007 he sat as an appeal judge at the UN Special Court for Sierra Leone.

In 2010 Robertson unsuccessfully defended Julian Assange. the founder of Wikileaks, in extradition proceedings in the UK.

A United Nations tribunal has severely criticised Uzbekistan's judges, its security services and the state's Prosecutor General for committing torture and the unfair trial of Kadyr Yusopov, formerly a leading diplomat who was the country's representative to the Organisation for Security and Cooperation in Europe (OSCE) and to UN organisations. It has demanded his immediate release from a prison sentence imposed after a secret trial for treason. Mr Yusopov had developed, after his retirement, a mental illness as a result of which he attempted suicide.

Geoffrey Robertson QC who brought the case on behalf of Mr Yusopov and his family said" This is a most damning criticism of a country that is pretending to the West that it respects the rule of law but is in reality allowing its secret police and its lickspittle judges to behave brutally. The conduct of its security police was disgusting as they tried to force a confession from a man recovering from a mental breakdown and then for 5 months denied him all contact with his family and his lawyer of choice. The judges behaved like legal lickspittles, refusing to investigate the torture to which he had been subjected. On these findings, the Prosecutor General should resign as he is clearly guilty of dereliction of duty.

"ROUTE SIXTY – SIX: -

U.S. Route 66 or U.S. Highway 66 (US 66 or Route 66) also known as Will Rogers Highway, the Main Street of America or the Mother Road, was one of the original highways in the U.S. Highway System. The highway, which became one of the most famous roads in the United States, originally ran from Chicago, Illinois, through Missouri, Kansas, Oklahoma, Texas, New Mexico, and Arizona before terminating in Santa Monica in Los Angeles County, California, covering a total of 2,448 miles (3,940 Km.)

US 66 served as a primary route for those who migrated west, especially during the Dust Bowl of the 1930's, and the road supported the economy of the communities through which it passed.

DISCLOSURE: information has been obtained and quoted from Wikipedia and BBC.

AFGHANISTAN IS FOR AFGHANS AND THAT DOESN'T MEAN ONLY THE DOGS!

The three Mi5 agents, Bill Parsons, Jack 'Dumpey ' Delaney and Rebecca James, an Australian from Sydney, are in the office of ' C ', the head of Mi5.

C starts the conversation with "Well my old friends and good mates you're all coming out of retirement again!" He then passes envelopes to them and writes a note saying 'I can't talk about this here as we still suspect that there are moles in Mi5, Mi6 and SOE. Therefore, take your envelopes, which have all the details of your next mission, read them and destroy them. '

C concludes with "If there are any questions let me know!"

"Not at this stage!" States Parsons.

The Mi5 agents then decide to retire to the Rose and Crown for a drink or two.

When there, Rebecca James opens here envelope and has a squiz.

"Bloody heck and stone the crows and starve the lizards we're off to flippin' Afghanistan!" Declares Bec.

"What's wrong with that!" Emphasises Jack.

"Well, it's full of Afghans for a start and I suppose AFGHANISTAN IS FOR AFGHANS AND THAT'S NOT ONLY THE DOGS. However, most of them seem to walk around stoned on opium, heroin and marijuana. Besides all they seem to grow is opium poppies and marijuana. "Says Bec.

"Well, they also grow saffron. "Interjects Bill.

"Yeh, at up to $1147 a kilo" replies Bec with her rejoinder. "And who wants yellow food anyway "says Bec with a temporary conclusion.

"I think they also grow a fair bit of fruit and vege. "Says Jack. putting another 'nail in the coffin' of Rebecca James.

"Oh well, cest la vie!" Says Bec. "Time for another round!" As Bill drags on his cigarette before the barmaid says "No Smoking Sir!"

Bill replies with "Sorry Jacquie, I was forgetting myself. "As he rubs his left ear- lobe.

Bec continues to read her letter from C whilst sipping on her pint of Fosters.

"You know C says that he doesn't know of any spies in Afghanistan yet, but I'll bet a Bungarra's body there are some there who are just as good as spies. Like, they slow down the supply of opium, heroin and marijuana so the price is bumped up and then there are those who put additives in the drugs to bulk them up which is not good for the junkies, and they also bump up the price of the saffron, not that that is a big deal as far as I'm concerned!" Says Bec.

"Yeh, well what are we supposed to be doing there!" says Jack.

"O.K., well then I'll read on McDuff!" States Bec.

"Apparently we're supposed to fly to Kabul and checkout the opium and heroin suppliers there to ascertain who they are and then try and curtail them. "States Bec.

"Yeh, that's all very well but I'll bet the CIA and the rest of the Yanks have done that already!" Replies Jack.

"Mmm, you're probably right! I'll check with C and find out "says Bill.

Bill texts C immediately and C's reply states "Yeh, the CIA have done a fair bit but we don't necessarily agree with them as some of them have a habit of partaking of drugs themselves and I know you lot are more reliable, so go to it and give me your report ASAP."

Bill, Jack and Rebecca then come out with "ITS GAME ON IN AFGHANISTAN!"

So the three Mi5 agents arrive in Kabul and check in at the Safi Landmark Hotel at 1st Street, Ahmed Zahir Road, Charahi Ansari, Kabul 1001. The hotel and the rooms were more than they expected, and they all had a bit of a siesta and arranged to meet for pre-dinner drinks at 5: 00 p.m.

At five they all meet in the cosy bar and have a few pre-dinner drinks. Of course, by now they have all read, memorised and destroyed their messages from Mi5.

Their dinner is quite sumptuous with a lazy Susan containing Kofta (meatballs), Kaddu Buranee (sweet pumpkin), Ashak (vegetable and chive filled dumplings topped with tomato and yoghurt sauces), Aush (handmade noodles), Bishak (small turnovers with fillings of potatoes, herbs and minced meat), Kabuli Palaw (meat and stock and herbs added to rice, fried raisins, slivered carrots and pistachios, Qorma (stew with chateau rice), Mantu (dumplings filled with onion and ground beef), another type of Ashak (dumplings filled with leeks), Kebab (lamb with fat from the lamb's tail to add extra flavour), Quroot (a reconstituted dairy product made from sheep or goat milk), Nan bread and Doogh (a cold drink made by mixing water with yoghurt and then adding fresh or dried mint and crushed cucumber).

Bec says "Well look at that! That'll keep us busy for a while and keep the kangaroos hoppin'! However, we also need something alcoholic!" So, she promptly asks the waitress for a round of Fosters for everyone.

After much eating and drinking, with little talking it then progresses to a couple of bottles of Howard Park pinot noir and then they are all ready for bed with their stomachs full.

The next morning after breakfast, which was not so sumptuous, they decided to venture out to see what they could see.

They were immediately confronted by the scream of three RAAF 18 A Hornets and six 2F-35A Lightning 11's from the USA flying about as low as they could, apparently in an effort to avoid Taliban radar.

"Geez, the Aussies and the Yanks are in town!" Says Bec as she clasps her hands over her ears.

"You're right there "says Bill Parsons as he and Jack Delaney do the same.

"Let's have a coffee at this café and look out for drug runners whilst we sip. "Says Jack.

"Good idea Caribou!" Says Bec. Bill agrees.

The town square of Kabul was full of men and children flying kites of all shapes and colours, riding the thermals and set on the backdrop of a vivid blue cloudless sky. Bill, Jack and Bec thought it was a marvellous sight.

However, a little distance away they sighted a thief being dealt with in the people's own form of justice, which was to hack off both of his hands, which was not such a marvellous sight to see! But that's the way it is in Afghanistan.

Bec says "Jeepers, if that's the way they treat thieves, I hate to think what they do when a bloke rapes a shiela! That's probably best not thought about!"

"Touche!" Confer Bill and Jack.

It is only a matter of minutes before they see some dealing in the streets.

Jack says "Lets nab them!"

Bill replies quickly with "No man! They are only the pawns in this game it's better to wait and see where they go and see who their suppliers are and move forward from there. I'll bet ten quid we can trace it to some cartel that is headed by a big multi-national drug company in the US that will deny everything and say they are squeaky clean and then slap a multi - million dollar lawsuit on us!"

"Do we want to go down that track? "questions Jack.

"Depends on how strong our morals are mate! Speaking on my behalf I'd do it because I feel it's the right and proper thing to do."

Bec and Jack confer and reply with "O.K. let's do it!"

So, they continue to observe the druggies in Kabul and then follow a couple of dealers out into the Taliban's fields of opium poppies and marijuana crops.

They Park their grey Jeep Renegade at a distance and proceed on foot until they are close enough to observe proceedings whilst looking through their binoculars.

The three Mi5 agents notice that the two Afghan drug

runners meet up with a couple of men who have North American accents. One is about six foot two inches tall and is smoking a cigar and wearing a Stetson hat and a checked long sleeve shirt with black corduroy trousers and brown riding boots. The other was shorter, about five foot ten inches and had a balding head and was wearing a plain blue long-sleeved shirt with blue Levi jeans and Nike sneakers. Rebecca James then took some photos of the men and the location with her Canon camera which was fitted with a high-resolution telephoto lens.

The four of them then entered a small, nearby shed and then appeared shortly afterward with each of the Americans holding plastic sachet bags with what appeared to be white powder in them. They then hopped into their red Grand Cherokee Jeep and opened a brief case that was labelled "Trusty P/ L "and placed the plastic bags inside and then drove off.

Parsons, Delaney and James then hastily ran to their Jeep Renegade and followed the dust trail at a distance, so as not to be spotted by the Americans.

Bec then sent the photos back to C and reported what was going on along with mention of Trusty P/ L.

C replies saying that the taller American is James Michigan and the other one is David Arnold and they have been on the CIA's drug suspects list for some time, but the CIA have not been able to make anything 'stick' on them. C also said that Trusty P/ L, as the name implies, is probably not so trusty and is a dodgey pharmaceutical company based in Michigan USA that is implicated in supply of illegal cocaine and heroin.

"Righto, let's get these mongrels!" says Bec vehemently.

"How do you propose to do that? "Questions Jack.

"Well, we'll drag them through every court in the USA if we have to!" Replies Bec.

"I hope you've got deep pockets "States Bill

"I won't actually be paying for it. It'll be the British government!" Replies Bec.

Rebecca James, Bill Parsons and Jack Delaney decide to engage lawyers in Washington, but they can't be engaged for four days so they decide to hire a car and drive Route 66. They hired a red Mustang 500 Shelby GT from Hertz in Chicago and set forth. Funnily enough, just as they start the engine the radio starts blurting out - "If you ever plan to motor west, Travel my way, take the highway that is best. Get your kicks on route sixty - six. It winds from Chicago to LA, more than two thousand miles all the way. Get your kicks on rote sixty -six. Now you go through Saint Looey, Joplin Missouri, And Oklahoma City is mighty pretty. You see Amarillo, Gallup, New Mexico, Flagstaff, Arizona, Don't forget Winona, King- man, Barstow, San Bernadino. Won't you get hip to this timely tip When you make that California trip. Get your kicks on route sixty-six. Won't you get hip to this timely tip: When you make that California trip, Get your kicks on route sixty-six, Get your kicks on route sixty-six, Get your kicks on route sixty-six." Travelling the 2,448 miles through St Louis, Missouri, Oklahoma, Arizona, New Mexico and Los Angeles and then up to Vancouver in Canada. From there they get the Canadian Pacific to Montreal. The three Mi5 agents then fly to Washington D.C. and approach the lawyers to prosecute Trusty P/L in the Supreme Court.

They locate the Supreme Court building with its Roman-esque style and eight frontal columns at One, First Street N.E. Washington D.C. and enter with their lawyers. The case is a drawn out affair which finally results in a win for the Brits but they are countered with a multi - million dollar lawsuit brought against then by Trusty P/ L.

"O.K. Bec what do we do now? "asks Bill.

"I'm going to get Geoffrey to deal with this!" States Bec.

"Geoffrey? "Questions Bill.

"Yes, Professor Geoffrey Robertson A.O., Q. C., L.L.B., Doctor of Laws, B. Civil Law (Oxford) , B.A., Rhodes Scholar (Oxford). He's a mate of mine from Sydney!"

That sort of left Bill and Jack dumbfounded for a while.

Bec texts Geoffrey Robertson and says that they are in a spot of bother with the lawsuit and asks if he can help them out.

Robertson texts back saying "Sure thing Bec, where are you staying in Washington? "Bec texts back "The Hyatt Place/ National Mall, 400 e St. SW Washington DC 20024-3246, room 200."

Robertson texts back saying, "O.K. I'll drop everything, and I'll be there the day after next."

The next day the three Mi5 agents have a relaxing day seeing the sites of Washington. The following day Robertson arrives and meets up with Parsons, Delaney and James at their hotel.

Robertson says in his rather Pommiefied voice "Hi Bec, long time no see."

Bec replies "G'day cobber, it must be at least three years when we were in Sydney."

"That's right, yes good old Sydney. Has it been two years since I was in the vicinity of the old coathanger and the singing sails of the Op House and King's Cross? Ahhhh memories "Reminisces Geoffrey Robertson.

Bec then introduces Bill and Jack to Robertson.

"Now, tell me all about this lawsuit!" States Robertson. Bec then tells him all about it. Robertson replies by saying "I think this will be best dealt with back in London where I can get all my mob back at Doughty Street assembled and onto it. My gut feeling is that this is eminently winnable!"

"Good – oh!" Says Bec "It's off to good old Blightey again!"

The next morning, they are all assembled at the Old Bailey with Robertson resplendent in his barristers gown and wig as he goes out to bat for Parsons, Delaney and James. The case is drawn out over three days, mainly because of delaying tactics and pontificating by the lawyers for Trusty P/L, but despite this the case is a win for Robertson, Parsons, Delaney and James. They then all retire to the Rose and Crown where Bec says. "Righto Geoffrey, the drinks are on us!"

Parsons and Delaney say "Too right!" Followed by "GAME OVER! MISSION ACCOMPLISHED IN AFGHANISTAN, AMERICA AND BRITAIN! NOW FOR RETIREMENT!"

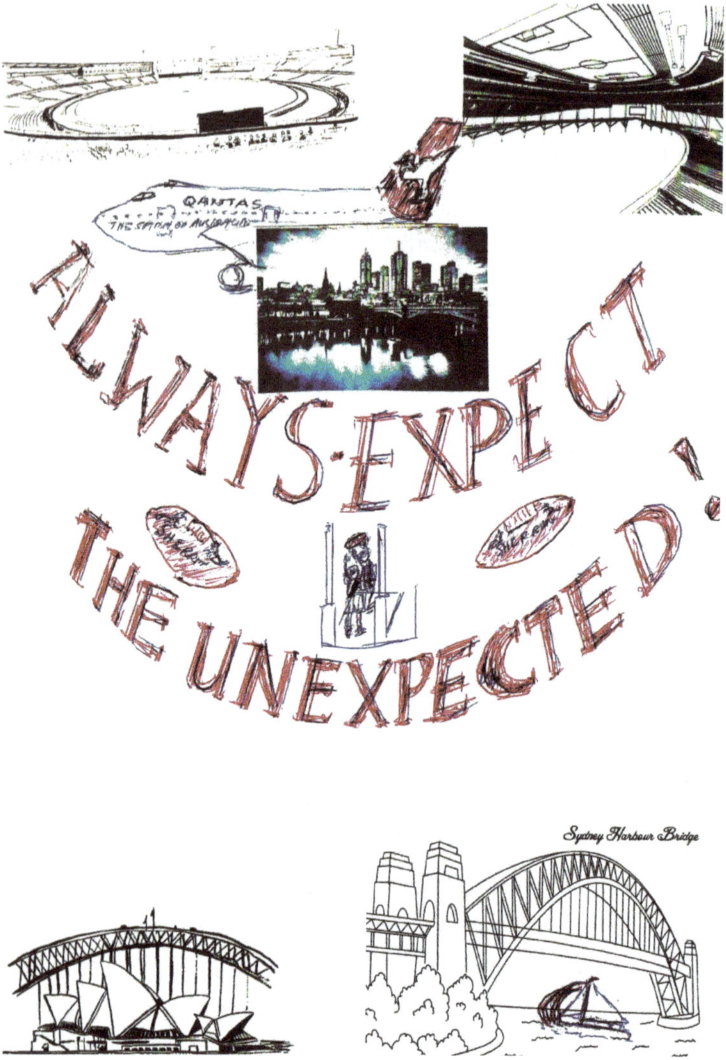

ALWAYS·EXPECT THE UNEXPECTED!

Sydney Harbour Bridge

9

SOUTHWARD HO!

PREFACE:

Antarctica is Earth's most southern continent. It contains the geographic South Pole and is situated in the Antarctic region of the Southern Hemisphere, almost entirely south of the Antarctic Circle, and is surrounded by the Southern Ocean. At 14,200,000 square kilometres (5,500,000 square miles) it is the fifth largest continent and nearly twice the size of Australia. It is by far the least populated continent, with around 5,000 people in the summer and around 1,000 in the winter. About 98% of Antarctica is covered by ice that averages 1.9km (1.2 miles; 6,200 ft) in thickness, which extends to all but the McMurdo Dry Valleys and the northernmost reaches of the Antarctic Peninsula.

Antarctica, on average, is the coldest, driest, and windiest continent, and has the highest average elevation of all the continents. Most of Antarctica is a polar desert, with annual precipitation of 200 mm (7.9 in) along the coast and far less inland; yet 80% of the world's freshwater reserves are stored there, enough to raise global sea levels by about 60 metres (200 feet) if it were to melt. The temperature in Antarctica has dropped to minus 87. 92 degrees Centigrade (minus 128.6 degrees Fahrenheit). Organisms' native to Antarctica include many types of algae, fungi, protista, and certain animals, such as mites, nematodes, penguins, seals and tardigrades (colloquially known as Water Bears or Moss Piglets, a phylum of eight legged segregated micro - animals). Vegetation, where it exists is tundra. Tundra is a type of biome where the tree growth is hindered by low temperatures and short growing seasons. The term tundra comes from Russian and Kildin Sami words meaning "uplands ", "treeless mountain tract". Tundra vegetation is comprised of dwarf shrubs, sedges, grasses, mosses and lichens. Scattered trees grow in some tundra regions. The tundra soil is rich in nitrogen and phosphorus.

Antarctica was the last region on earth to be discovered, likely unseen until 1820 when the Russian expedition of Fabian Gottlieb von Bellingshausen and Mikhail Lazarev on the ships 'Vostok 'and 'Mirny 'sighted the Finbul ice shelf. The continent remained largely neglected for the rest of the 19th century because of its harsh environment, lack of easily accessible resources, and isolation. In January 1840, land at Antarctica was discovered for the first time, almost simultaneously, by the United states Exploring Expedition, under a Lieutenant Charles Wilkes; and a separate French expedition under Jules Dumont d'Urville. The latter made a temporary landing. The Wilkes expedition, though it did not make a landing remained long enough to survey and map some 800 miles of the continent. The first confirmed landing was by a team of Norwegians in 1895.

Antarctica is governed by parties to the Antarctic Treaty System. Twelve countries signed the Antarctic Treaty in 1959 and 38 have signed it since then. The treaty prohibits military activities, mineral mining, nuclear explosions and nuclear waste disposal. It supports scientific research and protects the continent's ecology. Between 1,000 and 5,000 people from many countries reside at research stations scattered across the continent.

The first documented landing in Antarctica was by the American sealer John Davis. apparently at Hughes Bay, near Cape Charles in West Antarctica on 7 February 1821, although some historians dispute this. The first recorded and confirmed landing was at Cape Adare in 1895 by the Norwegian – Swedish whaling ship "Antarctic."

Explorer James Clark Ross passed through what is now known as the Ross Sea and discovered Ross Island in 1841. He sailed along a huge wall of ice that was later named the Ross Ice Shelf. Mount Erebus and Mount Terror are named after two ships from his expedition: HMS 'Erebus 'and 'Terror'.

Ernest Shackleton and three other members of his expedition made several firsts in December 1908 and February 1909: they were the first humans to traverse the Ross Ice Shelf, the first to traverse the Trans Antarctic Mountains, and the first to set foot on the South Polar Plateau.

Positioned asymmetrically around the South Pole and largely south of the Antarctic Circle, Antarctica is the southernmost continent and is surrounded by the Southern Ocean.

There are a number of rivers and lakes in Antarctica, the longest river being the Onyx and the largest lake, Vostok is one of the largest sub - glacial lakes in the world.

Antarctica is divided in two by the Trans Antarctic Mountains close to the neck between the Ross Sea and the Weddell Sea. The portion west of the Weddell Sea and east of the Ross Sea is called West Antarctica and the remainder is East Antarctica.

About 98% of Antarctica is covered by the Antarctic ice sheet, a sheet of ice averaging at least 1.6 Km (1 mile) thick. The continent has about 90% of the world's ice (and thus about 70% of the world's fresh water.) In most of the interior of the continent, precipitation is very low, down to 20 mm per year; in a few "blue ice "areas precipitation is lower than the mass loss by sublimation. Sublimation is the transition of a substance directly from the solid to the gas state without passing through the liquid state. In the dry valleys, the same effect occurs over a rock base, leading to a barren and desecrated landscape.

West Antarctica is covered by the West Antarctic Ice Sheet. The sheet has been of recent concern because of the small possibility of its collapse.

Vinson Massif, the highest peak in Antarctica at 4,892 metres is located in the Ellsworth Mountains. Antarctica contains many other mountains, on both the main continent and the surrounding islands. Mount Erebus on Ross Island is the world's most southernmost active volcano.

More than 100 million years ago, Antarctica was part of the super continent Gondwana. Over time, Gondwana gradually broke apart, and Antarctica as we know it today was formed around 25 million years ago, when the Drake Passage opened between it and South America.

PALEOZOIC ERA. (540-250 Ma) During the Cambrian Period, Gondwana had a mild climate. West Antarctica was partially in the Northern Hemisphere and during this period large amounts of sandstones, limestones and shales were deposited in Antarctica. East Antarctica was at the equator, where seafloor invertebrates and trilobites flourished in the tropical seas. By the start of the DEVONIAN PERIOD (416 Ma {million years ago}), Gondwana was in more southern latitudes and the climate was cooler, though fossils of land plants were known from this time. Sand and silts were laid down in what is now the Ellsworth, Horlick, and Pensacola Mountains. Glaciation began at the end of the DEVONIAN ERA (416 Ma), as Gondwana became centred on the South Pole and the climate cooled, though flora remained. During the PERMIAN PERIOD (298.9 Ma), the land became dominated by seed plants such as Glossopteris, a pteridosperm which grew in swamps. Over time these swamps became deposits of coal in the Trans Antarctic Mountains. Towards the end of the Permian period, continued warming led to a dry, hot climate over much of Gondwana.

MESOZOIC PERIOD (250 - 66 Ma)

As a result of continued warming, the polar ice caps melted and much of Gondwana became a desert. In Eastern Antarctica, seed ferns or pteridosperms became abundant and large amounts of sandstone and shale were laid down at this time. Synapsids, commonly known as "mammal - like reptiles

", which included species such as Lystrosaurus, were common in Antarctica during the EARLY TRIASSIC (Triassic period – 252 – 201 Ma). The Antarctic Peninsula began to form during the JURASSIC PERIOD (206- 146 Ma). Ginkgo trees, conifers, Bennititales, horsetails, ferns and cycads were plentiful during this period. In West Antarctica, coniferous forests dominated through the entire CRETACEOUS PERIOD (146 - 66 Ma), though southern beech (Nothofagus) became more prominent towards the end of this period. Ammonites (extinct relatives of sea creatures such as the modern nautilus) were common in the seas around Antarctica, and dinosaurs were also present. It was during this era that Gondwana began to break up.

The cooling of Antarctica occurred stepwise, as the continental spread changed the oceanic currents from longitudinal equator - to - pole temperature - equalizing currents to latitudinal currents that preserved and accentuated latitude temperature differences. Africa separated from Antarctica in the JURASSIC, around 160 Ma, followed by the Indian subcontinent in the early CRETACEOUS (about 125 Ma). By the end of the Cretaceous, about 66 Ma, Antarctica (then connected to Australia) still had a subtropical climate and flora, complete with a marsupial fauna. In the EOCENE EPOCH, (about 40 Ma) Australia - New Guinea separated from Antarctica, so that latitudinal currents could isolate Antarctica from Australia, and the first ice began to appear. Around 25 Ma, the Drake Passage opened between Antarctica and South America, resulting in the Antarctic Circumpolar Current that completely isolated the continent. The ice began to spread, replacing the forests that until then had covered the continent. Since about 15 Ma, the continent has been mostly covered with ice.

Geologically, West Antarctica closely resembles the Andes mountains of South America.

The main mineral resource found on the continent is coal. The Prince Charles Mountains contain significant deposits of iron ore. The most valuable resources of Antarctica lie off-shore, namely the oil and gas fields found in the Ross Sea in 1973. Exploitation of all mineral resources is banned until 2048 by the Protocol on Environmental Protection to the Antarctic Treaty.

According to a study published by PHYS.org there has been a significant increase in uranium concentrated in Antarctica. Uranium particles in Australia are being carried by the wind and are being deposited in Antarctica's Detroit Peninsula. Since World War II the rise in Southern Hemisphere uranium has been attributed to mining in Australia, Namibia and South Africa.

The first traces of lead (Pb) pollution were carried by wind from Australia in 1889 and Australia is the primary source

. Antarctica is the coldest of the Earth's continents. It was ice-free until about 34 million years ago, when it became covered with ice. The lowest natural air temperature ever recorded was minus 89.2 degrees Centigrade at the Russian Vostok Station in Antarctica on 21 July 1983. Temperatures reach a minimum of between minus 80 degrees Centigrade and minus 89.2 degrees Centigrade and reach a maximum of between 5 and 15 degrees Centigrade.

Antarctica is a frozen desert with little precipitation; the South Pole receives less than 10 mm per year on average.

The aurora australis, commonly known as the southern lights, is a glow observed in the night sky near the South Pole created by plasma - full solar winds that pass by the Earth. Heavy snowfalls are common on the coastal portion of the continent, where snowfalls of up to 1.22 metres in 48 hours have been recorded. At the continent's edge, strong katabatic winds off the polar plateau often blow at storm force. Katabatic (from the Greek word Katabasis which means "descending ") winds are drainage winds that carry high - density air from a higher elevation down a slope under the force of gravity. Such winds are sometimes called 'Fall Winds '. Some of Antarctica has been warming up; particularly strong warming has been noted on the Antarctic Peninsula. Over the second half of the 20th century, the Antarctic Peninsula was the fastest -warming place on Earth. There is some evidence that surface warming in Antarctica is due to human greenhouse gas emissions. There is a large area of low ozone concentration or "ozone hole "over Antarctica. The hole, reoccurring every spring since the 1970's, was detected by scientists in 1985. This hole covers almost the whole continent and was at its largest in September 2006; the longest lasting event occurred in 2020. The ozone hole is attributed to the emission of CFC's or chlorofluorocarbons into the atmosphere, which decompose the ozone into other gases. Ozone depletion may have a dominant role in governing climatic conditions in Antarctica and the wider area of the Southern Hemisphere. Ozone absorbs large amounts of ultraviolet radiation in the stratosphere. Ozone depletion over Antarctica can cause a cooling of around six degrees Centigrade in the local stratosphere. This cooling has the effect of intensifying the westerly winds which flow around the continent (the polar vortex) and thus prevents outflow of the cold air near the pole.

Invertebrate life in Antarctica includes microscopic mites like the Alaskozetes antarcticus, lice, nematodes, tardigrades, rotifers, krill and springtails. Antarctic krill, which congregate in large schools, is the keystone species of the ecosystem of the Southern Ocean, and is an important food organism for whales, seals, leopard seals, fur seals, squid, icefish, penguins, albatrosses and many other birds.

Few terrestrial vertebrates live in Antarctica, and those that do are limited to the sub -Antarctic Islands. Some species of marine animals exist and rely, directly or indirectly, on the phytoplankton. Antarctic sea life includes penguins, blue whales, orcas, colossal squids and fur seals. The emperor penguin is the only penguin that breeds during the winter in Antarctica; it and the Adelie penguin breed farther south than any other penguin. The Weddell Sea, a "true seal ", is named after Sir James Weddell, commander of British sealing expeditions in the Weddell Sea. The leopard seal is an apex predator in the Antarctic ecosystem, and they migrate across the Southern Ocean in search of food.

About 1,150 species of fungi have been recorded from Antarctica, of which about 750 are non - lichen forming. Their thick – walled and strongly melanised cells make them resistant to UV light.

About 300 million years ago Permian forests started to

cover the continent, and tundra vegetation survived as late as 15 million years ago, but the climate of present day Antarctica does not allow extensive vegetation to grow. A combination of freezing temperatures, poor soil quality, lack of moisture, and lack of sunlight inhibit plant growth. The flora of the continent largely consists of bryophytes. There are about 100 species of mosses and 25 species of liverworts, but only three species of flowering plants, all of which are found in the Antarctic Peninsula.

The Protocol on Environmental Protection to the Antarctic Treaty came into force in 1998, and is the main instrument concerned with the conservation and management of biodiversity in Antarctica. A major concern is the risk to Antarctica from unintentional introduction of non – native species from outside the region.

The Antarctic Treaty bans military activity on Antarctica, including the establishment of military bases and fortifications, military manoeuvres, and weapons testing. Military personnel or equipment are permitted only for scientific research or other peaceful purposes.

There is no current economic activity in Antarctica outside of fishing off the coast and small - scale tourism. Although coal, hydrocarbons, iron ore, platinum, copper, chromium, nickel, gold and other minerals have been found, they have not been in large enough quantities to exploit.

The International Association of Antarctic Tour Operators (IAATO) set landing limits and closed or restricted zones on the more frequently visited sites. Antarctic flight seeing sights (which did not land) operated out of Australia and

New Zealand until, the fatal crash of Air New Zealand flight 901 in the Mount Erebus disaster in 1979, which killed all 257 people aboard. Qantas resumed commercial, overflights to Antarctica from Australia in the mid – 1990's.

By ship one can go to Buenos Aries, Argentina or Punto Arenas, Chile. The majority of voyages depart from Ushuaia about a 3 ½ hours direct flight from Buenos Aries. The voyage then traverses the famous Drake Passage. and usually takes 1 ½ days. Alternatively, one can voyage from Hobart, Australia to Invercargill, New Zealand and then to Cape Adare in Antarctica.

Each year, scientists from 28 nations conduct experiments not reproducible in any other place in the world. In the summer more than 4,000 scientists operate research stations; this number decreases to just over 1,000 in the winter. McMurdo Station, which is the largest research station in Antarctica, is capable of housing more than 1,000 scientists, visitors and tourists.

Since the 1970's an important focus of study has been the ozone layer in the atmosphere above Antarctica. With the ban of CFC's in the Montreal Protocol of 1989, climate projections indicate that the ozone layer will return to 1980 levels between 2050 and 2070.

Sir Charles Kingsford – Smith, MC, AFC (9/2/1897-8/ 11/1935) often called by his nickname "Smithy" was an early Australian aviator. In 1928, he made the first transpacific flight from the United States to Australia. He also made the first non - stop flight crossing of the Australian mainland, the first flights between Australia and New Zealand, and the first eastward Pacific flight crossing from Australia to the United States; and, also made a flight from Australia to London, setting a record of 10.5 days.

Born 9/2/1897, Brisbane, Queensland, Australia. Died 8/ 11/ 1935 aged 38 in the Andaman Sea when his plane crashed in the sea of Burma. He was known for the first non - stop crossing of the Australian mainland and the Trans-Pacific flight from England to Australia air race. He was awarded the Knight Bachelor, the Military Cross, the Air Force Cross and the Segrave Trophy, awarded for outstanding skill, courage and initiative on land, water or in the air and he was in the Australian Flying Corps. In 1986, Kingsford - Smith was inducted into the International Air and Space Hall of fame at the San Diego Air and Space Museum.

Rose Bay, Sydney, Australia is a harbourside eastern suburb of Sydney. It is located seven kilometres east of the Sydney CBD in the local government areas of Waverly Council and the municipality of Woolahra. It is a highly desirable suburb with a dynamic village life and a good mix of shops and cafes. However, Rose Bay is one of the worst swimming beaches in Sydney as it is susceptible to human fecal matter pollution and the microbial water quality is not always suitable for swimming. The Australian aboriginal name for Rose Bay is "GINNAGULLAH". Rose Bay has extensive views of the Sydney Opera House and the Sydney Harbour bridge. It is the centre for Sydney's Jewish community and has Royal Sydney Golf Club and course and Woolahra Golf Club and course in its municipality, as well as the somewhat "toffey "suburb of Vaucluse.

Stammering (Stuttering). A famous Briton who stuttered was King George VI who went through years of speech therapy, most successfully under the Australian speech therapist Lionel Logue, for his stammer. Logue used techniques like singing, swearing and cessation of smoking in the endeavour to stop King George's stammer.

Another notable case was that of British Prime Minister Winston Churchill. Churchill claimed, perhaps not directly discussing himself, that "sometimes a slight and not unpleasant stammer or impediment has become of some assistance in securing the attention of the audience". However, those who knew Churchill and commented on his stutter believed that it was or had been a significant problem for him. His secretary, Phyllis Moir, commented that "Winston Churchill was born and grew up with a stutter "In her 1941 book "I was Winston Churchill's Private Secretary". She also noted about one incident, "It's s-s-simply s-s-splendid ", he stuttered as he always did when excited. Louis J Alber, who helped to arrange a lecture tour of the United States, wrote in Volume 55 of the American Mercury (1942) that "Churchill struggled to express his feelings but his stutter caught him in the throat and his face turned purple" and that born with a stutter and a lisp, both caused by a defect in his palate, Churchill was at first seriously hampered in his public speaking. It is characteristic of the man's perseverance that, despite his staggering handicap he made himself one of the greatest orators of our time.

For centuries "cures "such as drinking from a snail shell for the rest of one's life, hitting a stutterer in the face when the weather is cloudy, strengthening the tongue as a muscle, and various herbal remedies were used.

Proposed causes of stuttering have included tickling an infant too much, eating inappropriately during breast feeding, allowing an infant to look in a mirror, cutting a child's hair before the child speaks his or her first words, having too small a tongue, or the "work of the devil."

Some remedies that have been tried are singing the words, swearing, speech therapy and cessation of smoking.

Antarctic Research Stations: -

MCMURDO STATION is a United States Antarctic research station on the south tip of Ross Island, which is in the New Zealand – claimed Ross Dependency on the shore of McMurdo Sound in Antarctica, It is operated by the United States on the shore of McMurdo Sound in Antarctica. All personnel and cargo going to or coming from Amundsen - Scott South Pole Station pass through McMurdo. By road, McMurdo is 3 Kilometres from New Zealand's smaller Scott Base.

The station takes its name from its geographic location on McMurdo sound, named after Lieutenant Archibald McMurdo of HMS Terror. Under the command of British explorer James Clark Ross, the Terror first charted the area in 1841. Scott established a base camp close to this spot in 1902 and built a cabin there that was named Discovery Hut. On March 3, 1962, the U.S. Navy activated the PM – 3A nuclear power plant at the station. The reactor generated 1.8 MW of electrical power and reportedly replaced the need for 1,500 gallons of oil daily. As a result of continuing safety issues (hairline cracks in the reactor and water leaks), the US Army Nuclear Power Program was decommissioned in 1972. McMurdo is the world's most southerly harbour.

MAWSON STATION, commonly called Mawson, is one of three permanent bases and research outposts in Antarctica managed by the Australian Antarctic Division (AAD). Mawson lies in Holme Bay in MacRobertson Land, East Antarctica in the Australian Antarctic Territory, a territory claimed by Australia. Established in 1954, Mawson is Australia's oldest Antarctic station and the oldest continuously inhabited Antarctic station of the Antarctic Circle. Mawson was named in honour of the Australian Antarctic explorer Sir Douglas Mawson. It is a base for scientific research programs including an underground cosmic ray detector, various long-term meteorological aeronomy and geomagnetic studies, as well as an ongoing conservation biology studies, in particular of nearby Auster rookery, a breeding ground for emperor and Adelie penguins. It houses approximately 20 personnel over winter and up to 60 in summer. It is the only Antarctic station to use wind generators for over 70% of its power needs, saving over 600,000 litres of diesel fuel a day.

DISCLOSURE: - information has been obtained and quoted from Wikipedia.

SOUTHWARD HO!

It is January the fifteenth 2025 in London, England and it goes without saying that the weather is cold, wet, windy and miserable. Luckily the three Mi5 agents Rebecca Joyce, Bill Parsons and Jack 'Dumpey 'Delaney are in the heated office of the head of Mi5, C.

C's opening gambit is "Well my old mates, funnily enough you're coming out of retirement again!"

Rebecca Joyce quickly counters his opening gambit, almost akin to taking his Queen by saying. "I didn't realise we'd had a retirement. If we, did it was the shortest in history!"

Bill and Jack reiterate "Here, Here!"

He then gives them envelopes which detail their next assignment because as he says "We've still got this Tapidae Eulipotyphia in our ranks. To you who are uneducated that is a moldwarp or a moldywarp, and that again is a MOLE!"

As is customary the three of them retire to their local watering hole, the Rose and Crown, but before parting they ask C if he would like to join them.

He replies "No thanks folks I've got an appointment with the P.M. in an hour. So I'll go and see Boris and find out if he's having a "bad hair day "or not!"

This brings a smile and a chuckle to the faces of the three agents, and they all say "Fair enough. We'll see you next time."

So once again when they are at the Rose and Crown, and

they have ordered the first round of drinks Beccie is eager to open her envelope and does so forthwith.

"Bloody heck! We're off to the Antarctic. That's south of Oz and colder than here! I think I'll invite Cumberband down and he can talk to the penguins"

"Yeh what's with that bloke, he's supposed to be an actor, so you think he'd be able to say PENGUINS!" States Jack.

Bill and Jack then say, "GAME ON IN ANTARCTICA."

C has arranged their flight from London to Sydney with Qantas leaving Heathrow, London at 8:35 p.m. and arriving at Kingsford - Smith International Airport, Sydney at 6:10 p.m. Sydney time a duration normally of 22 hours and 55 minutes.

They all duly depart Heathrow on another cold, wet, windy, miserable day aboard Qantas flight QF 2 bound for Sydney. Shortly after takeoff they converse for a while and then Bec and Jack decide to get some shuteye but Bill who can't really sleep on planes decides to go to the rear of the plane to get a cup of coffee from the hostess.

"G'day Bill, I saw from the passenger list that you lot were all on board". Said Katie Barlow.

"Yeh, Hi Kate we're spending a few days in Oz staying at Bec's shack in Sydney before tripping down to Antarctica. "Replies Bill." Oh, Kate's shack in Nose Bay. "She replies, somewhat sarcastically.

Bill questions "Nose Bay? Is that another Australianism? "

"Well sort of but it is a sort of a play on words with a double meaning. Nose instead of Rose, I guess that's Aussie humour, but Nose also because Rose Bay is sometimes "on the nose !" as it is often contaminated with human fecal matter which somehow or another seems to come from the stormwater drains, so don't go swimming there!"

"O.K. we'll bear that in mind!" States Jack.

The rest of the flight is uneventful and after a period of about twenty hours and thirty minutes the plane circles over the great expanse of Sydney Harbour with the bridge and Opera House in full view in the vivid sunlight before QF2 lands at Sir Charles Kingsford - Smith International Airport.

They then collect their luggage from the carousel and get a taxi to Bec's shack in Rose Bay.

Bec says to the taxi driver "Number 321 New South Head Road, it's just out of Vaucluse near O'sullivan road, mate, and you can take the direct route too, it should be about seven K's!"

"O.K., love I'm with you there!" Replies the taxi driver.

So, in twenty minutes they are at Bec's beach shack. They alight from the taxi and grab their luggage and walk up to her beach shack.

"Blimey!" says Jack "This is some shack, as you put it!"

There before them was a huge, obviously architect de-signed building comprising what appeared to be five bed-rooms, a lounge, a dining room, kitchen, two bathrooms and toilets with a huge balcony / verandah with extensive views of the ocean and Rose Bay with Rose Bay wharf to their right and Point Piper to their left.

Bec says "Well folks make yourselves at home for a couple

of days and enjoy the warmth of the Australian sun before we head off to Antarctica!"

"Righto", says Bill "But I think I wouldn't mind staying here."

Jack says "D'accor!"

"Well!" Exclaims Bec. "What shall we do today, we could go and watch the Pomes and the Aussies play the next Test at The Sydney Cricket ground or a mate of mine's got a yacht and we could go sailing!"

Jack interjects with "Hey, Bec I thought that Pomes were the Prisoners of Mother England and so you Aussies are in fact POMES".

"Yeh, well as far as I'm concerned I don't give a pinch of pelican poop about that and you Brits are still and always will be POMES to me, so stick that up your Khyber!"

"Righto!" says Jack "I have no reply to that!"

"Just as well "Replies Bec, let's go for this sail!"

They make their way to the Rose Bay Yacht Club and find Bec's mate's yacht which has the name "Bennie's Toe 30 "as it is a Benetau Oceanis 30.1. The boat is still on its trailer, so they launch it at the ramp and hop aboard and tack off with a 20 metre per hour Southerly pushing them along into Sydney Harbour.

Bec cracks the customary Fosters for one and all and then says "Lets hoist the spinnaker and give this thing a bit of a shake - up and give these black Kevlar sails a bit of colour."

This was immediately done and the old Bennie's Toe 30 looked a magnificent sight sailing past the Sydney Opera

House and under the old "Coat Hanger" with its red and white striped spinnaker full of New South Wales air along with the myriad of other yachts sailing on the harbour. .

Bec says "Here comes another Benetau and I think its "The Sidewalk Café"

Jack says "It's pretty fast for a sidewalk café!"

"Yeh! and your pretty funny too, it must be this Aussie humour rubbing of on you mate!" says Bec "It used to be owned by Jack Baxter from Albany in Western Australia and had the fastest time in one of the Sydney to Hobarts but had a one hour penalty imposed on it for almost colliding with the Yankee yacht "Comanche ", so she's pretty rapid. I think I would have completed the collision with the Yanks and put them out, although in reality most of the Septic Tanks are O.K. Jack Baxter died a little time ago and I don't think "Sidewalk "has been sold so it's probably still in the family. I'll ask Marco Guintoli who is a good bloke, and he lives in Albany and sailed in "Sidewalk "in one of the Hobarts."

She adds "Well what are we going to do in Antarctica besides frrrreeeezzzzze!" through clenched teeth and lips.

"Well C reckons we need to check out the Russians down there. "says Jack

"Hmph, check them out! I can tell you what they'll be up to – no good! They'll be mining that Uranium and lead in the Antarctic Peninsula even though there is an embargo until 2048 with the Protocol on Environmental Protection to the Antarctic Treaty. However, that doesn't mean anything to the Ruskies and you know they don't give a wombats rear about any sort of protocol so forget that!"

Bill Parsons answers with. "Well, I don't know what a wombat's rear looks like but I'm guessing it's only attractive to another wombat, male or female. However, you are right about the Russians!"

"Too right I am Cobber! And wombats are quite cute little fellows but watch out for their claws, they 're designed for digging and not for being cuddled by humans. Likewise with koalas, they look cute and all they do is sleep in blue gum trees and occasionally wake up to eat and piss on humans who cuddle them. Can't really blame them for that, though. Come to think of it there are some humans that I wouldn't mind doing it to but it might be considered somewhat unlady – like."

"D'accor!" Says Jack whilst Bill characteristically twirls his black moustache and simultaneously rubs his left ear - lobe.

"I believe C's paid out, or more correctly The British Government, meaning the POMMIE taxpayers have paid our fare on the" Silversea" which is an Antarctic Luxury Cruiser with a strengthened hull and 12 Zodiacs along with a great restaurant with a full glassed area that allows sweeping ocean views and it leaves from Hobart, Tasmania, Australia and cruises to the Antarctic Peninsula via King George Island, Antarctic Sound and then onto the Antarctic Peninsula for six days then onto South Shetland Island and back to Hobart, Tasmania via King George Island. So, it sounds good except it will be cold, although only when we are outside and we can rug - up."

"Sounds great! I can hardly wait "Says 'Dumpey ' Delaney.

"Well, you won't have to wait long because we're off at sparrow's fart tomorrow!" States Bec.

Next morning, they get a cab to Sir Charles Kingsford – Smith International airport and board Qantas Jetstar flight JQ 721 for Hobart, Tasmania and in two hours they have landed at Hobart airport and notice that the ambient temperature is markedly colder than what they were used to in Sydney.

They get a cab and the driver says "Morning folks. Where to?"

Bec answers with "To the Grand Chancellor thanks mate!"

"Right you are!" He replies.

He drives them to the Grand Chancellor and being a Saturday, they pass the Salamanca Markets which are full of people accompanied by its old sandstone warehouses with narrow streets and colonial era cottages. The city's backdrop is the 1210 metre high Mt. Wellington with sweeping views, plus hiking and cycling tracks. The frontage to the Grand Chancellor is the Derwent River and nearby is the Cascade Brewery and the Wrest Point Casino.

After checking in Jack says. "O.K. we should be able to fill in a day here, let's get started!"

Bill says "And I'm not going to that Wrest Point Casino as I got fleeced and ripped off at that one in Hong Kong!"

"Yeh, well we can go but you don't have to bet. "States Jack.

"I suppose so, but I can't smoke there so it's not going to be much fun for me "Replies Bill.

So their day in Hobart was spent watching a Sheffield Shield match between Tasmania and Western Australia and the evening at the Wrest Point Casino with Bill not gambling and not smoking and not really enjoying himself at all so he was glad to board the "Silversea "next morning with the rest of the Mi5 gang and head for Antarctica.

They all noticed when they went outside on deck that the temperature was declining most rapidly as they proceeded further South.

Much later on they sighted their first iceberg and marvelled at the fantastic colouration of this mass of ice.

"First port of call is King George Island "States Bec.

"Mmmm, what's there? "Says Bill as he draws on a cigarette whilst out on deck, then twirls his moustache and rubs his left earlobe which he noticed was rather cold.

Bec googles about King George Island and reads out a rather lengthy reply to Jack and Bill.

"King George Island is the largest of the Shetland Islands lying 120 kilometres off the coast of Antarctica in the Southern Ocean. The island was named after King George III.

King George Island has three major bays, Maxwell Bay, Admiralty Bay and King George Bay. Admiralty Bay has three fiords and is protected as an Antarctic Specially Managed Area under the Protocol on Environmental Protection to the Antarctic Treaty.

The coastal areas of the island are home to a comparatively diverse collection of vegetation and animal life including elephant, Weddell and leopard seals and Adelie, Chinstrap and Gentoo penguins. Several other seabirds, including Skuas and Southern Giant Petrels nest on the island during the summer months.

Human habitation is limited to research stations belonging

to Argentina, Brazil, Chile, China, South Korea, Peru, Poland, Russia, Uruguay and the United States. They carry out research into areas as diverse as biology, ecology, geology and paleontology. The Chilean station on the Fildes peninsula is operated as a permanent village with an airstrip.

Port Thomas lighthouse at Arctowski Station is the most southerly lighthouse in the world. The Antarctic Peninsula and its surrounding islands are considered to have the mildest living conditions in Antarctica. July averaging minus 6.5 degrees Centigrade and 1.5 degrees Centigrade in the warmest areas. Average precipitation is 729 mm per annum. So, there you have it!" Concludes Rebecca.

Shortly afterwards the Silversea hoves within sight of King George Island and in half an hours' time it is entering Admiralty Bay with its magnificent scenery of deep water and fiords.

As a Chilean Lockheed C-130 Hercules drones overhead,

Bec relates the history of how on the ninth of December 2019 a Chilean Air Force C-130 Hercules military transport aircraft crashed in the Drake Passage while en-route to Base Presidente Eduardo Frei Montalvo, a Chilean military base on King George Island. The flight originated from Santiago International Airport, Santiago, Chile. 38 people, all on board were killed.

Bill says to Bec and Jack "So this is Antarctica? "

Bec replies "Well yes and no, it is Antarctica but where we are on King George Island there is more vegetation than on the Antarctic Peninsula and more precipitation and it's a bit warmer too but we should be there in another hour or so depending on how many icebergs there are around the place."

An hour and fifteen minutes pass by when Antarctica hoves in sight on the starboard side and the three Mi5 agents and all the passengers are rugged up on deck to view it. Shortly thereafter anchorage is made and the passengers and some of the crew board Zodiacs and land in Antarctica after negotiating their way around numerous icebergs with their wondrous chroma and hues of white and blue

They all noticed the Soviet Submarine with all the secrecy and surreptitiousness of a secret Soviet Strategic submarine sitting on the silky satin surface of the Southern Sea shored up in the safety of the sound.

On the beach there was a dead Blue Whale that was being feasted on by leopard seals and walruses, but they noticed and commented that there were no White Pointers and indeed no sharks. Bec said "Yeh, there are no White Pointers as the Great White is generally found in shallow waters and they would struggle with the crossing of the deep ocean surrounding the southern continent, thus there are no sharks in Antarctica.

However, they did notice the stench of the dying Blue Whale and the smell coming from the various nearby penguin rookeries and their associated ablutions.

Bec said "It somehow reminds me of when we were up in the Alps in Australia at Charlotte's Pass near Kosciuszko's Peak at 2,228 metres and my father had just had a radical prostatectomy with the quadruple whammy of 1) Urinary incontinence, 2) Ejaculatory incontinence, 3) Erectile dysfunction and 4) although he always jokingly says that it's no big deal - a shortened penis. Also, as I hesitate to say with the cold and the running water of the nearby pristine Snowy River where there was movement at the station and the mountain ponies run, he had to have a piss in the Snowy River which therefore is no longer pristine!"

Anyhow, back at McMurdo Station they enter the building and are immediately confronted by a tall person of about six feet three inches if he's an inch and about two axe handles wide across the shoulders whose name is Tex and from his drawl and the rest of the information, they have obtained they conclude he is a Texan and he's also smoking a Marlboro. However, he speaks with a stammer.

Bec says "G'day Tex, what's this stammer all about? Did your Mum tickle you too much as a baby, or did she eat inappropriately during breast feeding, or did she allow you to look in a mirror or do you have a small tongue or maybe it is the work of the devil!"

Tex tries to answer with "D-d-d- ammed i-f-f-f I-i-i-I k-k-know. B-b-but i-i-i-it's a p-p-p-pain i-i-i-n t-t-the b-b-butt. "As he sticks his large nicotine stained and furry tongue out."Have you tried singing? Asks Bill "I-i-i d-d-don't t-t-think y-y-y-ou w-w-want t-t-t-o h-h-hear m-m- me s-s-s-sing!" States Tex. "C'mon, give it a try "Says Jack.

To the tune of America, The Brave Tex gives forth "Well, here we are down in Antarctic freezing away!"

"Bravo, bravo, bravo! Encore, encore, encore!!! That was great "exclaim the three Mi5 agents. Tex continues singing

"Well, I guess I'll just have to sing my life away!"

"And give up those fags!" Exclaims Bec.

"Allright, allright, allright on to more important matters, what are these commies doing down here and what are we going to do about them?"

"As you've said, we can bet they're up to no good! 'Says Jack.

"That's for sure, cobber! Says Bec.

Tex sings "Well you know what, there's a whole lot of uranium down here on the peninsula that blows in from Australia and South Africa and there's this old decommissioned nuclear power station that the U.S. abandoned back in 1972. It's possible they may want to start that up again and use the uranium here even though they're not allowed to mine in Antarctica, but I can't see that will be considered by them."

"No way, I think you may be onto something there Tex, but how do we stop them? "Questions Bec.

"Also, if they do start the plant what do they do with the uranium? "Asks Jack.

"Probably refuel that nuclear sub on the harbour for starters and then transport it to Russia. "says Bill.

"Mmm, maybe we better get onto them instead of standing around talking and singing. "She says as she eyeballs Tex.

"Well, I suggest we sit here in the warmth of Mawson's hut along with all these other Aussies, that will make you feel right at home Joycee and observe that sub and the Russians. "Says Bill Parsons.

"Right you are mate, sounds good to me, anything to get out of the cold and those lazy katabatic winds that go right through you!" Remarks Bec.

Tex lights up another Marlboro and without thinking forgets to sing his remark "h-h-h-ere c-c-come t-t-t-he R-r-russians!" They then notice four Russians jump into a nearby snowmobile and head inland. The Mi5 agents do likewise with their snowmobile and follow at a distance.

"It looks like they are heading towards the Detroit peninsula. "Says Bill.

"Yeh, most likely after that uranium!" Says Jack.

Sure enough that was what they were doing, so bill videos it on his phone for documentary evidence. He then sends it to the Australian Antarctic Division who send it onto the Australian Federal Police. The Federal police replied to Bill saying that they were sending a contingent to Antarctica and they should be there in two days to arrest the Russians for illegally mining in Antarctica. The incumbent Australian government were informed and they in turn informed the Russian High Commissioner so that they would not be surprised by the arrests.

After a shootout on the Detroit Peninsula with AK – 47's blazing and some poor shooting, as no-one was hit,

the four Russians were duly arrested and transported back to the mainland. The Australian government engaged the Australian human rights lawyer Geoffrey Robertson AO, QC,Visiting Professor at Queen Mary University, U.N. War Crimes Judge, Master of the Bench - Middle Temple , Rhode's Scholar (Oxford), Bachelor of Civil Law (Oxford), Bachelor of Arts (Sydney). They were tried and convicted with the help of Bill Parsons testimony and video evidence, so it was 'fait accompli '. Robertson had injunctions applied to the Russians so that they could not come to Australia or Antarctica for the term of their natural lives and they were deported back to Russia and no doubt feted by Vladimir Putin and engaged as spies elsewhere.

After arriving back in Sydney Bill, Jack and Rebecca sought solace at their local in Rose Bay and said in unison "GAME OVER! MISSION ACCOMPLISHED IN ANTARCTICA. "Jack and Bill added "Let's head for home and retirement again!"

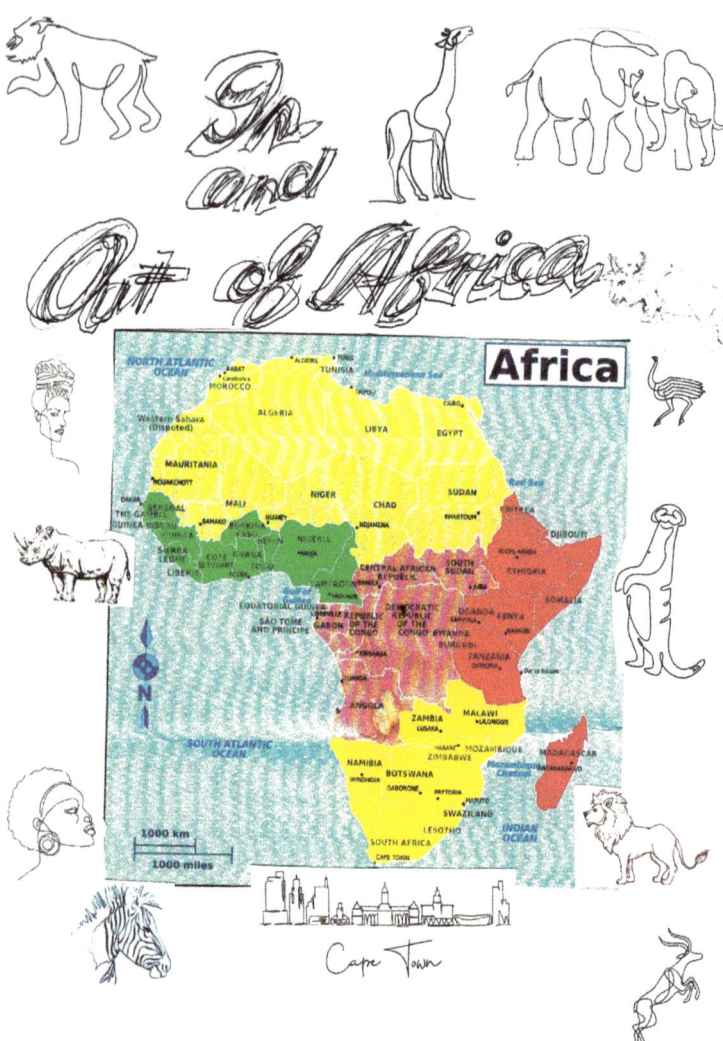

In and
Out of Africa

Africa

Cape Town

10

IN AND OUT OF AFRICA!

PREFACE:

AFRICA, the second largest continent (after Asia), covering about one - fifth of the total surface of the Earth. The continent is bounded on the west by the Atlantic Ocean, on the north by the Mediterranean Sea, on the east by the Red sea and the Indian Ocean, and on the south by the mingling waters of the Atlantic and the Indian Oceans. Africa's total land area is approximately 11,724,000 square miles and the continent measures about 5,000 miles from north to south and about 4,600 miles from east to west. Its northern extremity is Al-Ghiran Point, near Al-Abyad Point (Cape Blanc), Tunisia; it's southern extremity is Cape Aghulas, South Africa; its farthest point east is Xaafuun (Hafun) Point, near Cape Gwardafuy, Somalia; and its western extremity is Almadi Point, on Cape Verde, Senegal. In the northeast, Africa was joined to Asia by the Sinai Peninsula until the construction of the Suez Canal.

Paradoxically, the coastline of Africa – 18,950 miles in

length – is shorter than that of Europe, because there are few inlets and few large bays or gulfs. Off the coasts of Africa, a number of islands are associated with the continent.

Of these, Madagascar, one of the largest islands in the world, is the most significant. Other smaller islands include the Seychelles, Socotra, and other islands to the east; the Comoros, Mauritius, Reunion, and other islands to the southeast; Ascension, St. Helena, and Tristan de Cunha to the southwest; Cape Verde, the Bijagos Islands, Bioko, and Sao Tome and Principe to the west; and the Azores and the Madeira and Canary Islands to the northwest.

The continent is cut almost equally in two by the Equator, so that most of Africa lies within the tropical region. bounded on the north by the Tropic of Cancer and on the south by the Tropic of Capricorn. The Romans, who for a long time ruled the North African coast, are said to have called the area south of their settlements Afriga, or the land of the Afrigs – the name of a Berber community south of Carthage.

The whole of Africa can be considered as a vast plateau rising steeply from narrow coastal strips and consisting of ancient crystalline rocks. The plateau's surface is higher in the southeast and tilts downward toward the northeast. In general, the plateau may be divided into a southeast portion and a northwest portion. The northwest part, which includes the Sahara Desert and that part of North Africa known as the Magrib, has two mountainous regions – the Atlas Mountains in northwest Africa, which are believed to be part of a system that extends into southern Europe, and the Abhaggar downward in a scarp - the Drakensburg Range. One of the most remarkable features in the geologic structure of Africa is the east African Rift System, which lies between 30 and 40 degrees East. The rift itself begins northeast of the continent's limits and extends southward from the Ethiopian Red Sea coast to the Zambezi River basin.

Africa contains an enormous wealth of mineral resources, including some of the world's largest reserves of fossil fuels, metallic ores, and gems and precious metals. This richness is matched by a great diversity of biological resources that includes the densely lush equatorial rainforest of central Africa and the world - famous populations of wildlife of the eastern and southern portions of the continent.

SOUTH AFRICA - Officially known as the Republic of South Africa is the southernmost country in Africa. With over 60 million people, it is the world's 23rd- most populous nation and covers an area of 1,221,037 square kilometres. South Africa has three capital cities: executive Pretoria, judicial Bloemfontein and legislative Cape Town. The largest city is Johannesburg. About 80% of South Africans are of Black African ancestry, divided among a variety of ethnic groups speaking different African Languages. The remaining population consists of European (White South Africans), Asian (Indian South Africans and Chinese South Africans), and Multiracial (Coloured South Africans) ancestry.

It is bounded to the south by 2,798 kilometres of coastline of Southern Africa stretching along the South Atlantic and Indian Oceans; to the north by neighbouring countries of Namibia, Botswana, and Zimbabwe; and to the east and northeast by Mozambique and Eswatina (formerly Swaziland); and it surrounds the enclaved land of Lesotho. It is the southern-most country on the mainland of the Old World, and the most populous country located entirely south of the equator. South Africa is a biodiversity hotspot with a diversity of unique biomes and plant and animal life. South Africa is a multiethnic society encompassing a wide variety of cultures, languages and religions. The country is one of the few in Africa never to have had a coup d'etat, and regular elections have been held for almost a century.

However, the vast majority of South Africans were not disenfranchised (deprived of the right to vote) until 1994.

On 31 May 1961, the country became a republic follow-ing a referendum (only open to white voters) which narrowly passed; the British dominated Natal province largely voted against the proposal. Queen Elizabeth II lost the title of the Queen of South Africa. And the last Governor - General, Charles Robert Swart, became State President.

In the late 1970's, South Africa initiated a programme of nuclear weapons development. In the following decade, it produced six deliverable nuclear weapons.

South Africa is located at the southernmost region of Africa, with a long coastline that stretches more than 2,500 kilometres and along two oceans (The South Atlantic and the Indian). It is about the same size as Columbia, twice the size of France, three times as big as Japan, four times the size of Italy and five times the size of the United Kingdom. The interior of South Africa consists of a vast, in almost most places flat, plateau with an altitude of between 1,000 metres and 2,100 metres, highest in the east and sloping gently downwards towards the west and north and slightly less noticeably so to the south and southwest. This plateau is surrounded by the Great Escarpment, whose eastern, and highest, stretch is known as the Drakensburg. South Africa has a generally temperate climate because it is surrounded by the Atlantic and Indian Oceans on three sides, because it is located in the climatically milder Southern Hemisphere, and because its average elevation rises steadily towards the north (toward the equator) and further inland.

Numerous mammals are found in the Bushveld (a sub-tropical woodland ecoregion occurring in Botswana and Zimbabwe.) including lions, African leopards, South African cheetahs, southern white rhinos, blue wildebeest, kudus, impalas, hyenas, hippopotamuses, and South African giraffes. A significant extent of the Bushveld exists in the north - east including Kruger National Park and the Sabisand Game Reserve as well as in the Waterburg Biosphere (The Waterburg is a mountainous massif of approximately 654,033 hectares in Limpopo Province, South Africa. The average height of the mountain range is 600 metres with a few peaks up to 2,000 metres above sea level).

With more than 22,000 different higher plants, or about 9% of all the known species on Earth, South Africa is particularly rich in plant diversity. The most prevalent biome in South Africa is the grassland, particularly on the Highveld, where the plant cover is dominated by different grasses, low shrubs, and acacia trees, mainly camel-thorn (Vachellia erioloba.)

THE SERENGETI NATIONAL PARK: - Is a national park in Tanzania that stretches over 14,763 square kilometres.

It is located in the Mara and Simiyu regions and contains 15,000,000 hectares of savannah. It is well known for the largest annual animal migration in the world of over 1.5 million blue wildebeest and 250,000 zebra and for its numerous Nile crocodile and honey badger. The Park includes the neighbouring Ngorongo Conservation Area and Maasai Mara National

Reserve in bordering Kenya. The name "Serengeti "is an approximation of the word siringet used by the Maasai people for the area, which means "the place where the land runs on forever."

The Park covers 14,750 square kilometres of grassland plains, savannah, riverine forest, and woodlands. the park lies in northwestern Tanzania, bordered to the north by the Kenyan border, where it is continuous with the Maasai Mara National Reserve. To the southeast of the park is the Ngorongoro Conservation Area, to the southwest lies the Maswa Game Reserve, to the west are the Ikorongo and Grumeti Game Reserves, and to the northeast and east lies the Loliondo Game Control Area. Together, these areas form the larger Serengeti ecosystem. The Serengeti plain is extremely varied, ranging from savannah to hilly woodlands to open grasslands. The region's geographic diversity is due to the extreme weather conditions that plague the area, particularly the potent combination of heat and wind. Many environmental scientists claim that the diverse habits in the region originated from a series of volcanoes, whose activity shaped the basic geographic features of the plain and added mountains and craters to the landscape.

The Serengeti National Reserve is a lion stronghold. The African bush elephant and the African buffalo herds have all somewhat recovered from population declines.

JOHANNESBURG: - informally known as Jozi, Joburg, or The City of Gold, is the largest city in South Africa, classified as a megacity, and is one of the 100 largest urban areas in the world. It is the provincial capital and the largest city of Gauteng, which is the wealthiest province in South Africa. Johannesburg is the seat of the Constitutional Court, the highest court in South Africa. Most of the major South African companies and banks have their head offices in Johannesburg. The city is located in the mineral rich Witwatersrand range of hills and is the centre of large-scale gold and diamond trade.

The city was established in 1886 following the discovery of gold on what had been a farm. Due to the extremely large gold deposit found along the Witwatersrand, within ten years, the population had grown to 100,000 inhabitants.

A separate city from the late 1970's until, 1994, Soweto is now part of Johannesburg.

Originally an acronym for "South-Western Townships ", Soweto originated as a collection of settlements on the outskirts of Johannesburg, populated by native African workers from the gold mining industry. Soweto, although eventually incorporated into Johannesburg, had been separated as a residential area for blacks only (no whites allowed), who were not permitted to live in other white designated suburbs of Johannesburg. The metropolis is an alpha global city as listed by the Globalization and World Cities Research Network. In 2019, the population of the city of Johannesburg was 5,635,127. making it the most populous city in South Africa.

The main Witwatersrand gold reef was discovered in June 1884 on the farm Vogelstruisfontein by Jan Gerritse Bantjes that triggered the Witwatersrand Gold Rush and the founding of Johannesburg in 1886. Mines near Johannesburg are among the deepest in the world. with some as deep as 4,000 metres.

Johannesburg is located in the eastern plateau of South Africa known as the Highveld, at an elevation of 1,753 metres. The former Central Business District is located on the southern side of the prominent ridge called the

Witwatersrand (English: White Water's Ridge) and the terrain falls to the north and south. By and large the Witwatersrand marks the watershed between the Limpopo and Vaal Rivers as the city is drained by the Jukskei River while the southern part of the city including most of the CBD, is drained by the Klip River. The north and west of the city have undulating hills while the eastern parts are flatter. The city is often described as Africa's powerhouse, and as a modern and prosperous African city. It's city centre has a rectangular grid pattern. Streets are narrow and filled with high rises built in the mid-to late 1900's.

Johannesburg is home to some of Africa's tallest structures, such as the Sentech Tower, Hillbrow Tower, the Carlton Centre and Ponte City Apartments.

Johannesburg's climate is a sub-tropical highland climate. The 2011 population of Johannesburg was, 4,434,827 people.

Blacks account for 73% of the population, followed by whites at 18%, coloureds at 6% and Asians at 4%.

Johannesburg is the economic and financial hub of South Africa, producing 16% of South Africa's gross domestic product, and accounts for 40% of Gauteng's economic activity.

Johannesburg has not traditionally been known as a tourist destination, but the city is a transit point for connecting flights to Cape Town, Durban and the Kruger National Park.

Johannesburg is served principally by OR Tambo International Airport for both domestic and international flights.

APARTHEID: Apartheid, was a system of institutionalized racial segregation that existed in South Africa and South West Africa (now Namibia) from 1948 until the early 1990 ' s. Apartheid was characterized by an authoritarian political culture based on baaskap (boss- hood or boss-ship), which ensured that South Africa was dominated politically, socially and economically by the nation's minority white population. According to this system of social stratification, white citizens had the highest status, followed by Asians and Coloureds, then black Africans. The economic legacy and social effects of apartheid continue to this day.

Broadly speaking, apartheid was delineated into 'petty apartheid ', which entailed the segregation of public facilities and social events, and 'grand apartheid ', which dictated housing and employment opportunities by race. The first apartheid law was the Prohibition of Mixed Marriages Act, 1949, followed closely by the Immorality Amendment Act of

1950, which made it illegal for most South African citizens to marry or pursue sexual relationships across racial lines. The Population Regulation Act, 1950, classified all South Africans into one of four racial groups based on appearance, known ancestry, socioeconomic status, and cultural lifestyle: "Black ", "White ", "Coloureds" and" Indian ", the last two of which included several sub – classifications. Places of residence were determined by racial classification. Between 1960 and 1983, 3.5 million black Africans were removed from their homes and forced into segregated neighbourhoods as a result of apartheid legislation, in some of the largest mass evictions in modern history. Most of these targeted removals were intended to restrict the black population to ten designated "tribal Homelands ", known as bantustands, four of which became nominally independent states. The government announced that relocated persons would lose their South African citizenship as they were absorbed into bantustands.

Apartheid sparked significant international and domestic opposition, resulting in some of the most influential global social movements of the twentieth century. It was the target of frequent condemnations in the United Nations and brought about an extensive arms and trade

embargo on South Africa. During the 1970's and 1980's, internal resistance to apartheid became increasingly militant, prompting brutal crackdowns by the National Party government and protracted sectarian violence that left thousands dead or in detention. Some reforms of the apartheid system were undertaken, including allowing for Indian and Coloured political representation in parliament, but these measures failed to appease most activist groups. Between 1987 and 1993, the National Party entered into bilateral negotiations with the African National Congress (ANC), the leading anti- apartheid political movement, for ending segregation and introducing majority rule. In 1990, prominent ANC figures such as Nelson Mandela were released from prison.

Apartheid legislation was repealed on 17 June 1991, pending multiracial elections held under a universal suffrage set for April 1994.

Universal suffrage gives the right to vote to all adult citizens, regardless of wealth, income, gender, social status, race, ethnicity, political stance, or any other restriction subject only to minor exceptions.

Apartheid is an Afrikaans word meaning "separateness ", or "the state of being apart "literally" apart-hood".

Black people were not allowed to run businesses or professional practices in areas designated as "white South Africa "unless they had a permit - such being granted only exceptionally. They were required to move back to the black "homelands "and set up business and practice there. Blacks could never acquire land in white areas. In the homelands, much of the land belonged to a" tribe ", where the local chieftain would decide how the land had to be used. This resulted in whites owning almost all the industrial and agricultural lands and much of the prized residential land.

The population was classified into four groups: African, White, Indian and Coloureds. The coloured group included people regarded as being of mixed descent, including of

Bantu, Khoisan, European and Malay ancestry. Khoisan is a catch-all term for the non- Bantu indigenous peoples of Southern Africa. Many were descended from people brought to South Africa from other parts of the world, such as India, Sri Lanka, Madagascar and China (funnily enough) as slaves and indentured workers.

Voting rights were denied to Coloureds in the same way that they were denied to Blacks from 1950 to 1983.

However, in 1977 the NP caucus approved proposals to bring Coloureds and Indians into central government. In 1982, final constitutional proposals produced a referendum among Whites and the Tricameral Parliament was approved.

Tricamerism is the practice of having three legislative or parliamentary chambers. It is contrasted with unicamerism and bicamerism, both of which are far more common. The term was used in South Africa to describe the Parliament established under the Apartheid regime 's new South African Constitution.

South Africa's policies were subject to international scrutiny in 1960, when the UK Prime Minister Harold Macmillan criticized them during his Wind of Change speech in Cape Town. Weeks later tensions came to a head in the Sharpeville Massacre, resulting in more international condemnation.

The Sharpeville Massacre occurred on 21st of March 1960 and it was an incident in the Black township of Sharpeville, near Vereenigning, South Africa, in which police fired on a crowd of Black people, killing or wounding some 250 of them.

About 69 Blacks were killed and more than 180 wounded, some 50 women and children being among the victims.

It was a result of a peaceful protest regarding South African policies of apartheid. The enforcement of Pass Laws and the reissue of laws that restricted the movement of Black Africans in White areas in South Africa initiated a protest in Sharpeville.

THE IVORY TRADE: - The ivory trade is the commercial, often illegal trade in the ivory tusks of the hippopotamus, walrus, narwhal, mammoth, and most commonly, African and Asian elephants.

Ivory has been traded for hundreds of years by people in Africa and Asia, resulting in restrictions and bans. Ivory was formerly used to make piano keys and other decorative items because of the white colour it presents when processed but the piano industry abandoned ivory as a key covering material in the 1980's in favour of other materials such as plastic. Also, synthetic ivory has been developed which can also be used as an alternative material

for making piano keys. Elephant ivory has been exported from Africa and Asia

for millennia with records going back to the 14th century BCE. Transport of the heavy commodity was always difficult, and with the establishment of the early- modern slave trades from East and West Africa, freshly captured slaves were used to carry the heavy tusks to the ports where both the tusks

and their carriers were sold. The ivory was used for piano keys, billiard balls and other expressions of exotic wealth. At the peak of the ivory trade, pre - 29th century, during the colonization of Africa, around 800 to 1,000 tonnes of ivory was sent to Europe alone. By the 1970's, Japan consumed about 40% of the global trade; another 40% was consumed by Europe and North America, often worked in Hong Kong, which was the largest trade hub, with most of the rest remaining in Africa. China, yet to become the economic force of today, consumed small amounts of ivory to keep its skilled carvers in business

The African elephant, 1980's poaching and illegal trade: - In 1942, the African elephant population has been estimated to be around 1.3 million in 37 range states, but by 1989, only 600,000 remained. Although many ivory traders repeatedly claimed that the problem was habitat loss, it became glaringly clear that the threat was primarily the international ivory trade. Throughout this decade, around 75,000 African elephants were killed for the ivory trade annually, worth around 1 billion dollars. About 80% of this was estimated to have come from illegally killed elephants. The international deliberations over the measures required to prevent the serious decline in elephant numbers almost always ignored the loss of human life in Africa, the fuelling of corruption, the "currency" of ivory in buying arms, and the breakdown of law and order in areas where illegal ivory trade flourished. The debate usually rested on the numbers of elephants, estimates of poached elephants and official ivory statistics.

Solutions to the problem of poaching and illegal trade focused on trying to control international ivory movements through CITES (Convention on International Trade in Endangered Species of Wild Fauna and Flora).

Throughout the debate which led to the 1990 ivory ban, a group of southern African countries supported Hong Kong and Japanese ivory traders to maintain trade. This was stated to be because these countries claimed to have well - managed elephant populations and they needed the revenue from ivory sale to fund conservation. These countries were South Africa, Zimbabwe, Botswana, Namibia and Swaziland. They voted against the Appendix One listing and worked to reverse the decision. The two countries leading the attempt to overturn the ban immediately after it was agreed were South Africa and Zimbabwe. On 16 November 2017, it was announced that US President Donald Trump had lifted a ban on ivory imports from Zimbabwe implemented by Barack Obama.

China and Japan bought 108 tonnes of ivory in a one - off sale in November 2008 from Botswana, South Africa, Namibia and Zimbabwe.

China's increased involvement in infrastructure projects in Africa and the purchase of natural resources has alarmed many conservationists who fear the extraction of wildlife body parts is increasing.

Claims of a link between terrorism and the ivory trade have been made by a number of public officials and media outlets. NGO reports cited an anonymous source within the militant organization Al- Shabaab who claimed that the group engaged in the trafficking of ivory. The claim that Al-Shabaab received up to 40% of its funding from the sale of elephant ivory gained further attention following the 2013 Westgate shopping mall attack in Nairobi, Kenya.

International trade in Asian elephant ivory was banned in 1975 when the Asian elephant was placed on Appendix One of the Convention on the International Trade in Endangered Species. By the late 1980's it was believed that only around 50,000 remained in the wild. Trade in Walrus ivory has taken place for hundreds of years in large regions of the northern hemisphere, involving such groups as the Norse, Russians, and other Europeans, the Inuit, the people of Greenland and Eskimos.

The people of Greenland have likely traded narwhal ivory amongst themselves prior to any contact with Europe and for hundreds of years since, the tusks have moved from Greenland to international markets. In the 1600's, the Dutch traded with the Inuit, typically for metal goods in exchange for narwhal ivory tusks, seal skins and other items. Trading continues today between Greenland and other countries, with Denmark by far being the leading purchaser.

Canada has an international export ban of narwhal tusks from 17 Nunavut communities imposed by the Canadian federal government. The Inuit traders in the region are challenging the ban by filing an application with the Federal Court.

SERONERA WILDLIFE LODGE is located on the migratory route of the wildebeest, and it provides front-seat viewing of this extraordinary natural phenomenon. The lodge is artfully constructed around a rocky outcrop from glass and timber elements, perfectly blending into its surroundings;

next to the lodge several waterholes attract, day and night, the most amazing animals, providing a unique opportunity for a close encounter with the Big Five Cats. Seronera Lodge is only five minutes away from the departing point of the hot air balloon safaris, which offer a thrilling birds-eye perspective of the vast plains of the Serengeti.

From its privileged location, the Seronera 's 75 rooms afford stunning views of over a million wildebeest as they migrate from Kenya to Lake Victoria to escape the drought.

LAKE MANYARA WILDLIFE LODGE is in a small breathtaking National Park with an immense natural richness – there are over 300 bird species, including the thousands of flamingos that tint the soda waters of the Lake pink and the famous tree-climbing lions, which for unknown reasons sleep in the branches of the acacia trees.

DISCLOSURE: information has been obtained and quoted from Wikipedia and Hotels and Lodges Tanzania.

IN AND OUT OF AFRICA!

London 2026, the three Mi5 agents Bill Parsons, Jack 'Dumpey 'Delaney and the Australian Rebecca Joyce are finally enjoying their retirement. They are spending the inclement days, which is more often than not the case, playing squash, drinking at the Rose and Crown, reading and spending time with their families. On the clement ones they often walk, ride their bicycles or play golf or tennis. Today they are playing golf and have just finished their game and are sitting in the club house adding up their scores and signing their cards when all their mobile phones ping.

They check them and find a text from C, the head of Mi5, requesting them all to come to his office at nine tomorrow morning. Bec says "Oh, well that's the end of our retirement, so drink up and let's have another round!"

"Righto!" Answer Bill and Jack.

At nine o'clock, on the dot,

they are in C's office.

"Well my fine feathered friends you're off to Africa!"

"Freakin' Afreeka! Well I suppose it will be warmer than freezing' frigid Antarctica, unless you're takin' us up to the top of Kilimanjaro, boss!" Blurts Bec.

"That's a possibility, who knows where you lot will end up!" States C.

"As usual here are your envelopes giving your assignments. "Commands C.

"No David's!" Says Bec.

"Come again?" Questions C.

"Oh, it was something that happened whilst we were at Uni. There was this dental student called David Murray who was always responding to things by saying "No Worries!" . So, "No Worries!" became "No David Murray's!" which of course with Aussies became "No David's!""

"I think I see now, mate. "says C.

"No wuckers!" Replies Bec.

"I'm not going there!" Responds C.

Their meeting then terminates and as has become usual the three Mi5 agents retire to the Rose and Crown. They order a round of beers and open and read their envelopes.

They all exclaim "GAME ON IN AFRICA!"

Bec says "I don't know about this Africa thingo. I had a mate at high school by the name of Ken Jackson and he became an accountant, a stockbroker and a furniture manufacturer. I don't really see any relationship there, but what the heck! With his work he spent a bit of time in Africa and he always said "Don't go to Africa Bec it's a nation of misery!" So, as I've said I don't know about this one."

"Yeh, well I can see where you're coming from but there is some relationship between accounting and furniture manufacturing and between accounting and stockbroking, but that's about it. "Says Jack.

Bill just draws on his cigarette and twiddles with his left earlobe and makes no comment.

C also advises in their envelopes that he has booked them with South African Airlines to fly from Heathrow,

London to Johannesburg

leaving at 9:15 a.m. Greenwich time flying business class.

Jack says "Why in the hell has he booked us to Jo'burg when our destination is Cape Town? "

Bill replies "Because SAA don't fly to Jo'burg direct, but BA do."

"So why didn't we fly with BA then!" Is Jack's rejoinder.

"Beats me!" exclaims Bill "

They may be cheaper. ""That would be right!" Bec.

The three of them board South African Airways at Heathrow for their flight to Africa and after an uneventful 11 hours they touch down at Johannesburg International Airport for 30 minutes before transferring for their flight to Cape Town which takes 2 hours 10 minutes. After grabbing their suitcases they take a taxi from the airport to their accommodation at the Primi Seacastle Hotel which is directly situated on the beach with Table Top Mountain as a majestic backdrop. It is a four star luxury hotel with panoramic views of Camps Bay and its surroundings and is about ten minutes from the CBD.

"Well, this very nice, reminds me of Bondi a bit but the surfs not as good! Also Camps Bay is a one of the safer districts in Cape Town "Bec

Probably, but the white pointers are just as good, I'll bet!" Replies Jack.

"I'm not aiming to find out mate!" Says Bec.

"Actually, there are charter boats that you can go on and dive, in a cage, with them. "Says Bill.

"Righto, I think the day is relatively free tomorrow, let's do that!" Quips Jack.

That evening they all spent an enjoyable evening dining and wining in the Primi Seacastle and pondering what their next assignment will beach will have to let us know soon because even though it's nice here in Cape Town we can't hang around here for ever. "Says Bill.

Almost fatefully, their phones

chime and a text appear from C from Mi5 asking one of them to ring him.

Bill does so immediately and C replies. "Howdy mate, I should have put this in your envelopes, it was a bit of an oversight on my part, but your next assignment is to check out some KGB and German agents who are presently in Durban. I'll text the details Bec and bear in mind that this will probably all be compromised by this damn mole."

"Righto, Bwana!" Replies Bill, still in African mode.

As they have a bit of free time in Cape Town, they decide to go out on a Shark boat for a bit of an adventure. They buy their tickets and board the good boat "Rickety "and set forth for their rendezvous point five miles offshore.

They have left the surf behind but there is still quite a swell which is allright when they are making headway however when they reach their destination and start drifting Jack is feeling decidedly squeamish.

Bill says "You're looking a bit greenish around the gills mate. Never mind you'll feel better once you hurk!"

"I think that's probably so! Jack". "I'll probably feel a bit better when this stinking pig offal and guts go overboard too!"

"Righto, we'll do that now "Replies Bill.

He and Rebecca promptly attend to that which makes Jack feel slightly better.

They then start banging on the aluminium shark cage to try and further attract some Great Whites.

Within ten minutes three of them appear and they are all a good size ranging from about 9 to 5 metres.

The three Mi5 agents hop into the cage with their underwater cameras and get some great photos of the Great Whites. After ten minutes they all hop out back onto the "Rickety "and export their photos to their families and to Cat Mi5.

C texts back. "Great mate, looks like a good lot of fish and chips there."

Bec texts back, correcting him

by saying "Actually, they're not fish but I get your drift C for chip."

When they have finished feeding the sharks, and Jack the fish, they decide to head back to shore.

Jack says, "Thank goodness for that I'm feeling a bit better now that we're heading for terra firma."

With a following sea and full throttle, they were back on land within an hour and grabbed a cab to the Primi Seacastle. When they are there Bec googles to find a place to have lunch. "Hey, this place looks all right. It's called the Waterkloof Tasting Lounge and is out in Old Sir Lowry's pass road in Somerset West Cape Town. It has a biodynamic winery with views of fields and peaks and the views of False Bay may be the best in Western Cape. They say they have a premium wine tasting which is great value and gives tasting of six wines. I'll make a booking around 12:30. Says Bec enthusiastically.

"Righto!" Reiterates Bill and Jack.

Their taxi pulls up outside the vineyard at 12:15 and they alight and walk-in. A staff member shows them to their table, and they all take a seat. Bill then orders a bottle of their Riesling and three glasses. When this arrives shortly thereafter he pours wine into the glasses and says "Bottoms up!"

"Right, we're off go Durban tomorrow to see what these Germans and Russians are up to. "Says Bill.

"Well one things for sure, they won't be up to any good and it will probably be illegal for another. "Says Beccie.

"What time do we set off tomorrow? "Questions Jack. "On board at 9:00 a.m. matey!" Replies Bec.

They then all peruse their menus and catch the waiter's eye and order their lunch. "I'll have half a dozen natural oysters followed by grilled swordfish and sticky date pudding for sweets. "Starts Bec.

Jack and Bill say "That sounds pretty good, I'll have the same."

"Oh we better have another une bouteille of that Reisling please kind sir. "Adds Rebecca.

The wine arrives promptly and the meal within ten minutes. "What a lovely place. "Says Jack. "Beautiful views, good wine, presumably good food although the company leaves a bit to be desired."

"Funny, I was just thinking the same thing!" Says Bec with a smile.

"O.K., this trip tomorrow. Cape Town to Durban is about 70 minutes, I don't know how long the stopover is, but then fly to Seronera, which is apparently the Maasi word meaning the place of the bat- eared fox. From Seronera we take a taxi into the Serengeti. That all takes about another 17 hours. Seronera is a small settlement in the Serengeti

National Park and it has an airstrip and is best known as the big cat capital of Africa, so watch it when we're camping.

"Why don't we arrange a hot air balloon ride over the Serengeti? It would be awesome!" States Bec.

"Great idea. "Says Bill.

"I'll Google it now "Says Bec. "Done!" She adds. "They'll pick us up at 7 O 'clock on the day following our arrival in Seronera fellas."

The day of their departure for the Serengetti arrives and after about 17 hours of travel they arrive in Seronera.

They arrive at their accommodation at the Seronera Wildlife Lodge and settle in.

"This is an amazing place. "Says Jack. "I've never seen so many animals at close range."

"Yeh, it's incredible but we won't be here for long as we're off on that balloon trip tomorrow and I think they pick us up at sparrow's fart "Says Bill.

"You know it may be funny, but I've never seen or heard a sparrow fart!" Says Bec.

"Maybe you need to get your eyes and hearing tested "Says with a smile.

It's fairly warm so they all decide to take a dip in the pool.

When they are in Bec decides to do a few laps of the pool, then they all get out and sit at a table at the poolside.

"This is fabulous "Says Bec." Much better than Nose Bay!"

"Yeh, I'll drink to that. "Says Bill as he gestures to the waiter.

"Yes Sir, what will it be?"

Questions the waiter. "Three Pina Coladas please and make them big ones."

Replies Bill.

They then proceed to have their drinks whilst looking over the great expanse of the Serengeti and notice a hot air balloon wafting along in the distance.

After finishing his drink Bill says "I'm a bit peckish. How about some toasted sandwiches for lunch?"

"Yeh, righto!" Reply Bec and Jack.

The order was placed, and it arrived in ten minutes.

Jack says "Bon Appetite!" BiBon Appetito!" And Bec says "Bog in!"

They all start hoeing into their sandwiches and shortly finish them.

Bec says "Hey, that was all right, how about some more Pina Coladas!"

"Sure thing!" Say Bill and Jack. "We're only going up in a balloon tomorrow at sparrow's fart, I believe Bec "As he gives her a wink and a smile. "And I think that's a lot of hot air."

"Forever the comedian "Says Bill.

"Yeh, well even so after these Pinas I think an early night might be in order. "Continues Bill.

"Darn tootin!" Says Bec. "Especially if we are gettin' up at farrow's. "She adds as she gives Bill a wink and a smile.

Six O' Clock the next morning arrives pretty rapidly and

they have breakfast at the Lodge and prepare for the arrival of the taxi to take them down the road a bit to the take – off for the hot air balloon.

Within minutes they were in the basket of the hot air balloon, waiting for it to be fully fired up for take-off.

When this was done the anchors were lifted and they were airborne, drifting along with a slight westerly breeze.

Their elevation changed from treetop to about 3,000 metres depending on what their guide/pilot, Roger, wanted them to see. Whatever the height was they had magnificent views of the Serengeti, the land that never ends, and the animals who were unaware of their presence and carried on with their usual normal habits.

Before too long they came across a herd of elephants that appeared to be milling around and stomping at the ground stirring up the dust whilst trumpeting loudly.

"What in the Dickens is going on here!" Exclaims Bill.

"There are four blokes down there brandishing rifles, and it looks like they are cutting off their tusks for the ivory trade "Says Bec.

"By George, you're right!" Exclaims Bill. "Take this thing in lower Roger. "Bill says to the pilot "And I'll zoom in and get some photos of them and send them to C and see if we can find out who they are. He peremptorily does so and also alert the Serengeti Park rangers about what is going on, however they are situated miles away and say it will take some time to get there.

In a few minute C texts back to Bill saying that two of them are agents from Germany and big-game fanatics and the other two are Russian Federal Security Service (FSB {formerly The Foreign Intelligence Service -SVR which was formerly the KGB – The committee for Russian State Security}). C thinks that the Russians may also be going to take over South Africa's nuclear facilities and hiJack their plutonium.

Bill says "O.K., there's not much else we can do at the moment except to keep track on these guys and alert the rangers as to their whereabouts."

He immediately alerts the rangers who say. "Righto

Bwana we'll send in another group from the West so that we will have a sort of pincer attack on them. Thanks for alerting us, Sir."

As the afternoon unfolded, the Germans and Russians were rounded up and handcuffed and the ivory confiscated. The dead elephant was butchered and cut up for pet meat, so it did at least serve a useful purpose.

Bill, Jack and Beccie did not wait around for the trial of the prisoners but did hear that they were duly convicted and sentenced to fifteen years goal with no chance of ever entering Africa legally again.

Bill, Jack and Rebecca headed for Jo 'burg and then to Britain where Jack and Bill were, once again, going to take their retirement from Mi5 and Rebecca was going to go back to Sydney, Australia for her annual vacation and then back to London to see what C had in store for her.

As they boarded the plane they said in unison. "GAME OVER! MISSION

ACCOMPLISHED IN AFRICA!"

Mi5   Mi5

SOE   SOE

BILL PARSONS , JACK.DELANEY, REBECCA.JAMES

ROUTE
US
56

ROUTE
US
66

I Love to Go to
America!

11 █

I LOVE TO GO TO AMERICA!

PREFACE:

U.S. Route 66 or U.S. Highway 66 (US 66 or Route 66), also known as the Will Rogers Highway, the Main Street of America or the Mother Road, was one of the original highways in the U.S. Highway System. US 66 was established on November 11, 1926, with road signs erected the following year. The highway which became one of the most famous roads in the United States, originally ran from Chicago, Illinois, through Missouri, Kansas, Oklahoma, Texas, New Mexico, and Arizona before terminating in Santa Monica in Los Angeles County, California, covering a total of 2,448 miles. It was recognized in popular culture both by the hit song "(Get your Kicks on Route 66 ") and the Route 66 television series which aired on CBS from 1960 to 1964. In John Steinbeck's classic novel, "The grapes of Wrath" (1939), the road" Highway 66" symbolized escape and loss.

US 66 served as a primary route for those who migrated

west, especially during the Dust Bowl of the 1930's and the road supported the economies of the communities through which it passed. People doing business along the route became prosperous due to the growing popularity of the highway, and those same people later fought to keep the highway alive in the face of growing threat of being surpassed by the new Interstate Highway System.

US 66 underwent many improvements and realignments over its lifetime but was officially removed from the US Highway System in 1985 after it had been replaced in its entirety by segments of the Interstate Highway System.

From the outset, public road planners intended US 66 to connect the main streets of rural and urban communities along its course for the most practical of reasons; most small towns had no prior access to a major national thoroughfare.

Much of the early highway was gravel or graded dirt. Due to the efforts of the US Highway 66 Association, US 66 became the first highway to be completely paved in 1938.

The beginning of the decline for US 66 came in 1956 with the signing of the Interstate Highway Act by President Dwight D. Eisenhower who was influenced by his experiences in 1919 as a young Army officer crossing the country in a truck convoy (following the route of the Lincoln Highway), and his appreciation of the highway network as a necessary component of a national defence system.

Over the years, US 66 received numerous nicknames. Right after US 66 was commissioned, it was known as "The Great Diagonal Way "because the Chicago – to – Oklahoma City stretch ran northeast to southwest. Later, US 66 was advertised by the US Highway 66 Association as "The Main Street of America "US 66 was unofficially named "The Will Rogers Highway" in 1940.

B. 'Banjo 'Paterson (1864 – 1941) is rightly recognized as Australia's greatest storyteller and most celebrated poet, the boy from the bush who became the voice of a generation. He gave Australia it's unofficial national anthem, 'Waltzing Matilda ', and treasured ballads such as 'The Man from Snowy River ', 'The Geebung Polo Club' and ' Clancy of the Overflow ', vivid creations that helped to define Australia's national identity.

But there is more, much more to Banjo's story that straddled two centuries and saw Australia transform from a far – flung colony to a fully-fledged nation.

Born in the Australian bush, as a child Banjo rode his pony to a one-room school along a trail frequented by outlaw Ben Hall. As a young man he befriended Breaker Morant and covered the second Boer War as a correspondent reporter. He fudged his age to enlist during World War I, ultimately driving an ambulance before commanding a horse training unit during that conflict. Newspaper editor, columnist, foreign correspondent and ABC broadcaster, he knew countless luminaries of his time, including Rudyard Kipling, Winston Churchill, Field Marshall Haig and Henry Lawson. The tennis ace, notorious ladies 'man, brilliant jockey and celebrated polo player was an eye -witness to many key moments in Australian history and saw the Australian racehorses Carbine and Phar Lap race.

CLANCY of the OVERFLOW: -

Clancy is a character that comes out of Paterson's imagination but based on people he has probably met. That bushman was none other than his great grandfather, Thomas Clancy, and overseer and drover who was based in central New South Wales, Australia from the 1860's to the 1880's.

The Overflow is an area in New South Wales which contains many sheep and cattle stations.

DINGO: -

The dingo (Canis familiaris) is an ancient lineage of dog found in Australia. Its taxonomy classification is debated; as far as the variety of scientific names presently applied in different publications, it is variously considered a form of domestic dog not warranting recognition as a subspecies of dog or wolf or a full species in its own right.

The dingo is a medium – sized canine that possesses a lean, hardy body adapted for speed, agility and stamina. The dingoes three main coat colourations are tan, black and tan, or creamy white. The skull is wedge - shaped and appears large in proportion to the body. The dingo is closely related to the New Guinea Singing Dog and The New Guinea Highland Wild Dog. Their lineage split early from the lineage that led to today's domestic dogs and can be traced back through the Malay Archipelago to Asia.

The earliest known dingo fossil, found in Western Australia, dates back to 3,450 years ago. However, genomic analysis indicates that the dingo reached Australia 8,300 years ago but the human population which bought them remains unknown. Dingo morphology hasn't changed over the last 3,500 years; this suggests that no artificial selection has been applied over this period.

The dingo's habitat covers most of Australia, but they are absent in the south-east and Tasmania and an area in the southwest. As one of Australia's largest extant (still existing) terrestrial predators dingoes prey on mammals up to the size of red kangaroos, in addition to birds reptiles, fish, crab, frogs, insects and seeds. The dingo's competitors include the native quoll, the introduced red fox and the feral cat. A dingo pack usually consists of a mated pair, their offspring from the current year, and sometimes offspring from the previous year.

There are indications that dingoes were under some form of domestication by Aboriginal Australians. When livestock farming began expanding across Australia in the early 19th Century, dingoes began preying on sheep and cattle.

The dingo plays a prominent role in the Dreamtime stories of Aboriginal Australians; however, it rarely appears depicted in their cave paintings when compared with the extinct thylacine also known as the Tasmanian Wolf or the Tasmanian Tiger.

NAZI WAR CRIMINALS: -

After Allied forces defeated Germany in World War II, Europe became a difficult place to be associated with Adolf Hitler 's Third Reich. Thousands of Nazi officers, high – ranking party members and collaborators - including many notorious war criminals – escaped across the Atlantic, finding refuge in South America, particularly in Argentina, Chile and Brazil.

Argentina, for one, was already home to hundreds of thousands of German immigrants and had maintained close ties to Germany during the war. After 1945, Argentina's President Juan Peron, himself drawn to fascist ideologies, enlisted intelligence officers and diplomats to help establish "rat lines", or escape routes via Spanish and Italian ports, for many in the Third Reich. Also giving aid: the Vatican in Rome, which in seeking to help Catholic war refugees also facilitated fleeing Nazis - sometimes knowingly, sometimes not.

As thousands of Nazis and their collaborators poured into South America, a sympathetic and sophisticated network developed, easing the transition for those who came after. While no definitive evidence exists that Hitler himself escaped his doomsday bunker and crossed the ocean, such a network could have helped make it possible.

Some of the most notorious Nazi war criminals were: -

Adolf Eichmann. He was the world's most wanted Nazi. He was the architect of Hitler's "Final Solution "to exterminate the Jews from Europe.

After World War II ended, Eichmann went into hiding in Austria. With the aid of a Franciscan monk in Genoa, Italy, he obtained an Argentinian visa and signed an application for a falsified Red Cross passport. In 1950 he boarded a steamship to Buenos Aires under the alias Ricardo Klement. Eichmann lived with his wife and four children in a middle – class Buenos Aires suburb and worked in a Mercedes – Benz automotive plant.

JOSEF MENGELE

Was second only to Eichmann as a target of Nazi hunters, the doctor nicknamed the "Angel of Death "conducted macabre experiments among the prisoners at Auschwitz prison camp. An SS officer, Mengele was sent at the start of World War II to the eastern front to repel the Soviets and received an Iron Cross for his bravery and service. There, he used the prisoners – particularly twins, pregnant women and the disabled – as human guinea pigs. Mengele even tortured and killed children with his medical experiments.

In 1949 with the help of a Catholic clergy member he fled via Italy to Argentina where he owned a mechanical equipment shop. He lived in various Buenos Aires suburbs but after hearing of Eichmann's capture, went underground first in Paraguay and then in Brazil. Nazi hunters pursued him for decades, but Mengele ultimately drowned off the Brazilian coast in 1979, felled by a stroke.

WALTER RAUFF

Was an SS colonel who was instrumental in the construction and implementation of the mobile gas chambers responsible for killing an estimated 100,000 people during World War II. He oversaw the modifications of trucks that diverted their exhaust fumes into airtight chambers in the back of the vehicles capable of carrying as many as 60 people. The trucks were driven to burial sites, and along the way victims would be poisoned and /or asphyxiated from the carbon monoxide. He gained a reputation for utter ruthlessness and was infamous for the indiscriminate execution of both Jews and local partisans.

Allied troops arrested Rauff at the end of the war. He escaped from an American POW camp and hid in Italian convents. After serving as a military adviser to the president of Syria in 1948, he fled back to Italy and escaped to Ecuador before settling in Chile.

Never captured, Rauff worked as manager of a king crab

cannery and actually spied for West Germany between 1958 and 1962. He died in Chile in 1984.

FRANZ STANGL

Was nicknamed the "White Death "for his proclivity to wear a white uniform and carry a whip, the Austrian born Stangl worked on the Aktion T- 4 euthanasia program under which the Nazis killed those with mental and physical disabilities. He later served as the commandant of the Sobobor and Treblinka death camps in German -occupied Poland. More than 100,000 Jews are believed to have been murdered during his tenure at Sobobor before he moved to Treblinka, where he was directly responsible for the Nazis second - deadliest camp, where 900,000 were killed.

After the war, Stangl was captured by the Americans but escaped to Italy. Assisted by the Nazi -sympathizing bishop Alois Hudal, Stangl travelled to Syria on a Red Cross passport before sailing to Brazil in 1951.

He was employed by Volkswagen in Sao Paulo, and he was arrested in 1967 after being tracked down by Simon Wiesenthal, a holocaust survivor and well - known Nazi hunter. Extradited to West Germany, Stangl was tried and found guilty of the mass murder of 900,000 people. Sentenced to life imprisonment, he died of heart failure in 1971.

JOSEF SCHWAMMBERGER

Was an Austrian Nazi, who was an SS commandant in

charge of three labor camps in the Jewish ghettoes of Nazi -occupied Poland during World War II. In 1943 he organized the mass execution of 500 Jewish prisoners at the Przemysi camp. He personally executed 35 people at Przemysi, shooting them in the back of the neck, and dispatched Jews to the Auschwitz death camp. In Mielec in 1944, he cleansed the city of Jews. "His path was littered with corpses ", said the Nazi hunter Simon Wiesenthal.

Arrested in Austria in 1945, Schwammberger escaped to Italy in 1948 and months later arrived in Argentina, where he lived openly under his own name and received citizenship.

Sought by West Germany for extradition in 1973, Schwammberger went into hiding but was eventually arrested by Argentine officials in 1987 after an informant responded to the German governments $ 300,000 reward. He returned to West Germany to stand trial. Witnesses at the trial said they had seen Schwammberger throw live prisoners onto bonfires, kill Jews kneeling beside mass graves and slam children's heads against walls "because he didn't want to waste a bullet on them". In 1992, he was found guilty of seven counts of murder and 32 cases of accessory to murder and sentenced to life imprisonment. Schammberger died in prison in 2004 at the age of 92.

ERICH PRIEBKE

Was a mid - level SS commander and member of the Gestapo who participated in the 1944 Ardeatine Caves massacre in Rome in which the Nazis slaughtered 335 people in retaliation for the killing of 33 German SS members by Italian partisans. Priebke admitted killing two of the Italians but claimed he was only following orders. Priebke also signed off on the transport of 2,000 Roman Jews to Auschwitz and served as the Nazi go -between with the Vatican.

He escaped from a British prisoner of war camp on New Year's Eve in 1946 by cutting through barbed wire while his guards were drunk. With the help of Bishop Alois Hudal, Priebke fled to Argentina on a falsified Red Cross passport in 1948. He settled in Patagonia where he operated a delicatessen and worked at a German school, living under his own name

Priebke was extradited to Italy in 1994 where he was convicted of war crimes and sentenced to life imprisonment where he died in 2013 aged 100.

GERHARD BOHNE

Was a lawyer and SS officer who headed the Third Reich's Work Group of Sanatoriums and Nursing Homes and was responsible for the administrative logistics of Hitler's Aktion T- 4 Euthanasia Program. He carried out a systematic extermination in order to purify the Aryan race and avoid state expenditures on those with mental and physical disabilities. All told the program killed some 200,000 Germans with incurable diseases, mental illness and other handicaps. Bohne was thrown out of the Nazi Party after submitting a report accusing his agency of fraud and corruption.

He fled to Argentina in 1949 disguised as a "technician "for the military under the country's president, Juan Peron.

After a coup deposed Peron, Bohne returned to Germany and was indicted by a court in Frankfurt in 1963. Released on bail, Bohne once again fled to Argentina where he was finally extradited three years later as the first Nazi war criminal surrendered by Argentina, declared unfit to stand trial, Bohne survived another 15 years before his death in 1981.

NAZI WAR CRIMINALS STILL ALIVE: -

Oskar Groenig. A former SS junior squad leader who was sentenced to 4 years in prison charged with 300,000 cases of accessory to murder.

Helmuth Leif Rasmussen. Served as a guard in Belarus's Bodruish camp where 1,400 Jews were killed.

Gerhard Sommer allegedly helped massacre 560 civilians including 119 children in Tuscany.

Alfred Stark was accused of ordering the execution of 117 Italian prisoners of war in Greece in 1943 - part of the slaughter of nearly 9,500 officers of the Aqui Division.

John Robert Riss was sentenced to life imprisonment in Rome for the 1944 massacre of 184 civilians in Tuscany.

Aglimantis Dailide, allegedly arrested 12 Jews who were presumably executed.

Helmut Oberlande, served in the infamous Nazi Death Squad, estimated to have murdered 23,000 Jewish civilians. He lived in Canada and became a Canadian citizen, but this was revoked because of his Nazi war crime history. Oberlande died on September 20th 2021, aged 97.

He was part of a Nazi Death Squad that executed 40,000 people, mostly Jews.

DISCLOSURE: Information has been obtained and printed from Wikipedia, History, Google, A B" Banjo" Paterson. Grantlee Kieza's book "Banjo".

I LOVE TO GO TO AMERICA!

It is London, England. It is summer 2024. Although if you're an Australian, like the Mi5 agent Rebecca Joyce who is from Sydney, Australia, you would not call it summer! To put it mildly the weather is cold, wet, windy and the sky is grey and sullen.

Bill Parsons and Jack 'Dumpey 'Delaney, retired Mi5 agents, are finally enjoying their retirement, spending their days generally playing squash, tennis when the weather allows, golf and reading.

Today, however they are doing another of their favourite pastimes at their local rubbidy-dub the Rose and Crown.

Rosie, the affable barmaid, greets them with "Mornin, gents what'll it be?"

"Mornin. Rosie, just the usual, a couple of pints of Guinness, thanks!"

Jack and Bill have a seat and the Guinness arrives lickety-split and they are downed the same.

"Another couple of pints of Guinness thanks Rose!" Requests Jack. They also arrive lickety -split but are downed a bit more slowly this time.

Bill characteristically twirls his black moustache and rubs his left ear lobe between his left thumb and index finger and thoughtfully says to Jack. "You know, mate things have been a bit quiet lately. I haven't heard anything from C about spies or the like. I think I might trip off to the US and Canada for a change of scenery. Do you want to be in it? "Asks Bill.

"Yeh, sure thing but I think I'll go solo and leave the wife at home, with this retirement thingo there's not much dough coming in!" Replies Jack.

"I understand where you're coming from mate, likewise. "Says Bill.

"I think we could hire a red Mustang Shelby GT convertible, that should impress someone!" Says Bill.

"Yeh. I'd say the shallow end of the gene pool!" Adds Jack.

"You've got a point there. Anyway, we could hire one and drive across Route 66, say east to west and go up to Vancouver and get Canadian National Railways from Vancouver through the Rockies to Levis, Quebec."

"Sounds like a plan Stan. "Replies Jack.

"Well, I'll get C to arrange our flights and then we'll be off! I'll also let Bec know. "States Bill.

C subsequently arranges their flights departing Heathrow on Saturday leaving at 2:55 p.m. and advises them by text.

On receiving C's text reply Bill, says to Jack "Bloody heck, he's got us leaving Heathrow at 2:55 in the morning which is pretty uncivilized. That means we get into Chicago at about 9:49 p.m. which I guess is not too bad, so long as our accommodation is arranged. I'd better see to that! And I'll advise Bec."

Saturday comes and they wing it with Virgin Atlantic to Chicago's O'Hare International Airport, named after "Butch "O'Hare who was the US Navy's first Medal of Honour recipient during World War II. They arrive after about nine hours in the air and after retrieving their luggage they get a cart to the Hotel Chicago which is a Hilton Hotel and check in.

Bill thinks 'Now I'll have to Google Hertz to find out when and where we can pick up this Mustang.'

He subsequently does that and finds out that Hertz Car Rental have an outlet at O'Hare International.

Bill says "That's good we can pick it up at Hertz here."

Jack replies. "Good, that probably won't Hertz a bit as the British taxpayers will be paying for it!"

So they walk over and pick up their Mustang and start it up with the glorious sound of that V8 warbling away and quite coincidentally as they turn on the radio it is playing "Route 66."

So they take off on their next adventure, travelling through Illinois, Missouri, Oklahoma, Kansas, Missouri, Texas, New Mexico, Arizona and California. Whilst passing through northern Arizona they stopped and were amazed by the Grand Canyon.

In California they went to The Santa Monica Pier which is the western terminus of Route 66 and had the obligatory selfies taken to document the occasion of completing Route 66. They then drove to their accommodation at Shutters on the Beach which features two ocean - front restaurants and an outdoor swimming pool and spa and is 14.5 km. from Los Angeles International Airport.

Bill, Jack and Rebecca Joyce, an Mi5 agent from Sydney, Australia are having lunch at one of the ocean front restaurants at Shutters when Bill says "You know whilst we are in California we should go for a ski as there is excellent skiing at Heavenly, Squaw Valley, Alpine Meadows, Mammoth Mountain, Kirkwood and North Star just to name a few".

Jack says "Well we've got a week or so here. Why don't we try them all?"

Bill replies "Righto, I'll get onto booking accommodation and ski runs as it can get a bit crowded on some of them at times!"

Bec says "This California is an amazing place, it has so much sunshine, like Oz, but it has all this snow as well. I mean we do have a bit in Oz up by Kosciusko's side which reminds me of Banjo Paterson's The Man From Snowy River but more on that later".

She continues with "Then they have this great Lake Tahoe where you can go water skiing, so let's do that now!"

They then proceed to line up a ski boat, a Bayliner with a huge Mercruiser inboard-outboard.

Bill and Jack get up first on double skis as they are used to snow skiing. Bec gets up solo on a single ski which she soon jettisons and goes barefooting sort of just to prove she is an Australian and then she does a lap of Lake Tahoe to rub it in.

On landing she says "O.K., break out those Fosters!" Which they immediately do.

After downing one Bec says. "Now about this Man from Snowy River!" And she starts with a full rendition of Banjo Paterson's poem.

"THERE WAS MOVEMENT AT THE STATION, FOR THE WORD HAS PASSED AROUND

Bec continues the poem through to the end …

AND THE STOCKMEN TELL THE STORY OF HIS RIDE."

Bill says "Very good Bec, a most stirring poem!"

"Hear, hear!" Adds Jack.

"But, wait, there's more!" Adds Bec and she goes into a rendition of "The Man From Kaomagma".

"THERE WERE MOTIONS ON THE STATION – FOR A WOG HAD PASSED AROUND …

Undaunted, Bec carries on with the whole verse in its entirety: -

"THE GEEBUNG POLO CLUB GOES LIKE THIS …

'BUT I DOUBT HE'D SUIT THE OFFICE, CLANCY, OF "THE OVERFLOW".

Bill and Jack say "Encore! encore!"

But Bec says "Sadly fellas there's no more at the moment as my little ole eyes are beginning to close."

Bill says "Allright, I think we had better have an early night tonight as we've got a long haul tomorrow from LA to Redding which will take us about 8 hours, depending on the traffic. I suggest we stay overnight there and then trip to Roseburg which is about 4 ½ hours. From there through Portland and up to Seattle is about a six-hour haul. So, all in all there is a fair bit of driving coming up!"

"Yeh, but it won't be too bad with the three of us sharing the driving!" States Bec.

"That's true. "Jack adds. So, the three Mi5 agents leave sunny California and its ski fields behind and set out in their red Shelby GT Mustang for the environs of Seattle.

After a few days of uneventful driving, they enter the city limits of Seattle with the hood up on the Mustang.

"So, this is Seattle. Overcast and spitting rain. I think we should head back to LA!" States Bec.

"Yeh, I'm with you Bec. "Agrees Jack.

Bill says "Well, I suggest we shack up here for the night and then head for Vancouver and catch the ferry over to Vancouver Island for a couple of days, then head back to Vancouver and catch the Canadian Pacific to the east coast!

Bec says "Okee dokey matey blockey let's leg it down to the pawn shop! How do you spell pawn / porn? "

Bill and Jack think without saying it 'What in the heck have we got here? Are all Australians like this? '

The drive to Vancouver and passing through the USA / Canada border was uneventful and after staying in Vancouver they sailed on the ferry with their Mustang to Vancouver Island.

They spent a couple of days there and were in admiration of the island and its scenery.

They then sailed back to the mainland and booked their

passage on the Canadian Pacific through the Rocky Mountains and the great Prairie Provinces, then past the Great Lakes and into Levis to end their Canadian Pacific journey.

Whilst on the train Bill said "Well, we're off to South America next and there were quite a few Nazis who fled to South America. I might do a bit of research into that!"

He immediately Googles History and gets an article on "The 7 Most Notorious Nazis Who Defected to South America"

"You know folks these Nazis were murderous bastards without sense or soul and the Roman Catholics at the Vatican weren't much better!' He says emphatically.

"What's the go with the Vatican? "Queries Bec.

"Well, the Vatican gave aid to the Nazis fleeing to South America, sometimes knowingly and sometimes not. Also, Volkswagen and Mercedes were not innocent in these matters as they employed Adolf Eichmann and Franz Stangl. "Recites Bill.

They were interrupted by a ping on Bill 's mobile and a following text from C, the head of Mi5, saying "Seeing as you are all going to South America I shall assign you to see if you can pick up and arrest a few Nazi defectors who are down there and have not been apprehended such as Helmuth Rasmussen, Gerhard Sommer, Alfred Stark and Aglimantis Dailide."

They all simultaneously say "Righto! Game on in South America!"

Shortly they booked their flights from Toronto to Buenos Aires for the 14 ½ hour flight.

When on board the three Mi5 agents initially watched "True Grit "by the Cohen Brothers and Spielberg and then Jack and Bec drifted off to sleep whilst Jack went and had a beer and a talk with the Hosties at the back of the Virgin Atlantic's Boeing 787.

Bill says "I think I'll contact C and find out where Rasmussen, Stark, Sommer and Dailide are residing so we can nab them."

C texts back and says Rasmussen and Stark are in Buenos Aires where Rasmussen is the VW agent and Sommer and Dailide are the Mercede's agents. Whereas Stark is in Argentina in the Atlantic coast.

"Oh, well we shall see a bit of South America. Couldn't they have gone a bit further south though, say Tierra del Fuego where it might be even colder and wetter, Geez!" Quips Bec.

On landing in Buenos Aires, they get a cab to the Four Seasons hotel and check in.

"Tomorrow we'll check out the VW and Mercedes dealers and observe Rasmussen, Sommer and Dailide's movements!" States Bill.

The following day they do that and conclude that it won't be too difficult to arrest them.

Bill says "I better check with C and find out whether he has alerted the local police and Interpol about all of this."

Which he promptly does. C replies in the affirmative.

The next day, with the help of a couple of detectives from the Buenos Aires police Rasmussen, Sommer and Dailide are arrested and charged with being Nazi war criminals, tried and sentenced to life imprisonment.

Bec says "Righto, mission accomplished in BA, now off to Argentina, hopefully without crying!"

The boys say 'Game on in Argentina!"

They subsequently book their flight to Santa Cruz in Argentina with Aerolineas Argentinas. After a 3 1/4 hour flight they touch down in Rio Gallegos, the capital of Santa Cruz in Patagonia province. From the airport they get a taxi to the Hotel Patagonia which is in Zapiola Av. near the Gallegos River. On arrival, there they check in and then meet for a cup of coffee to talk over their strategy with capturing Stark who is the Mercedes Benz dealer in Santa Cruz.

After checking him out at the Mercedes dealership in conjunction with the local constabulary they apprehend Stark and charge him with being a Nazi war criminal whereupon he is rapidly dealt with through the justice system and duly sent to life imprisonment in Santa Cruz.

Bill, Jack and Bec then retire to the Hotel Patagonia and sink a few drinks.

Bec quips "Strewth! This place reminds me of Hotel California where you can check out but never leave!"

Bill and Jack say "Well, we're checking out and leaving tomorrow and going home to Britain because it's MISSION ACCOMPLISHED AND GAME OVER IN SANTA CRUZ!"

MISS PARSONS, DELANEY AND JAMES NEXT ADVENTURE IN ALASKA.

ARCTIC, ARCTIC ARCTIC, ITS COLD, COLD COLD AT THE NORTH POLE !

BRR BRR BRR!

12

ARCTIC, ARCTIC ITS COLD, COLD, COLD AT THE NORTH POLE !

PREFACE :-

The word Arctic comes from the Greek word "arktikos" meaning "near the Bear, northern" and from the word " arktos" meaning bear. It literally means referring to the northern constellation of the Bear. First recorded in 1350 – 1400 from the Greek "arktos "the Great and Little Bear Constellations are only visible in the Northern Hemisphere.

The Arctic is the most unusual region on our planet, and it is not surprising that it is called enigmatic and mysterious, because the region is hiding many miracles. The Arctic has a unique nature the great expanses of ice and snow, huge icebergs of the most incredible and bizarre forms, drifting in the Arctic Sea.

Winter temperatures average below minus 50 degrees

Centigrade Polar bears live in the Arctic near the North Pole. In total, only 4 million people live in the Arctic. Reindeer (Caribou), Walruses, Beluga Whales, Arctic Hares, Arctic Foxes, Grey Wolves, Canadian Lynx, Ermines, Rough Legged Hawks, Peregrine Falcons, Gyr Falcons, and Snowy Owls are some of the animals that live in the Arctic.

Projections show that the area of land and sea that falls within the Artic Circle is home to an estimated 90 billion barrels of oil, an incredible 13 % of Earth's reserves. It is also estimated to contain almost a quarter of untapped global gas resources, 1,1, 609 billion cubic feet of natural gas and 44 billion barrels of undiscovered natural gas liquids.

Expansion of oil and gas drilling in the Arctic could be extremely damaging. Direct contact with spilled oil would kill Polar Bears but an invisible threat could persist for years as toxic substances lingering in ice or water may impact the entire food web of the Arctic

ecosystem for years to come. The U.S. President, Joe Biden, prevented drilling in the Arctic National Wildlife Refuge.

Companies involved in oil and gas in the Arctic include: - Royal Dutch Shell, Exxon Mobil, Chevron, British Petroleum (BP), Conoco Phillips, Husky Oil and Repsol Uranium in the Arctic: - The Arctic contains large deposits of Uranium, generating intense interest from mining companies and raising concerns that a mining boom of Uranium could harm the caribou and other animals at the centre of Inuit life . The Canadian government has made it clear that Arctic mining will be one of the cornerstones of the country's economic future. Kazakhstan has the world's largest reserves of

Uranium at 304,000 metric tonnes followed by Canada with 275,000 metric tonnes.

List of companies mining Uranium in the Arctic: -

- Greenland Minerals.
- Nex Gen Energy.
- Denison Mines.
- Filo
- Trilogy Metals.
- Fission Mining. MI5 is British Military

Intelligence Section Five. Its principal function is national security in the United Kingdom. It identifies, and contains threats to national security as well as threats to the economic wellbeing of the United Kingdom which arise from overseas. Its boss is known as 'C' – for Control. Tradecraft: - Within the intelligence community Tradecraft refers to the techniques, methods and technologies used in modern espionage (spying) and generally, as part of intelligence assessments. This includes general topics or techniques (dead drops, for example), or specific techniques of a nation or organization (the particular form of encryption {encoding}) used by the National Security Agency, for example: -

- Agent handling is the management of espionage agents, principal agents, and agent networks (called "assets") by intelligence officers , who are typically known as case officers.

- Analytical tradecraft is the body of specific methods for intelligence analysis.
- Black bag operations are covert or clandestine entries into structures or locations to obtain information for human intelligence operations. This may require breaking and entering, lock picking, safe cracking, key impressions, finger printing, photography, electronic surveillance (including audio and video surveillance), mail manipulation ("flaps and seals"), forgery ,and a host of other related skills. Concealment devices are used to hide things for the purpose of secrecy or security. Examples in espionage include dead drop spikes for transferring notes or small items to other people and hollowed out coins or teeth for concealing suicide pills.
- Cryptography is the practice and study of techniques for secure communication in the presence of third parties (called adversaries). More generally, it is about constructing protocols that block adversaries.
- A cut-out is a mutually trusted intermediary, method, or channel of communication, facilitating the exchange of information between agents. People playing the role of cut-outs usually only know the source and destination of the information to be transmitted but are unaware of the identities of any persons involved in the espionage process. Thus, a captured cut-out cannot be used to identify members of an espionage cell.
- A dead drop or "dead letter box "is a method of espionage tradecraft used to pass items between two individuals using a secret location and thus does not require

them to meet directly. Using a dead drop permits a case officer and agent to exchange objects and information while maintaining operational security. The method stands in contrast to the "live drop ", so called because two persons meet to exchange items or information. "Drycleaning" is a countersurveillance technique for discerning how many " tails ", (following enemy agents) an agent is being followed by, and by moving about, seemingly oblivious to being tailed, perhaps losing some or all of those doing surveillance .

- Eavesdropping is secretly listening to the conversation of others without their consent, typically using a hidden microphone or a "bugged" or" tapped" phone line.

- False flag operations is a covert military or paramilitary operation designed to deceive in such a way that the operations appear as though they are being carried out by entities, groups, or nations other than those who actually planned and executed them. Operations carried out during peace -time by civilian organisations, as well as covert government organisations, may by extension be called false flag.

- A front organization is any entity set up and controlled by another organisation, such as intelligence agencies. Front organisations can act for the parent group without the actions being attributed to the parent group. A front organisation may appear to be a business, a foundation, or another organisation.

- A honey trap is a deceptive operation in which an attractive agent lures a targeted person into a romantic liaison and encourages them to divulge secret information during or after a sexual encounter. Interrogation is a type of interviewing employed by officers of the police, military, and intelligence agencies with the goal of eliciting useful information from an uncooperative suspect. Interrogation may involve a diverse array of techniques, ranging from developing a rapport with the subject, to repeated questions, to sleep deprivation or , in some countries torture. A legend refers to a person with a well-prepared and credible made-up identity (cover background) who may attempt to infiltrate a target organisation, as opposed to recruiting a pre-existing employee whose knowledge can be exploited.

- A limited hangout is a partial admission of wrongdoing with the intent of shutting down further inquiry.
- A microdot is text, or an image substantially reduced in size onto a small disc to prevent detection by un-intended recipients or officials who are searching for them. Microdots are, fundamentally, a steganographic approach to message protection. In Germany after the Berlin Wall was erected, special cameras were used to generate microdots that then were adhered to letters and sent through the mail. These microdots often went unnoticed by inspectors, and information could be read by the intended recipient using a microscope.
- A onetime pad is an encryption technique that cannot be cracked if used correctly. In this technique, a plain-text is paired with random, secret key (or pad).
- One way voice link is typically a radio -based

communication method used by spy networks to communicate with agents in the field typically (but not exclusively) using shortwave radio frequencies. Since the 1970's infrared point to point communication systems have been used that offer one-way voice links, but the number of users was always limited. A Numbers Station is an example of a one-way voice link, often broadcasting to a field agent who may already know the intended meaning of the code or use a one-time pad to decode. These numbers of stations will continue to broadcast gibberish or random messages according to their usual schedule; this is done to expend the resources of one's adversaries as they try in vain to make sense of the data, and to avoid revealing the purpose of the station or activity of agents by broadcasting solely when needed. Steganography is the art or practice of concealing a message, image, or file within another message, image, or file. Generally, the hidden message will appear to be (or be part of) something else: images, articles, shopping list, or some other cover text. For example, the hidden message may be in invisible ink between the visible lines of a private letter. The advantage of stephanography over cryptography alone is that the intended secret message does not attract attention to itself as an object of scrutiny. Plainly visible encrypted messages – no matter how unbreakable – will arouse interest and may in themselves be incriminating in countries where encryption is illegal (such as China and Egypt). Surveillance is the monitoring of the behaviour, activities, or other changing information, usually of people for the purpose of influencing, managing, directing, or protecting them. This can include observation from a distance by means of electronic equipment (such as Internet traffic or phone calls); and it can include simple, relatively no – or low – technology methods such as human intelligence agents watching a person and postal interception. The word surveillance comes from a French phrase for "watching over " "sur " meaning "from above " and "Eviller" means " to watch".

- TEMPEST is a National Security Agency specification and NATO certification referring to spying on information systems through comprising emanations such as unintentional radio or electrical signals, sounds, and vibrations. TEMPEST covers both messages to spy upon other and also how to shield equipment against such spying. The protection methods are also known as emission security (EMSEC), which is a subset of communications security (COMSEC).

- IN POPULAR CULTURE, in books of such authors as thriller writer Grant Blackwood, espionage writer Tom Clancy, and spy novelists John le Care' , characters frequently engage in tradecraft , e.g. , making or retrieving items from " dead drops"." dry cleaning", and wiring , using , or sweeping for intelligence gathering devices , such as cameras or microphones hidden in the subject's quarters, vehicles, clothing, or accessories.

DISCLOSURE: - Information has been obtained and used from Wikipedia and Google.

"Well Jack here we are in Anchorage, on our retirement at last!" Says Bill Parsons.

"Yeh! "Replies Jack Delaney another MI5 agent. "It's cold and there's three foot of snow everywhere with Grizzly bears and Caribou plodding down Fourth Ave. Let's go and have a beer to warm the cockles of our hearts!'

They find a nearby pub, which wasn't difficult and order a couple of pints of Arctic Rhino and down them rapidly and so order another couple of Head Buzzard IPA's just for something different.

"Hey, these are alright!"

Exclaims Jack.

"Too Right! "Replies Bill. "You know what Jack there are a lot of oil and gas companies in town like Conoco Phillips Proprietary Limited and Chevron and also uranium miners. Do you know what Proprietary Limited means?"

"No idea Caribou! "Replies Jack. "But I'll bet Bec does, She knows everything, but she's not retired like us so she's not here."

"Yeh, well I don't know whether she knows everything It's just that she's got her

mobile and Dr. Google seems to know everything!"

"Good point! "Says Bill. I think I'll text her and find out."

Bec James replies "A proprietary limited company is a separate legal entity. It will be liable for its own debts. This ensures that claims against the company can only be paid by using assets owned by the company. This gives a layer of protection for directors and shareholder's personal assets. They pay a corporate tax rate of 27.5% in Australia which is significantly lower than the highest marginal tax rate for individuals of 47%. I hope you're enjoying the cold up there, its 35 degrees and sunny here in Sydney!"

"Thanks for that Bec, I think I'll start up a proprietary company! "Exhorts Jack.

"Well it doesn't look like we'll be playing tennis today." Says Jack. "Yeh, well your right there! "Replies Bill." but we could put our racquets on our feet in all this snow."

"You know mate there are reports in the local rag about some Germans killing Polar bears and taking their coats and leaving the rest out there and presumably the wolves are devouring the remains" "I don't know, what is it with Germans? It seems some of them have just got to kill something. You know Adolf Hitler was the same and wanted to get rid of all the Jews. "Says Jack.

"You know live Polar bears cost about $420,000 and high grade skins used to go for $20,000 but now they are about $5,000 "Says Bill.

"I think I'll get onto C and see if he has anymore information about these Germans and if he wants us to do anything, seeing as we're here!" Explains Bill.

C replies by text to Bill and says that the Germans are Gerhard Tafel and Maxwell Schmitt and they belong to a group of neo-Nazi upstarts who may be quite dangerous so he said he'll also get Rebecca James and Jack O'Halloran and the CIA and FBI onto them as well because they will need to be watched 24/7 and he also suspects that they are going to have some dealings with Uranium mines in Alaska.

O'Halloran flew into Anchorage the next day and met up

with Parsons and Delaney. Rebecca arrived in two days' time from Sydney, rugged up to the nines and none too happy about having to leave sunny Oz for Alaska.

"Righto, where are these Germans? When we find them it's GAME ON IN ALASKA!"

It didn't take the MI5 agents long to find the rowdy Germans who were at Humpy's Great Alaska Alehouse at 610 W. 6ᵗʰ Avenue downing a few pints of Heineken .

The MI5 agents and the CIA agents enter Humpy's and grab a table and some drinks and observe the Germans." They don't look too dangerous ." Says Jack. "Looks can be deceptive says "Bec.

"Yeh, I think we'll wait and see on this one." Quips Bill. After an hour of drinking Heineken's the Germans leave and are followed at a distance by the MI5 and CIA agents. The Germans hop into a snowmobile and head out into the hinterland of snow and mountains. The MI5 and CIA agents do similarly, however they realise that they will be readily observed by the Germans, however they are well equipped with guns and ammunition and they are all crack shots. After about an hour's travelling the Germans halt and pull up in the vicinity of an Alaskan Uranium mine and alight from their snowmobile and continue on foot armed to the teeth with AK47's and Lugers ,seemingly without regard for their pursurers.

Bill Parsons says "Mmm, doesn't look like they are going in there to have a picnic! You all had better get those AK 47's ready"

They immediately check to see that their AK47's are

loaded, engaged and ready to fire and then raise them to their shoulders and advance towards the Uranium mine site, ready to face the unknown. The Germans storm the mine with a barrage of machine gun fire and screams of anguish from the mine site staff as they are all gunned down. The MI5 and CIA agents hurry towards the mine through the thick snow . When they get there they are confronted with cross fire from the Germans and luckily no MI5 or CIA agents are wounded but they manage to dispose of the Germans who had already bundled up ten bars of Uranium.

Bec James says "MISSION ACCOMPLISHED AND GAME OVER IN ALASKA!"

Jack O'Halloran quickly adds " Not so quickly Bec, I hereby ask for your hand in marriage."

Which she readily accepts.

Jack says "Hey Bill you're a marriage celebrant why don't you marry them here and now?"

"Good idea Jack." Says Bill. And so it was done there in Anchorage, Alaska. Rebecca James and Jack O'Halloran became man and wife "I think my last name will be James – O'Halloran." Says Bec "Does that mean you have two fathers? "Questions Jack Delaney. "Well, actually yes, Mr. Comedian. my Dad and Jack's   Dad?"

So Bill and Jack continued with their retirement in Alaska and the O'Halloran's went back to Sydney, Australia and got on with their lives. However in a strange twist of fate Jack O'Halloran was tried and found guilty of treason as his relationship with Rebecca turned out to be a "Honey Trap

Operation "and he was attempting to find out information about Australian /U.S. intercontinental cruise missiles.

Fini .

Casablanca

FORT KNOX

BETWEEN

Airbus A350

Airbus A350

MOROCCO

AND A HARD

PLACE

OHIO CLASS NUCLEAR SUBMARINE

FORT KNOX, MAINE, USA

New York

13

BETWEEN MOROCCO AND A HARD PLACE!

PREFACE:

Morocco, officially the Kingdom of Morocco, is the north-westernmost country in the Maghreb region of North Africa. It overlooks the Mediterranean Sea to the north and the Atlantic Ocean to the west, and the disrupted territory of Western Sahara to the south. Morocco also claims the Spanish exclaves of Ceuta, Melilla and Penon de Velez de la Gomera, and several small Spanish - controlled islands off its coast. It spans an area of 446,550 square Km., with a population of roughly 37 million. Its official and dominant religion is Islam, and the official languages are Arabic and Berber; the Moroccan dialect of Arabic and French are also widely spoken. Moroccan culture and identity are a vibrant mix of Berber, Arab, and European cultures. Its capital is Rabat, while its largest city is Casablanca.

Inhabited since the Paleolithic Era over 90,000 years ago, the first Moroccan state was established by Idris 1 in 788.

It was subsequently ruled by a series of independent dynasties, reaching its zenith as regional power in the 11th and 12th centuries, under the Almoravid and Almohad dynasties, when it controlled most of the Iberian Peninsula and the Maghreb. In the 15th and 16th centuries, Morocco faced external threats to its sovereignty, with Portugal seizing some territory and the Ottoman Empire encroaching from the east. The Marinid and Saadi dynasties otherwise resisted foreign determination, and Morocco was the only North African nation to escape Ottoman domination. The Alaouite dynasty, which rules the country to this day, seized power in 1631, and over the next two centuries expanded diplomatic and commercial relations with the Western world. Morocco's strategic location near the mouth of the Mediterranean drew renewed European interest; in 1912, France and Spain divided the country into respective protectorates, reserving an international zone in Tangier. Following intermittent riots and revolts against colonial rule, in 1956 Morocco regained its independence and reunified.

Since independence, Morocco has the fifth-largest economy in Africa and wields significant influence in both Africa and the Arab world; it is considered a middle power in global affairs and holds membership in the Arab League, the Union for the Mediterranean, and the African Union. Morocco is a unitary semi-constitutional monarchy with an elected parliament. The executive branch is led by the King of Morocco and the Prime Minister, while legislative power is vested in the two chambers of parliament: the House of Representatives and the House of Councillors. CASABLANCA: - Is the largest city of Morocco. Located on the Atlantic coast of the Chaouia plain in the central - western part of Morocco, it is the second largest city in the Maghreb region and the eighth largest in the Arab world. Casablanca is Morocco's chief port and one of the largest financial centres in Africa. In 2019 the city had a population of about 3.7 million in the urban area and over 4.27 million in the Greater Casablanca.

Casablanca is regarded as the economic and business centre of Morocco, although the national political capital is Rabat.

The port of Casablanca is one of the largest artificial ports in the world, and the second largest port in North Africa, after Tanger – Med Casablanca also hosts the primary naval base for the Royal Moroccan Navy.

When Sultan Mohammed ben Abdallah (c, 1710 – 1790) rebuilt the city after its destruction in the earthquake of 1755, it was renamed "ad – Dar al -Bayda' "(The White House").

The area which is today Casablanca was founded and settled by the Berbers by at least the seventh century BC.

It was used as a port by the Phoenicians and later by the Romans. In the early 15th century, the town became an independent state once again, and emerged as a safe harbour for pirates and privateers, leading to it being targeted by the Portuguese, who bombarded the town which led to its destruction in 1468. The Portuguese used the ruins of Casablanca to build a military fortress in 1515,

As Portugal broke ties with Spain in 1640, Casablanca came under fully Portuguese control once again. The Europeans eventually abandoned the area completely in 1755 following an earthquake which destroyed most of the town. In the 19th century, the area's population began to grow as it became a major supplier of wool to the booming textile industry in Britain and shipping traffic increased. Casablanca is situated on the Atlantic coast of the Chaouia Plains, which have historically been the breadbasket of Morocco.

Casablanca has a hot-summer Mediterranean climate. The cool Canary Current off the Atlantic coast moderates temperature variation, which results in a climate remarkably similar to that of coastal Los Angeles.

The Grand Casablanca region is considered the locomotive of the development of the Moroccan economy. One of the most important Moroccan exports is phosphate. Other industries include fishing, fish canning, sawmills, furniture production, building materials, glass, textiles, electronics, leather work, processed food, spirits, soft drinks, and cigarettes.

Casablanca's main airport is Mohammed V International Airport, Morocco's busiest airport. Regular domestic flights serve Marrakech, Rabat, Agadir, Oujda, Tangier, Al Hoceima, and Laayoune, as well as other cities.

DISCLOSURE: - Information has been obtained and quoted from Wikipedia and Google.

It is January 24, 2025, in Morocco. It is Hot. It is 42 degrees Centigrade in the shade. There has been no wind, although a slight zephyr (which the locals label 'The Doctor') is beginning to come in from the Mediterranean and the Atlantic heralding a bit of respite. However, the locals are used to this. But the Mi5 agents Bill Parsons, Jack 'Dumpey' Delaney from England are not used to this and are sweating profusely. Not so the other MI5 agent, Rebecca James, from Sydney Australia, as this weather is just like home.

They have been sent on assignment to Casablanca, Morocco by 'C', for control, the head of MI5 to search out a suspected terrorist group in Morocco.

Even though Morocco is an Islamic country, and they don't celebrate Christmas and also supposedly don't drink alcohol, the MI5 agents do. They have managed to locate the Sheraton Casablanca Hotel and Towers, Marriot Bonvoy Hotel in Casablanca. Situated at 100 Av. des Far, it is an upscale hotel in the financial district and a 4-minute walk from Manch'e Central train station and 3 kilometres from the Hassan II Mosque. It has modern rooms featuring Wi-Fi and flat screen T.V.'s along with safes, minibars and coffee makers. Upgraded rooms grant access to a lounge offering complimentary continental breakfast. Suites add separate lounges and marble bathrooms, and a two-bedroom suite has a kitchen.

Parking is free. There are three restaurants, one serving Japanese cuisine, as well as a sports themed bar, a cocktail bar and a nightclub. Other amenities include a gym., a seasonal outdoor pool and event facilities.

C has booked them into a two-bedroom suite and after

checking in they meet up in the lobby lounge and order drinks. Bec says "Well, here we are again fellas. C said that the Foreign Office were going to get MI6 to handle this one, but C said that MI6 would only botch it up, so he decided to get you two out of retirement as he said you were the best agents ever, and that includes MI5 and MI6."

"Hang on, Bec you're included in that!" Jack states emphatically.

"Thanks mate! But he didn't say that.

"I'm sure it was implied" Adds Bill.

"Righto" says Bill." However, we don't know who these terrorists are, how many and what they look like. So, it's like finding the proverbial needle in a haystack".

"Yeh, and sometimes you can find that by sitting on it" Says Bec.

"Yeh, well I'm sitting on my backside here and I can see a group of four Moroccans at that table over there who are deep in conversation and appear rather secretive. Bill, you speak Arabic, see if you can eavesdrop and get a bit of an idea of what they're on about." Says Rebecca.

"Sure, thing Bec, give me a sec."

Bill gives all his attention to listening to the Moroccan's conversation and shortly whispers "They are saying something about the USA and Fort Knox as far as I can make out!"

"I reckon they are our quarry then" says Jack.

"Okee -Doekee. it looks like it's GAME ON IN THE U.S.!"

Exclaims Bec. Bec whispers" Folks, group together and I'll make out that I'm taking a photo of you whilst I'll actually take a photo of those Moroccans and I'll send it off to C to find out if Mi5 know who they are."

The deed is done and C replies to Bec's phone with a text saying "They are allied to Al Qaeda and are fairly active terrorist suspects, their names are Ahmed Bakhti, Arif Hadj, Fatima Kharmrat and Amira Rosheen. I'll alert all the relevant authorities in Morocco and the U.S. to keep a watch and surveillance order on them 24/7."

"Righto! "Exclaims Bill. "This is looking interesting. We'll have to be on our toes with this lot! "

So, the Moroccans and the MI5 agents depart Casablanca on an Air France Airbus 380, which is the world's largest passenger airliner, but which is now vanishing due to its size and high operational costs and arrive at John F Kennedy International Airport 15 hours later at a respectable time of nine o'clock in the morning.

The Moroccans hail a yellow cab, and the MI5 agents take the next cab off the rank and Bill says "Follow that cab! "They all arrive at the Hilton Garden Inn at 136 West 42nd Street NHY 10036 which is also conveniently located near three subway stations.

The MI5 agents check in at the reception desk and find their room and have a shower and then meet in the lobby bar to discuss their plan of attack with the Moroccan's.

Bill says, "I think it best if we split up and tail and observe them separately, also just in case they split up too."

"Good idea." Says Jack Bec chimes in with "C sent a text saying that he has got the CIA on board and the hotel staff will let us know when the Moroccans are about to depart. So good night fellas and don't let the bed bug's bite. I'll see you in the morn.! "

Jack and Bill concur "Yes, see you then Bec! "

The day dawns bright and sunny but cold and they all have breakfast downstairs at the breakfast bar and note that the Moroccans are all there as well.

"Hurry up with that coffee Bill!" Exclaims Bec. "I think they are about to depart soon."

"O.K. Bec I'll get my skates on." Says Bill.

Just before they are about to depart Bill's phone rings. He says "Damn, who in the name of hell is this! "And answers it with a rather gruff tone. "Parsons here, what do you want?"

"Oh, hello Bill it's Jack O'Halloran from CIA. Have I caught you at a bad time?" Bill answers "Yes, sort of but what do you want anyway?"

O'Halloran is a single, 30-year-old, tall, fit, well-muscled Californian with fine angular facial features and a good mop of black hair which is anchored down with Californian Poppy hair oil with its distinctive popular scent and allure.

"Bill, MI5 have contacted us about your Moroccans, and we will help keep a watch on them as well. However, there are more Moroccans residing here in the U.S. that we have concerns about so we just wanted to alert you about them."

"Well, thanks for that, it will be most helpful as we have our hands full with this little lot! "States Parsons.

"Strewth, stone the crows and starve the lizards, they 're on the move! If we don't get movin' like a racehorse goanna they're gonna be the other side of the black stump at the back of Bourke! "Exclaims Bec.

"I dunno, we can't take you Aussies anywhere." Retorts Jack.

"That may well be, but we better get on Shanks's ponies, or we'll be left for dead out in the never-never! "Is Bec's reply to that.

They quickly follow the Moroccans and on their tail are two CIA undercover agents, unknown to the MI5 agents and presumably the Moroccans.

The Moroccans jump into a Yellow Cab and the entourage do the same into another cab with the words "Follow that cab!"

The Moroccans pull up at 224 East 43rd Street which is directly outside Avis Car Rentals. The Moroccans go inside and rent a blue Ford station wagon. After they had left the showroom Bill, Jack and Rebecca enter and say" We'll have whatever they had and where were they heading to? "

The receptionist replies "They are heading for Indianapolis, Indiana, Sir!"

"And how long does that take Ma'am?"

"About eleven hours, Sir"

"O.K. thanks for that! We 'll let Avis know when we are finished with the car wherever we are. Goodbye."

"Bec chimes in with "See you later alligator, or in a while crocodile in Oz."

They then depart in their green Ford station wagon and Bec texts C to let him know what's going on.

As they are following the Moroccans Bec exclaims" I think I know where they are heading!"

Bill and Jack question "Where?"

"To the Indi 500 racetrack and I know all about it, coz I've got Google. It's a 500-mile car race traditionally held over the Memorial weekend, which is as you know is this weekend, being the last weekend of May. The track is nicknamed the "Brickyard" as the surface was paved in brick in the fall of 1909. One yard of brick remains exposed at the start / finish line. The inaugural race was held in 1911.

The event is steeped in tradition with pre- race ceremonies, post - race celebrations and race procedure. The most note-worthy and most popular traditions are the 33-car field and lining up three wide for the start. The circuit is 2.5 miles long. So, there you are, courtesy of Dr. Google". States Bec.

Bill adds "Thanks for that Bec, most informative."

"Ditto!" Says Jack.

"Well." Says Bill. "Here we are in Indianapolis on Memorial weekend, so I guess we head for the track."

"Yes, maybe" says Bec but aren't you forgetting about our terrorists."

'Mmm, well maybe You are right, we'll track them first." Says Bill

They do so and as it turns out the Moroccans head to the Indi 500 track. The MI5 agents follow them into the arena, at a distance. When inside they come across Jack O'Halloran and the other FBI and CIA agents.

"G'Day Jack. How ya goin." Says Bec.

"Hi Ya Bec" says Jack in his American drawl.

Long-time no see! It must have been three years since we were in Cairns working with ASIO on those American - Chinese cocaine runners."

Bec replies "Yeh Jack, good to see you again. Yeh, it was three years ago up in FNQ!" As it turns out Jack and Bec had a bit of a relationship going on in Australia but because of logistical reasons it petered out

"I guess you lot are here watching these Moroccans and not because you are Indi fans." Says Jack.

"That's right" says Bill.

"Yeh, well we better get a bit of a move on because they have gone over to the other side of the arena and met up with another couple and by the look of their complexions and attire, they are Moroccans too, unless I'm mistaken. "

Bec says. "Let's get closer and I'll get a shot of them and send it off to C."

She immediately does so and shortly C replies with "They are more terrorist suspects who are resident in the US and are under a watch order."

O'Halloran confers with this.

Jack says. "You may or may not know but we've been watching the Moroccans who are US citizens and they have built up quite an arsenal of AK47's, rifles, grenades, rocket launchers and crossbows, all of which are legal here." Bec says.

"I'm damn glad they aren't in Australia. We had a massacre in Port Arthur, Tasmania in 1996 when 35 people were killed and 23 wounded and our P.M., John Howard bought in gun buybacks in 1996 and legislation so that only people who obtained a gun license could own a firearm. The Septic Tanks have their National Rifle Association and all their gun lobbies so it would be tantamount to political death if a President tried to veto them. Besides the Yanks are allowed to have tear gas in their possession and use it on their fellow citizens but they are not allowed to use it in war. They're also allowed to carry rocket launchers. Go figure that one out, Sport!" Before the Indi race is over the Moroccans split up and go their separate ways.

The MI5 and CIA agents confer and agree to split and follow the Moroccans.

The local Moroccans head for their homes in Indianapolis, whereas the other Moroccans

hopped into their vehicle and headed southwest.

Unknown to the FBI and CIA agents the local Moroccans had double backed from their homes to the Indi 500 track and placed and exploded bombs which tied up most of the U.S. CIA and FBI for some time.

However, Parsons, Delaney and James were not fooled by this and tailed the terrorist Moroccans at a distance.

Unknown to the MI5 agents, the Moroccans also had a large cache of weapons onboard.

Jack says "Hello where in the hell are they going? It looks like they're going into Brandenburg."

They follow them into the townsite of Brandenburg and note that they stop outside the tourist coach agency and buy tickets and then board the coach with their backpacks and a long thin parcel.

In ten minutes time the coach departs and the MI5 agents follow at a distance. The tourist coach enters Fort Knox and parks outside the main entrance. The passengers alight. The Moroccans quickly pull-out grenades, tear gas canisters and a rocket launcher and throw the grenades through the windows and follow them with tear gas canisters launched from the rocket launcher. This quickly activates the resident U.S. Army Cadet Command who give little resistance and are quickly mown down by the Moroccan's AK47's. The front doors of Fort Worth are knocked out by grenades and a couple of fork lift trucks are commandeered and driven into Fort Worth and all the bars of gold bullion are transported to the nearby Naval base at St. Norfolk which is the world's largest naval base, situated in southeast Virginia in Sewells Port Peninsula of Norfolk City and comprises an area of approximately 3,400 acres, where they are loaded aboard six nuclear submarines that have been easily commandeered from Garden Island which is situated off Perth, Western Australia. The MI5 agents are unable to do anything except observe as they are fearful of being gunned down too.

Bill contacts C to tell him what has happened. C replies that they will track these subs by satellite and let Bill know of their whereabouts. C also informs them that the Moroccans had stormed the Nuclear facility at Portsmouth and confiscated all their Uranium -235.

Jack says "These terrorists are dangerous!"

Bec replies with "Tell me something we don't already know Cobber!"

As soon as the gold bullion is loaded aboard the submarines and the Moroccans Bakhti, Hadj, Kharmrat and Rosheen are aboard they weigh anchor and submerge and head for Morocco. When the Moroccans think they are out of sight they surface and proceed at full speed for Casablanca.

MI5 are keeping them under surveillance and C texts their agents advising them to fly to Casablanca post haste. He also adds that he thinks that their intention is to raid Saudi and Kuwait oil and gas fields to exploit their supplies as Morocco is not well endowed with oil and gas. C has also engaged the British Navy and had a couple of destroyers and frigates steam to Casablanca to thwart the Moroccans in their stolen submarines.

On arriving in Casablanca, the British Navy engaged the submarines and overpowered them and capture the Moroccans. They are subsequently taken to England and tried in a court of law and found guilty of espionage along with many other charges and sentenced to life imprisonment, never to be released.

Bill, Jack, and Rebecca shout "GAME OVER, MISSION ACCOMPLISHED!"

Bill and Jack add "Now for retirement, but not for you Bec! "

Moscow

KGB PRISON MOSCOW

Moscow

London

ONCE A SPY ALWAYS A SPY!!

14 ▮

ONCE A SPY, ALWAYS
A SPY!

PREFACE:

Spies have been around for some time and they will probably be around forever. However the nature of spying has changed and nowadays seem to be more applicable to computer hacking and gaining ciber knowledge about nations and how there armed forces operate. For example. Edward Joseph Snowden (born June 21,1983) is an American former computer intelligence consultant who leaked highly classified information from the National Security Agency (NSA) in 2013 when he was an employee and subcontractor for the Central Intelligence Agency (CIA). His disclosures revealed numerous global surveillance programmes, many run by the NSA and the Five Eyes Intelligence Alliance with the co-operation of telecommunication companies and European governments , and prompted a cultural discussion about national security and individual privacy.

In 2013, Snowden was hired by an NSA contractor, Booz Allen Hamilton, after previous employment with Dell and the CIA. Snowden says he gradually became disillusioned with the programmes with which he was involved, and that he tried to raise his ethical concerns through internal channels but was ignored. On May 20, 2013, Snowden flew to Hong Kong after leaving his job at an NSA facility in Hawaii, and in early June he revealed thousands of classified NSA documents to journalists Glenn Greenwald , Laura Poitras , Barton Gellman, and Ewen MacAskill.

Snowden came to international attention after stories based on the material appeared in the Washington Post, The Guardian, and other publications. A subject of controversy, Snowden has been variously called a traitor, a hero, a whistleblower, a dissident, a coward, and a patriot.

In July 2013, media critic Jay Rosen defined the "Snowden Effect "as" Direct and indirect gains in public knowledge from the cascade of events and further reporting that followed Edward Snowden's leaks of classified information about the surveillance state in the U.S. "In December 2013, The Nation wrote that Snowden had sparked an overdue debate about national security and individual privacy. In Forbes, the effect was seen to have nearly united the U.S.

Congress in opposition to the massive post – 9/11 domestic intelligence gathering system . In its Spring 2014 Global Attitudes Survey, the Pew Research Centre found that Snowden's disclosures had tarnished the image of the United States, especially in Europe and Latin America.

DISCLOSURE:- information has been obtained and quoted from Wikipedia and The Guardian.

It is 2025. It is Kensington , London. It is cold, wet, windy with a sullen sky. The MI5 agents Bill Parsons, Jack 'Dumpey' Delaney are retired and living in London. The third MI5 agent, Rebecca James, an Australian from Sydney, Australia is still active and living in Kensington and

wishes she was back in Oz away from this Pommie weather.

Control, known as "C" for short, is the head of MI5 and has alerted Bill and Jack, bringing them out of retirement again, and Rebecca that they have concerns about a dentist working in Kensington by the name of Geoffrey Liddell. Liddell is tall, six foot two

inches, handsome, with blonde hair and blue eyes and a clean shaven face. He is muscular and athletic and a good sportsman having played rugby and cricket and obtaining Blue awards in both of these sports whilst at Oxford University. Whilst at Oxford he became aligned to Communism and has since stayed interested in that line of politics. He visits Moscow frequently and has a girl friend, Svetlina Karolinski, who works for the KGB. Consequently Bill contacts C to get the lowdown on Liddell and C relates the above information to the MI5 agents. So the three MI5 agents are asked by C to check him out. They locate his surgery and wait in their unmarked MI5 car which is a nondescript Ford Zodiac with a souped up V8, turbocharged motor and high performance suspension for high speed driving. However, for the time being there occupation is to sit and observe Liddell.

There is a sign outside his surgery premises saying ;

"Dr. Geoffrey Liddell M.D. Sc.) Kings College. London) B.D.Sc (Kings College. London)".However it is not so much what the sign says but what it doesn't say that is of importance. The sign doesn't say "Geoffrey Liddell, KGB agent and Russian spy".

After half an hour of observation Bill decides that he needs a cigarette and he goes to reach for his packet when Rebecca says "Pardon me Bill!"

Bill then takes his cue and hops out of the car and lights up his cigarette and takes a few puffs. Presently, a local postman comes along the footpath in his electric cart. Bill stops him and says " Excuse me sir. I'm Bill Parsons from MI5." He then shows him his I.D. and credentials and continues with "Could you please tell me if Dr. Liddell gets any or much overseas mail, especially from Russia?"

"Well, as a matter of fact he does! "Replies the postman, with a cockney accent. He

adds "He gets a lot from Moscow and some of it seems to be scented with, I would say a French perfume, like Dior or the like. "Bill says "Thankyou sir." And then lets the postman continue on his way.

Bill then rings C and informs him of what the postman had said.

Bec reminds Bill that posties in Britain had been riding bicycles on their rounds since

the 1800's and so the use of electric vehicles seemed like a backward step as far as the physical health of the posties was concerned.

Bill then stubbed out his cigarette and said he was going to make an appointment to go and see Liddell which he did straight away.

The dentist's receptionist said "That will be fine sir. He can see you in ten minutes. Would you please fill in this medical history form and then take a seat. Thankyou."

Bill does so and then takes a seat.

In fifteen minutes he is shown into the surgery and greeted by Dr. Liddell.

Liddell says "Ah, Mr. Parsons, how can I help you?"

Bill replies "I'm just in need of a checkup and possibly a scale and clean, please." "Sure, just hop up in the dental chair and I'll lay you back."

Bill does so and Liddell says "I see you work for a government department.

Which one would that be? "

Bill replies "Security." "Oh, mmm. Would that be MI5, MI6 or Special Branch?" Bill thinks. "He's onto me. I'd better play this carefully." So he says "I'm not allowed to divulge that "knowing full well that it would not throw Liddell of the scent.

Dr. Liddell then examines Bill's mouth and says "You're fine, just in need of a scale and clean and a topical fluoride treatment and by the way it would be a good idea if you gave up smoking because apart from the lung complications it is also detrimental to your periodontal health and can cause oral cancer which is not very pleasant!" "O.K." Replies Bill.

This is duly done then Bill says goodbye to Liddell, pays his account and then leaves.

Bill contacts C and tells him what had happened and said that he thought Liddell would do a runner to Russia and suggested that they put out an all points report so that Liddell could not leave the country. Wisely, Liddell does not do a

runner straight away, instead he leaves it for four weeks and in the meantime lets his hair grow longer and also grows a beard and dies his hair and beard black. However the observing MI5 agents have noticed this.

On the morning of Geoffrey Liddell's planned departure, he is arrested by police at Heathrow Airport and charged with being a KGB agent and a spy. He was duly convicted of

both charges and imprisoned for life , never to be released . Bill Parsons , Jack Delaney and Rebecca James celebrate by having a few drinks at the Rose and Crown and say altogether "GAME OVER, MISSION ACCOMPLISHED – ONCE A SPY ALWAYS A SPY!, BUT THIS SPY WILL SPY NO MORE!

Author Bio

Rodney James White was born in Perth, Western Australia on September 11, (9/11) 1947. He attended Manning Primary School and Wesley College in South Perth. He obtained a B.D.Sc. from the University of Western Australia in 1970 and first practised dentistry in the Pilbara of Western Australia as a government dentist under a WA government dental cadetship at the Tom Price Hospital for three years. He then worked for 43 years in private practice in Manning, a suburb of Perth, and is now retired. He married his wife Gail in Melbourne, Australia in 1970. They have three children, Julia, Brendan and Robert, and five grandchildren.

Printed in Australia
Ingram Content Group Australia Pty Ltd
AUHW011317080424
392747AU00010B/103